Absolute Zero

Misadventures from a Broad
A Prequel Based on the Val Fremden Midlife Mystery Series
Margaret Lashley

Note from the Author:

Absolute Zero is a full-length, stand-alone novel about something we've all longed to do—run away to Europe! It's also the funny, yet often heart-wrenching prequel to the hilarious Val Fremden Midlife Mystery Series.

Absolute Zero is not itself a mystery, per se. (Unless you count the mystery of why in the world we do the crazy things we do!) Actually, this novel is a satirical look at a midlife farce—reinventing yourself after forty. Just like life, the story is full of ups and downs. And it's told through the eyes of a sharp-witted, reluctantly redneck woman who's always played it safe—until now.

Freedom comes at a great price for Val. Will it be worth it in the end? Well, that's up to you....

Praise for the Val Fremden Midlife Mystery Series

"One of the best series I have read in YEARS!!!![1]"
"This is a knock-down hilarious series."
"Margaret writes with a "smirk" of a Cheshire cat. Fantastic read."
"These characters are so well written that you can almost see them in your mind while reading the book."
"A perfect blend of mystery and humor and the writing and editing are top rate."
"This series gets better with every book. The plot is great, the characters are zany and the situations in which Val finds herself are hilarious."
"If you want a fun, suspenseful, and downright crazy book to read this summer this is definitely your pick."
"If you haven't read any Val books you are truly missing out on a really great series."
"Love it! Margaret Lashley can write no wrong words. This series is fabulous."

---

1. *https://www.amazon.com/gp/customer-reviews/R1IHI9VSLPCO1M/*

   ref=cm_cr_dp_d_rvw_ttl?ie=UTF8&ASIN=B071KYVB8X

More Val Fremden Midlife Mysteries

"Life is a four-letter word. But it doesn't have to be a curse...."

Val Fremden

Chapter One

Sideswiped by unexpected turbulence, the commuter plane's wheels hit the tarmac hard and bucked three times like a kicking rodeo bull. The first bounce tossed my distant thoughts clear out the window and sent me skittering like a duck on ice into the present moment. I clutched both armrests in a death grip, as if they might save me from oncoming disaster. But it was too late. My life had hit the skids months ago.

"Whoa! That was a close one!" I said to the elegantly dressed woman in the seat next to me.

She eyed me strangely, as if she didn't understand. Then I remembered that there was a darn good chance she didn't. The realization made me squirm inside.

The plane settled down and taxied normally toward the terminal. For the pilots and crew, it was just another ordinary day. For me, though, it was anything but. I peered out of the small oval windowpane at the unfamiliar countryside surrounding the small airport. *This was for real. I'd gone and done it.*

The plane came to a halt. A mechanical bell binged. I looked around nervously. I slung my purse across my shoulder and sardined myself into the line of passengers inching their way down the narrow aisle. When I reached the plane's exit door, I paused hesitantly, like a convict who'd gotten free of her cuffs without anybody noticing. My mind swirled with excitement and abject terror. Goosebumps rushed across my body. The hair at the base of my neck pricked up like a scaredy-cat.

What the hell was I doing?

Mere days before, I'd slammed every single door—including the screened one—on my life back in Florida. The last chance to change my mind had come and gone, as unheeded as a speed limit sign at a NASCAR rally. Every safety net I'd ever known was thousands of miles away, across the Atlantic Ocean, out of sight and out of reach.

I took a deep breath to steady myself, then stepped off the plane into the complete unknown. I glanced back and waved goodbye to the *Air Italia* flight crew. I turned again and meandered down the gangplank behind a frail, elderly couple holding hands. Their long-standing marriage triggered flashbacks of my own, long-suffering one.

Seven weeks ago, I'd signed the final divorce papers ending fifteen years of matrimony to Jimmy Johnson, a man I no longer knew. I envisioned the beautiful house Jimmy and I had shared together. I'd sold it and my advertising business just days before the flight. After splitting the pot with Jimmy, I'd netted a hot-dang jackpot of $473,000. I pictured my best friend, Clarice Whittle. I'd left my Ford in her garage, along with a few boxes that held the final remains of the cranky, resentful woman I hoped this trip would get rid of for good.

I'd brought next to nothing with me. I'd left even less behind. No kids. No pets. No job. No husband. No responsibilities. No *nothing*.

I'd spend the last forty-one years in perpetual motion—Val Jolly's non-stop stint as dutiful daughter, long-suffering wife and brown-nosing business woman. I'd catered to everyone else's needs for as long as I could remember. Somewhere along the way I'd turned into a crabby, shrill woman that even *I* didn't like. I'd forgotten who I was and what *I* wanted. This trip was going be my chance for R&R&R—relaxation, re-invention, and (hopefully!) romance.

I was in Italy to try my hand at *living irresponsibly,* like my trampy cousin Tammy Jeter. She'd always done as she darn well pleased. Up 'til now, I'd thought she'd been selfish. Especially when she left Whitey Large and their five pit-bulls (One with puppies!) to run off with Tater Johnson. Turns out, that girl had had it right all along.

Unlike Tammy, I'd done everything society said I *should* do. I'd been a faithful wife. I'd worked my fingers to the bone. I'd racked up all the major merchandise. But instead of feeling victorious, I'd felt shackled like a poor old pack mule, burdened with an impossible load of stuff I couldn't work up the feelings to care about anymore. A big-old house full of junk to dust and polish. A never-ending stream of pointless tasks to juggle. A distant, thoughtless man to resent the hell out of....

If that's the American Dream, shoot this pack mule now and put me out of my sad-sack misery!

I sighed, then scolded myself for it. As of late, it had become an annoying habit.

"*Signora?*"

Someone tapped me on the shoulder. I turned around to find myself eyeball-to eyeball with a man who made Billy Meyers, our high-school homecoming king, look like a toad-frog.

"Yes?"

"Oh. English. Yes. You...move it? Yes?"

I looked around. I'd gotten lost in my thoughts and was clogging the exit line like a lump of greasy hair in a bathtub drain.

"Oh! Sorry!"

I scooted along the corridor connecting the plane to the terminal. I'd taken a fashion tip from Tammy and worn a short, flouncy brown skirt and a button-down, white cotton blouse. After two flights and twenty hours of traveling, my skirt was wrinkled to hell, and I'd spilled coffee all over my blouse. I'd come to Italy to find a new Romeo. What could I hope to catch with rag-bag bait like this? I drew in a deep breath to sigh again. But, to my surprise, I jumped and let out a high-pitched squeal instead. *A stranger had just pinched my bottom!* I blushed with embarrassment and...what was it? Yes! *Southern Pride!*

Screw that tired, old American dream. I wasn't in Florida anymore. I was in Italy!

I rubbed the pinched spot on my butt cheek and looked around. The Bari airport terminal wasn't even as big as Tallahassee's. I wanted to remember the exact moment my new life of irresponsibility had begun. I looked around at the happy people passing to and fro, so content with their lives. In front of me, a tiny little girl in a pink dress let go of a red balloon. My eyes followed it upward. I spied a sign that read: *Benvenuti a Bari.*

"Welcome to Italy, Val," I said out loud.

A sudden wave of giddiness washed over me. I burst out laughing. I never realized I could feel so...*light*. Like the balloon set loose by that child, I, Val Jolly, was at liberty to wander aimlessly, adrift in the world.

I was free.

I'D PICKED ITALY AS the starting point for my do-over life because, besides my home state of Florida, Italy was the only other place I'd ever been. Last year, my girlfriend Clarice Whittle and I'd won a five-day trip to Italy with a recipe we entered in *Southern Taste* magazine. It was a modern redo of the classic half-a-canned pear on a lettuce leaf. Instead of mayo in the center, we'd substituted Cheez Whiz mixed with a sure-fire crowd pleaser—crumbled bacon bits. We'd taken second place behind a brownie pie full of Skittles and marshmallow fluff.

Clarice and I'd had a big time visiting Rome and Naples, and that place where the volcano turned everybody into Cheetos—Pompeii. So it came natural that when I'd decided it was time to get out of Dodge, aka St. Petersburg, Florida, that I'd chosen Italy. Besides, in all the romance novels I'd ever read, Italy was the number one place where middle-aged, burned-out Caucasian woman like me went when their lives had turned to crap. So in my book, it came bona fide.

Before arriving in Bari, I'd landed in Rome on an overnight flight from Tampa. Naturally, the connecting flight to Bari had been overbooked. When I got up to the check-in booth, it looked like BOGO day at the Piggly Wiggly. There must have been thirty Italians yelling and making hand gestures at each other, the likes of which I'd never seen before. Like a nitwit, I'd run off to this foreign country only knowing three words of Italian, *si, no,* and *ciao.* So, I'd had no idea what was going on. I was just about to panic when some guy in a uniform grabbed my carry-on from my hand.

"Hey! Gimme that back!"

The guy eyed me like I was the last moron he could cope with for the day.

"Signora, *prego. Americana?*"

"Uh...*si.*"

"I must a take your bag. No room over the head."

He'd raised both hands over his head and moved them back and forth in a way that reminded me of Pastor Piddleton on TV. I couldn't help but giggle. Lucky for me, that softened him up some. He'd smiled and winked at me.

"I take your bag to pass away. Yes?"

I'd hoped he didn't mean that literally. Seeing as how I didn't think I had any choice in the matter, I'd agreed.

"Yes...si."

The man looped a red tag around the handle of my brown checkered bag and snatched it away from me again. I'd held my breath as he wheeled my little darling away. I'd cringed when he tossed it in a heap like contraband next to the gate. I'd even frowned at it apologetically as I passed by it on my way to board the plane. Only after I'd been seated had I remembered that my hairbrush and all of my makeup were inside that bag. *Dang it!* I'd planned on fixing my face before we landed in Bari. But thanks to that overbooked flight from Rome, it was not to be.

When we'd bounced down in Bari an hour later, I wasn't the only one who'd looked a little worse for wear. The city's tiny airport didn't even *try* to make a good impression. In fact, it looked more like a hangar than a real airport. Bari wasn't on the main tourist route, so I guess it wasn't used to catering to the insecurities of sophisticated redneck foreigners like me. Under the *Benvenuti a Bari* sign were a bunch more notices pointing left and right, but none of the words were in English. I was as lost as a drunk man's charm. So I followed the other passengers as they strolled along, hopefully toward baggage claim.

Along the way, screeching kids, style-conscious lovers and gift-laden grandmas rushed to greet their kin. I'd never seen so many hugs or heard so much hollering outside one of our family reunions. I was totally taken aback by how affectionate, *and loud,* a couple of dozen Italians could be. Compared to Florida, everyone there seemed so well dressed, too. Even the old men wore respectable jackets and hats. Considering my sorry state, I must have stuck out like a pig in a petunia patch.

Slept-in clothes. Two-day-old-makeup. Face it, Val. You look like a washed-up old cocktail waitress sneaking home from a one-night stand.

I looked down at my tragic blouse and grimaced. I tried to smooth my snarled, shoulder-length hair with my fingers. That's how my genuine Diamonettie ring got caught in the rat's nest at the back of my head. *Aww crap on a cracker!* I tried to pull the dang ring loose without making a spectacle of myself, but it just got worse the more I messed with it. I was just about to yank out a giant wad of my own hair when I heard a man's voice so close behind me it made my back arch.

"Prego, Signora," he said softly.

I felt his hand slip into my hair. He's fingers intertwined with mine as he gently worked the ring free from my hair.

"Thank you, sir!"

"*Ecco*," he replied.

I turned around. There, standing in front of me holding my ring in his elegant hand, was a knight in shining Armani. He was slim, about six feet tall, with wavy dark hair and smoldering brown eyes. *Just my type!* He wore a tailored suit and a devilish grin. *Oh, my goodness.* I wouldn't have been surprised if he told me he'd just dropped by on the way back to his castle.

"*Senta. Tutto va bene*, Signora." He handed me my ring.

"I...I'm sorry. I don't speak Italian."

"Ah." He smiled in a sexy, playful way that made my gut go limp. "I speak small English. You make a trip, si?"

"Si."

"Touristica, no?"

"Si."

"You stay in Bari?"

"No. Brindisi."

His face registered amused disappointment. "Ah. Too bad for me. We could be umm...*friends*, no? *Allora*. It is not to be." He smiled, kissed my hand, and turned his attention to the baggage carousel.

My mouth fell open like a barn door with a broken hinge. No American man had looked at me like that in at least a decade. Even when I was dressed to the nines! I caught my breath and looked down at my wrinkled brown skirt and coffee-stained blouse. *This was unbelievable! Eat your heart out, Tammy Jeter!* My heart thumped with a strange new aliveness. I tried in vain to stop a simply unstoppable grin. I scoured my mind, trying to remember a phrase from *Sex in Sorrento,* the romance novel I'd studied to prepare for my trip. What was it? Oh yeah. *Viva la dolce vita!*

Twenty minutes later, the handsome knight, along with his wife and kids and everyone else on the flight, were gone. I stood alone at baggage claim and watched the empty conveyor belt groan to a halt. Neither my suitcase nor my carry-on had made it to Bari with me. That weird, uncomfortable mixture of exhilaration and terror came rushing back. I clutched my purse a little tighter. It was all I had left besides the clothes on my back.

I bit my thumbnail and thought about Clarice. Suddenly, I remembered a moment we'd shared in Rome together last year. After eating too much pasta and drinking too much red wine, we'd found our way to the famous Trevi Fountain. Like the tourists we were, we'd both tossed a coin over our shoulders into its dark, blue waters.

"What'd you wish for?" I'd asked Clarice.

She'd laughed. "A man with a good job and all his teeth. How about you, Val?"

"I want to be somewhere where nothing reminds me of anything."

Well, like it or not, Val Jolly, you've just gotten your wish.

There I was, in a foreign land, with nothing but a passport, a purse and a pair of sweaty panties. I was on my own. Totally free. I could *do* whatever I wanted, and *be* whoever I darn well pleased. There was only one flaw in my plan. I had no idea what I wanted to do, or who I wanted to be.

I'd given myself three weeks to figure it out—as if reinventing my whole life was something I could do on a tight schedule.

Hey, I was an American. I had no idea how much I had to learn.

Chapter Two

I'd been in Italy for half an hour and was already about to drown in my own stupidity. The lost puppy look on my face must have said it all. A man in a beige uniform came over and took me gently by the arm. He ushered me to a window that read: *Ritiro Bagagli Perso*. In small print under it were the English words: Lost Baggage Claim. I'd sighed with relief.

Well, I chatted and gestured and did everything but sing *Boot Scootin' Boogie* with the surly clerk at the window, but nothing was going to break her foul mood. Finally, after a discussion as long and incomprehensible as one of Pastor Piddle's sermons, I put my John Handcock on five undecipherable forms and was told I was free to go.

I was free. Yay. Yeah. Hmmm....

I walked to the exit and stepped into the warm, summer breeze. A gust of wind caught my rumpled skirt and lifted it to my waist. I swatted at it wildly, trying to hold down first the front and then the back, but it was as hopeless as trying to keep ten kittens in a box. I heard a catcall and looked up. To my utter surprise, my shabby-ass Marilyn Monroe impersonation earned me a round of whistles from a construction crew nearby! My ears reddened and my lips curled into a naughty grin.

For some reason unbeknownst to me, in Italy, I was *hot!*

Oh, man! I was *definitely* not in Florida anymore. Back home, I couldn't get a rise like that if I stood on a street corner, naked, handing out hundred-dollar bills in a shiny red Camaro. *But I wasn't home. I was in a whole new world with a whole new set of rules....*

I leaned against the wall, admiring the crystal blue sky and keeping the back of my skirt down below my panty line. The heavenly smell of fresh-roasted coffee filled the air, threatening to lure me back inside to the airport coffee shop.

I took a step in that direction and noticed a thin, shabby-looking fellow moving toward me. He approached gingerly, pausing hesitantly every few steps, as if trying to make up his mind what to do. His white shirt and grey pants were clean, but threadbare. His shoes were worn down at the heel. He wasn't exactly threatening, but he *did* seem suspicious somehow.

All of a sudden, he took a giant step forward and jabbed his long, pointy nose within an inch of mine. I looked around for help, but the construction crew was on break. Naturally, there was never another man around when I needed one. I fought the urge to belt the old geezer with my purse. I could feel his hot breath on my face as he spoke.

"You are Val, no?"

I nearly fainted with relief. The weather-beaten old guy had to be the cab driver hired to pick me up.

When I was in Italy with Clarice last fall, we'd done a bunch of touristy things. This time around, I wanted to experience Italy like a local. There'd only been two problems with my plan. First, I didn't know a single soul in the whole country. Second, I didn't speak four words of Italian. Other than that, I was all set.

I'd googled around on the internet for what they called *immersion vacations* and found a budget, two-week program with an organization called World of Wow. Their brochure had promised the opportunity to "get a real taste of Italian culture." That had sounded good. The WOW trip also required a few hours of teaching English each week. That had sounded okay, too.

With WOW, I'd be on vacation, but I'd also have stuff to do. So I wouldn't get the DTs from having too much free time on my hands. Hopefully, the next two weeks would prepare me for the second phase of my adventure in living irresponsibly—a week-long Mediterranean cruise. It sailed out of Civitavecchia, Italy the same day that the WOW volunteer vacation ended. Clarice said she was coming on *that* trip with me—*if* she hadn't found that man with a good job and a full set of choppers by then. She'd turned her nose up at the volunteer work vacation, but she'd been chomping at the bit to meet me in Rome for that luxury cruise.

I'd booked both trips just three weeks ago on *Cheaper Beeper*, a last-minute closeout travel website. I wasn't broke by any means, but I'd earned every dime of my money myself, and didn't want to waste a penny. The cab driver was here to take me to Brindisi. The WOW brochure described it as "a small, seaside village about an hour's drive south of convenient Bari airport."

"Hello, sir. I mean...*ciao!* Yes...I mean *si*. I'm Val."

A gap-toothed grin cracked the seriousness of the old man's sun-hardened face. He grabbed my hand and nearly shook my arm out of the socket.

"*Bene! Sono Vittorio! Bene!*"

He let go of my mangled hand and spewed a torrent of Italian at me. I listened politely, then shot back with English. Sometime during this incomprehensible exchange, our smiling faces sagged. We'd both used up our entire second-language skills with our first words to each other. Thankfully, I'd already learned that in Italy—as in most parts of the world—a smile could get a person a long way.

Vittorio knew this trick, too. He grinned and went to work putting his entire body to use as a human translator. I watched intently as he acted out holding an invisible handle in his right fist, then turning it upside down and moving it to almost touch an imaginary thing he held between the pinch of his left thumb and index finger. After that, he moved his pinched-together fingers to his lips, which had formed an O, as if he were going to blow a kiss.

I hadn't slept in over twenty-four hours and had the attention span of a Georgia gnat. I didn't have any idea what the old man was up to, so I shrugged apologetically. Vittorio raised his eyebrow and he sniffed the air like a hound dog after a possum. I smiled weakly. He repeated the entire performance again, as I stood there dumbfounded. Frustrated, Vittorio twisted his mouth sideways, then pointed a thumb toward the airport entrance. He wafted his hands toward his face and sniffed again.

Finally, a lightbulb went off in my dimly lit wits. *Vittorio wanted to get a coffee at the airport coffee shop. Duh!*

"Coffee? Si!" I nodded enthusiastically.

The old man showed me the gap in his teeth again.

"Bene!"

I followed the old codger back inside the airport and up to the coffee shop counter. I stood, tongue out like a hungry waif, and watched as Vittorio held up one mummified-looking thumb and matching index finger and said, "Doo-ay."

The tired-looking barista gave a quick nod and began pulling and pushing weird gears and gizmos on a machine filched from *Willy Wonka's* chocolate factory. A minute later, two tiny white cups full of steaming, black mud landed on the counter in front of us.

"Benvenuta, Signora," Vittorio said. He raised his tiny cup at me, then slammed back the sludge in one gulp.

I followed his lead. The thick black brew burned like lava as it slid down my throat. The high-octane caffeine jolted my sleep-deprived brain like a mule kick to the noggin. *Whoa!* I set the cup down, closed my eyes and shook my head to clear it. When I opened my eyes again, the barista was staring at me.

"*Quattro euro,*" he muttered.

I looked over at Vittorio for help. The old cabbie took my purse from the counter, opened my wallet with his long, mummy fingers, and gave the barista two big silver coins from the change compartment.

"Less go-go," Vittorio said. He mimed holding a steering wheel, then turned and walked toward the airport exit.

I followed him hesitantly, suddenly unsure of myself. *Had I just been scammed? Was Vittorio a scam artist? What if this whole World of Wow thing was just one big scam, too? Aunt Patsy had warned me about this!*

As Vittorio led me through the nearly empty airport parking lot, I scrutinized him for tell-tale signs of being a serial killer. *Do they drink espresso over here?* The old man stopped at a dusty, dented black car that appeared to have been manufactured the same year I was born. *What did a European axe murderer look like, anyway?*

I pondered this question, along with whether or not to run for the Appian hills, but decided I was way too jetlagged and out of shape to make any credible effort at escaping. I resigned myself to my fate. I reached for the door handle, then jumped back with a start. There was a woman sitting in the back seat!

My eyebrows shot up an inch. Vittorio hadn't seemed in a rush at all, even though this other woman must have been waiting for us the whole time. I was shocked by his rudeness. Then I remembered something I'd learned during my visit with Clarice last fall. Italians were genetically incapable of being in a hurry.

I'd noticed only one exception to this rule, and that was when they got behind the wheel of a car. Italians in possession of a steering wheel instantly transformed into voracious demons, each with an insatiable need for speed. Traffic lights became suggestions. Sidewalks became open lanes. Horns became mechanical obscenities! This phenomenon was made doubly odd by the fact that, in every other aspect of their lives, time appeared to be of no significance to Italians whatsoever.

"WOW," said Vittorio, gesturing toward the woman in the back-seat.

I took another glance at her. WOW was right. I didn't know how long she'd been waiting, but it had been at least one minute over her limit. She looked ready to gnaw the upholstery. Her presence should have brought me relief. After all, it meant that I was no longer alone with Vittorio, the Vivisector of Venice. But it didn't. Somehow, she managed to seem even scarier than him.

I chose the devil I came with and climbed into the passenger seat next to Vittorio. When I turned to greet the woman, her spray-tanned skin and injection-swollen lips told me instantly that she was American.

"Hi, I'm Val," I said, trying to sound both cheerful and apologetic for making her wait.

"That's *my* name," she hissed, as if I had taken hers without her permission.

Her crinkled nose and pinched expression reminded me of that snotty lady who worked at *J.J.'s Bar'B'Que*. She always looked as if she smelled dog crap.

I turned back to face the windshield, my eyebrows an inch higher. I guess I wasn't the only one who could use a do-over life.

ON THE WAY TO THE HOTEL, Vittorio's deranged driving garnered grunts and grumbles from the woman in the backseat. The awkwardness of the situation made me antsy. To pass the time, I decided to secretly amuse myself by coming up with a pet name for the uptight woman in the rearview mirror. After conjuring up a few rather ungracious monikers like "crap-sniffer" and "panty-waddles," I settled on Val II. I figured the Roman numerals were apropos, given our current locality.

After settling that matter in my mind, I turned my attention to practicing Italian with the maniac at the wheel. I fished through my purse for my pocket-sized *Rick Steves Italian Phrase Book & Dictionary*. At least I still had *it*. I thumbed through it and came up with some gems for Vittorio.

"Do you believe in Santa Claus?" I asked with an innocent face.

Vittorio eyed me curiously, then tooted his horn at some unknown assailant.

"Want to hear me burp?"

I heard Val II snort derisively. I ignored her and tried to swallow air to make a fake burp. But my throat was scalded from the espresso. Vittorio shrugged, unimpressed.

"Got any candy?"

Vittorio ignored this comment completely and followed behind a motorcycle as it tried to squeeze into an imaginary lane between two cars. I decided to up the ante.

"I'm a lesbian."

That one got his attention. Vittorio shot me a look of horror and nearly lost control of the cab. His thin face contorted in pain. He clasped his hands together as if in prayer and moved them back and forth underneath his chin like a poodle begging for table scraps.

"No, no, no!"

He followed his monosyllable plea with a stream of Italian so passionate and imploring that I got worried he might lose hope and drive us off a cliff.

"Hey! Watch it up there!" Val II groused.

I pried Vittorio's locked hands apart and put them back on the steering wheel. He kept glancing at me wistfully until I laughed and shook my head no. I fumbled through my phrase book to find the right word to explain.

"*Scherzo*," I said. "Joke."

Vittorio's head jerked sideways to face me. His expression brightened, as if he'd stepped out of cold, dark shadow into warm sunlight. "Scherzo!" he echoed. He smiled and nodded his grey head. Then, with both eyes on the road, he reached over and gave my left thigh a quick squeeze with his boney fingers. A second later, the hand flew back to the wheel and pounded on the horn. "Stupido!" he yelled at the car ahead of us. He shook his head, shot a nasty-looking hand signal at the windshield and mashed the gas pedal to the floor.

"Why don't you can it, lady?" Val II griped. "Just let the guy drive, already, before he kills us all."

She sounded a lot like the woman I'd boxed up and ditched in Clarice's garage. That was someone I definitely *didn't* want to have along on my trip. I ignored Val II and let her words go unchallenged. Besides, I was too tired for a pissing match. My eyelids were growing heavier by the second.

I set my phrase book in my lap and watched the Italian countryside fly by. The gentle, rolling hills were blanketed in endless groves of ancient olive trees. Their thick, gnarled trunks were as distinctive as faces, giving each tree its own sort of personality. It was late afternoon, and the fading sun emphasized the pinkish hue of the red clay soil that clung to their twisted roots.

Every so often, an ancient, falling-down farmhouse of beige fieldstones broke the beautiful monotony of the silver-leaved olive trees. The grassy, abandoned yards that surrounded the tumbledown homesteads stood out like emerald oases, freckled with clusters of bright-red poppies.

The pastoral scenery was hypnotic. My eyes began to droop and I started to nod off every few minutes, only to be awoken by my own, pig-like grunts. After a particularly loud snort, I took a bleary glance over at Vittorio. His eyes were on the road, and there was no ax in his hand. I looked in the rearview mirror. Val II was fast asleep. Drool had collected at the base of her over-filled bottom lip and was dripping out like a leaky tap.

I shifted in my seat and glanced through my phrase book again. I'd been joking with Vittorio about the lesbian thing. But after searching the booklet for the right words, I told the old man something I was convinced was true.

"Vittorio. *No potere amore*," I said. "I'm no good at love."

Vittorio scoffed. "Scherzo, no?"

"No. No scherzo."

Vittorio's eyes grew wide. He crossed himself and shot a strange hand signal up toward the roof of the car.

"No. Impossible, bella, Signora." He slammed on the brakes, skidded to a stop and jammed the cab into park.

I flinched out of fear. *Why had he stopped? Was he was going to throw me out of the cab! Or...oh no! Maybe he was reaching for his ax!* I tried to read his expression, but Vittorio wasn't looking at me. He was staring straight ahead, motionless, as if he'd turned the meter off on himself, as well. I started to speak, but a rusty voice from the backseat beat me to it.

"Are we finally here? It's about time."

I looked out the window. It was nearly dusk, but I could still make out the cheerful, peachy-pink color of the Hotel Bella Vista, just as the brochure had advertised. I smiled, relieved, and opened the cab door.

Val II climbed out of the backseat and stretched her legs. I studied her for a moment and realized that besides our first names, we didn't have a lick in common. Sure, she was about five feet four inches tall, same as me. She also looked to be in her early forties. But there the resemblance ended.

Val II was a silicone-boobed, makeup-troweling, high-maintenance, Botox witch. A lipo surgeon had run amok on her skinny, hard-looking body. She'd had all the fat sucked out of the wrong places and injected into the right ones. As a result, she looked as real as a three-dollar bill printed in red ink. She and her kind were the arch enemies of every woman who'd ever had the lack of foresight to want to age gracefully. Just looking at her made me want to spit nails.

To top it off, even though her hair was cut in a shoulder-length bob like mine, it was a tacky, pinkish-orange color that could only come from a bottle. My hair was medium brown, and though it came from a bottle, too, I liked to think it was a shade within the range of human possibility.

"So tell me," Val II asked, eyeing me like I was a turd in a punch-bowl, "why did *you* sign up for a volunteer vacation in *Italy*?"

I eyed her cautiously, then decided to make a joke. "Oh. Easy," I said. "Because it beat the alternative. Sleeping on a filthy mattress in Botswana."

A wry grin forced its way across Val II's rubber-duck lips.

"You and I are gonna get along just fine," she said, and patted me on the shoulder like I was her minion.

I forced a fake smile. *Well, we'll just see about that.*

Chapter Three

Most normal people would probably consider a "volunteer vacation" an oxymoron. In other words, someone would have to be either an ox or a moron to pay for the privilege of working during precious time off from a regular job. But I didn't have a regular job. And, truth be told, I probably wasn't normal, either.

I mean, who else would ditch their life the way I had? I'd been president of my own small ad agency, and had made a pretty penny hawking udder balm and hoof-rot salve for Alberts Agro International. And my ex Jimmy hadn't been a bad guy. He just wasn't good at keeping his temper—or a job. Jimmy was, as my Grandma Violet used to say, "Unaffected by ambition."

I could've maybe lived with that. But about three or four years ago, the chemistry Jimmy and I once shared had fizzled out like a wet firecracker. He'd become a dud in bed, and wouldn't help out around the house, either. Jimmy's "underperformance" both at work and in the bedroom wasn't due to lack of brains or some physical ailment. I'd have cut him more slack if that had been the case. But it wasn't. The only thing Jimmy suffered from was pure, honest-to-goodness laziness. I got tired of taking care of him, and even more tired of him *not* taking care of me. I figured if I was going to live like a nun, I might as well fly the coop.

Past disappointments buzzed around my head like a swarm of angry bees from the second I woke up in my little room at the Hotel

Bella Vista. I reminded myself I wasn't in Italy to reminisce about the casualties of love and war. I was here to remember who I was, to reinvent myself, and, if possible, to finally get my pipes cleaned for the first time in like, *forever*. I snickered at the idea, and made myself blush.

Even though my luggage was missing in action, I still had all my travel documents. I'd carried them in my purse, thank goodness. I crawled out of bed to check for the thirteenth time that my pocketbook and passport were still on the nightstand. I pulled the cruise brochure out of a side pocket and studied the happy people on the front cover. Their smiles made me homesick for something I couldn't name. I stuffed the brochure back in my purse and sighed.

I checked the clock on the nightstand. It was almost 7 a.m. I was supposed to meet the other volunteers at 7:30. Without luggage, I'd been forced to sleep in the nude last night. It had been weird and unfamiliar, and I knew Grandma Violet would have disapproved. But I'd found it kind of thrilling, in a new, exotic kind of way. *Maybe that's how the Italians did it.*

I snuck, butt-naked, outside onto the balcony to retrieve my only set of panties. I'd rinsed them out in the bathroom sink last night. They were still damp. I had no choice. I pulled them on anyway, then slipped into my bra, wrinkled brown skirt, and coffee-stained white blouse. I fluffed my hair with my fingers and sighed. *Stop sighing!*

The full-length mirror in the corner taunted me like a piece of Eleanor White's chocolate cheesecake delight. I fought off the temptation to take a peek. I was better off not knowing. I stepped out into the hallway and clicked the door shut behind me. The smell of fresh-brewed coffee urged me on as I ambled toward the elevator.

AFTER AN UNSETTLING, jerky ride down three stories in an elevator the size and shape of an apartment refrigerator, the door opened begrudgingly and I stared into the Hotel Bella Vista's odd lobby. It was sparkling clean. But it most certainly wasn't what I'd call fancy. A mish-mash of contradicting styles gave it an eclectic, cobbled-together feeling. The traditional, coffered ceilings soared to maybe twelve feet high. On the east wall, gloriously tall wooden windows afforded a fabulous view of the pool area and the sea beyond.

The old-world, romantic feel of the building itself was in stark contrast to its furnishings. The prim, tailored curtains were of a garish, modern print. Huge, geometric shapes in red and blue competed fiercely with the sea view for attention. The square, low-backed, black-leather chairs and couches grouped along the walls looked as if they'd been manufactured in the 1960s, complete with spindly looking, stainless-steel legs.

One side of the lobby featured a sleek front desk of onyx-hued marble. In the middle of the reception area stood a barista-style coffee counter that doubled as a cocktail bar by night. It was constructed of dark, chocolate-stained wood and clear, plate glass. Curiously, there were no chairs at the bar. (I later discovered Italians typically stood while having an espresso or a beer.) An assortment of clear cocktail glasses hung at arm's reach above the bar's glass counter top, illuminated by the bluish light emanating from recessed ceiling lamps.

My kitten-heeled sandals made a hollow clicking sound as I walked across the lobby's terrazzo floor toward the Internet room. This was the rendezvous point stated on a flyer handed to me yesterday, along with my keys, by the drop-dead-gorgeous front desk manager, Antonio. I yanked open the oversized, wooden door. I wasn't sure what I'd expected to find, but my gut reaction told me I'd been wishing for something different. I unconsciously blew out a disappointed breath, then quickly forced a smile to compensate for my undeliberate rudeness.

Sitting around the oval, mahogany conference table were five completely unremarkable Caucasians. Probably all Americans. There were two men and, counting me, four women. I thought about complaining to the company about the lack of diversity. But how could I? I was as white and American and middleclass as the rest of them.

No one said a word as I stepped inside. The room was crowded with silent anticipation. I nodded respectfully and took a seat at the table.

As my fanny hit the cushion, the door flew open again. A short, plump woman bustled in. Her beige skirt and jacket were so tight she appeared to have swollen to maximum capacity while still inside them. Her jet-black hair was twisted carelessly into a loose bun. She exuded a harried, put-upon air. Sizeable sweat stains deepened the color of the fabric under her jacket armpits. She sighed loudly, then looked up at us, wide-eyed, as if she'd just become aware of our presence.

"*Buon giorno*. Good morning. I am Monica Mozzarelli," she said, as if for the millionth time this morning.

One of the guys in the group, a dumb-looking bald man, snickered loudly. I was instantly embarrassed to be an American. Monica Mozzarelli didn't seem to notice. Either that or she didn't give a crapoli.

"So, everybody, let's get to know each other, yes?" Ms. Mozzarelli nodded with minimum effort toward an old lady in an orange pantsuit. "You first."

"I'm Berta," the woman said in a crusty voice like a toad's croak. She was skeleton-thin and somewhere between seventy and a hundred and fifty years old. "I'm a psychologist. Retired. From Manhattan. I'm—"

"*I'm* a lawyer. Name's Frank Templeton, Esquire," interrupted a pompous-faced man of around sixty. He had a greying comb over atop his round head and a ruddy complexion compliments of high blood pressure. He looked as if he could blow at any minute.

Berta pursed her lips and shot Frank a hard glance that, in my book, only had one possible interpretation. *Two points for you, Berta.*

The man who'd snickered spoke next. "I'm Peter Axion, senior accountant with the IRS," he said in a half-apologetic, half-proud tone. "It's a dirty job, but someone's got to do it." Peter was tall, balding, and pasty. The perfect poster child for his profession.

I took my turn at bat and bunted. "I'm Val Jolly. I'm...." *Oh my gosh! What are you? Think of something!* "I'm a former...uh...I'm re-tired."

"My name is Val, too. Val *Finnegan.*" She said her last name as if it was better than mine. "I'm a professional beauty consultant from Ocala, Florida."

I noticed Frank eye Val II's fake boobs as the last woman introduced herself. She was a slim, tattooed, black-haired woman in her mid-twenties.

"I'm Tina Taylor. From Jersey." Her surly, dark-brown eyes glanced around the room with jaded curiosity. "What's up?"

At the end of the introductions, as if on cue, smug-looking Frank stood up, cleared his throat and puffed out his chest.

"I'll be taking charge," he announced. "I'm a veteran of volunteer vacationing. I know all of the correct procedures."

Frank. A control freak. What a surprise.

Everyone, including Monica Mozzarelli, seemed relieved someone else was going to take the lead. The weary Italian and blustery attorney got down to business, pairing up teams and organizing assignments. I got busy *doing nothing.* I had to sit on my hands and bite my tongue, but I did it. It was a strange feeling, not taking on responsibility. I hoped I could get used to it.

While I waited for my fate to be decided for me by strangers, I studied my fellow volunteers. Peter looked to be about my age, probably six feet tall. He had the kind of bluish-white skin that wouldn't tan, and a long face with thick, livery lips. Even though he had a lanky, athletic build, there was something awkward and ungainly about his body. I watched flop sweat glisten on his bald head as he tried to make small talk with Tina.

"Where'd you get those tats?" he asked the *Jersey Shore* wannabe.

"From the tattoo store," Tina replied curtly. She rolled her eyes and returned to chewing her black-polished, bitten-to-the-quick fingernails.

"Oh, right." Peter was undaunted by Tina's dismissive tone. The poor guy had to have been clueless not to get the hint. "I've been thinking about getting a tattoo myself."

"Yeah? You know it hurts like crazy."

For her young age, Tina's attitude came off surprisingly bitter, like my third-cousin Martin Mercer who'd once scaled a prison wall only to find an even higher one on the other side.

"But you IRS guys, I guess you're into pain."

As Peter pondered her meaning, I glanced over at Berta and did a double take. The old psychologist had been watching me watch everyone else! Berta shot me a dirty grin that made me feel oddly like a kid caught red-handed eating somebody else's candy.

"Okay, everyone, listen up!" barked Frank. "I've got your assignments here. Read 'em and weep."

Frank laughed stiffly at his own joke, then passed sheets of paper around the table. When I got mine, I read it and groaned. I'd been paired with Frank, the humorless, controlling, attorney-at-large. *Crap on a cracker!*

According to the list, Frank's and my assignment was at a technical school for kids who weren't going on to college, but wanted to learn vocational trades. The other volunteers were assigned to high schools. Berta got paired with Tina, Val II with Peter.

"It is Sunday, domenica," said Ms. Mozzarelli, with all the enthusiasm that could be stuffed inside half a cannoli. "So, you see, you all have the day free to enjoy the beauties of Italia." She hastily gathered up her things to make her getaway.

I wanted to ask Ms. Mozzarelli a question, but someone hooked me by the arm and stopped my traction. The frazzled Italian woman disappeared out the door. I turned around. It was Frank.

"Work starts tomorrow," he informed me, as if I was now one of his flunkey employees. "Let's meet in the lobby at 8 a.m. tomorrow morning. *Sharp*."

"Yes sir," I replied, matching Ms. Mozzarelli's enthusiasm to a tee.

WHILE THE OTHERS WENT off exploring the city, I spent my free Sunday afternoon poking around the Hotel Bella Vista and adjacent seashore. I liked to travel, but I'd been afflicted with perhaps the worst sense of direction to be bestowed upon a human being since my infamous Uncle Larry Jolly. One year, when he was nineteen years old, he'd gotten lost at the state fair for nearly three days. He'd survived on rainwater and half-eaten corndogs, according to Grandma Violet. I must've inherited his genes, because I'd been known to get myself all turned around on my way home from work, inside peoples' houses, and even in two-stall public restrooms.

When I'd arrived last night, I'd discovered that my hotel room was right in front of the elevator on the third floor. The ancient contraption grumbled and squeaked like a gaggle of angry geese every time somebody used it. That didn't bother me a lick. My room was a straight shot in. No confusing hallways or turns to navigate. If I hadn't been so ass-dragging tired, I'd have jumped for joy.

My bad sense of direction wasn't the only reason I didn't want to stray too far from the hotel. The other one was a tad more obvious than the first. I'd begun to look—and smell—worse than Uncle Larry did when Aunt Patsy had finally found him by the Tilt-a-Whirl eating half a chocolate moon pie he'd filched from a trash can.

It was just my luck that not a single blessed store in Brindisi was open on Sunday. I couldn't even buy a toothbrush! The horrors! I could almost see Grandma Violet rolling over in her grave when I went to bed last night with dirty teeth. This morning, my nasty breath was vile enough to melt a 64-pack of Crayolas. Almost as bad, my armpits and legs rivaled Sasquatch's. And my hair? Well, it was beyond mentioning in polite society.

And there was one more thing. I figured if I'd messed around and got lost, I was a *goner*. I didn't have a clue how to ask for directions in Italian. I decided to play it safe and keep close to home, so to speak.

With my Italian phrasebook in hand, I left the hotel and limped barefoot across the street. I scrambled like a badly-dressed, middle-aged circus chimp onto a cream-colored boulder a few yards from the sea. Sitting there all alone on that rock, I suddenly felt the hollow drum of loneliness begin to beat in my chest. I stared out into the water and sighed. *What was I doing here with all these strangers?* From my boulder-high perch, the Adriatic Sea took on a strange, artificial shade of blue that reminded me of...*Oh my gosh! Ty D Bol toilet cleaner!* My Grandma Violet swore by Ty D Bol, and had taught me to do the same. I relaxed and stared out at the hypnotic blue sea and felt like I'd found a little piece of home.

I WOKE TO THE SOUND of someone calling my name. I tried to get up but it felt like my spine was broken. The sky overhead was purplish blue. I realized I was still laying outside, on the boulder. The voice called my name again.

"Val Jolly?"

"I'm here!" I called back.

"*There* you are," Berta said. "You're late for dinner."

"Oh. Okay. Thanks. Be right there."

The skinny old woman watched as I slid gracelessly down the boulder like a handicapped sloth.

"Nice drawers," she said dryly.

I turned around to make a snide retort, but Berta's startled face stopped me in my tracks.

"What?" I asked.

"I hope you packed some aloe, kid. You're fried to a crisp."

Chapter Four

I've always been one of those annoying morning people. But I came by it honest. I spent the best part of my childhood in a place most people never noticed, even when they were driving right through it. Greenville, Florida was where my Grandma Violet and Grandpa Hue built their family farm back in the 1930s.

As a kid, I'd spent every summer there since I was old enough to remember. That was where I'd learned to pull my own weight. At the farm, as soon as a kid could walk, he or she'd get a list of chores to do. The summer when I was seven, the job had fallen to me to get up early and snatch a dozen warm brown eggs from under extremely suspecting hen's bottoms. Grandma would fry them up, two at a time, and serve them with grits and buttermilk biscuits. Grandpa, Pa for short, was always the first to get served. We kids never tired of laughing at Grandma Violet's joke when she'd say, "I'm fixin' to make possum eggs."

I loved the farm, but not farm boys. My starter marriage to Ricky Benjamin had gone south quicker than an autumn goose on the *Concord*. I'd filed for divorce *and* to get my maiden name back. It'd hardly seemed worth it to have to carry around a reminder of a union that hadn't lasted any longer than a tube of toothpaste.

I wasn't the first in my family to get divorced, but I *was* the first to run off to college afterward. The choice to get a higher education had set me apart from my family in ways I'd never expected. When

I moved to Tampa to attend university, in their eyes, I'd become a "fancy person." After I graduated, they'd started treating me oddly, like I was some kind of traitorous reality-show celebrity or something. Six years later, when I'd married Jimmy Johnson and kept my last name, my Aunt Patsy had held a prayer vigil for my soul. Going to Italy last fall had jet-propelled me to the status of "international fancy person." That time, even my cousin Tammy was jealous.

AT THE FIRST HINT OF morning light, my mind revved to life, in full gear, like it had since I was a child. "What's on the to-do list today?" my grey matter would ask. For the first time in forever, I didn't have much of an answer.

By 6:30 a.m., despite my sunburn, I'd already showered, ironed my yucky, coffee-stained blouse, and wriggled into my rinsed-out panties and skirt. I'd also snuck outside and spent an hour sitting on the rocks across the street from the hotel, staring out at the friendly Ty-D-Bol sea. I was grateful for the cool wind blowing across the water. It eased the throbbing heat that pulsed from my nuclear-red face, hands and the fronts of my legs.

With nothing but a buttered roll and a glass of wine for dinner last night, my throat ached from hunger. Italy was six hours ahead of Florida, so it was only half-past midnight back home. But my stomach didn't care.

The night clerk was exactly where he'd been when I'd snuck out an hour earlier. Dressed in an olive-green suit, the slim young man lay sprawled out on a black leather couch like a drunken wedding guest. I took a seat across from the couch and waited for him to wake up. He snored like a buzz saw. My empty stomach growled like a pit bull. At precisely 7:03, I couldn't stand it any longer. I woke him up by clearing my throat. Loudly.

"Ahem...." I grunted.

The man snuffled mid-snore, then opened one bleary eye. He looked at me, puzzled, as if he was wondering how I'd gotten into his dream. He blinked and looked at me again. To his disappointment, I was still there. He sat up and rubbed his eyes. I gave him my best apologetic look and tried out the Italian I'd been practicing all morning.

"*Mi dispiache*," I said. "Prego, cappuccino?"

He looked at me as if he hoped it was a scherzo. When he realized I was serious, he forced a weak smile and bobbed his head once. With Herculean effort, he dragged himself off the couch and stumbled toward the coffee counter. I followed behind him, my Southern guilt only slightly overruled by hunger. I stood at the barista bar and smiled so brightly at the poor guy he squinted as if to escape the glare.

He ran his fingers through his thick, dark hair and sighed. Then he turned and studied the huge, copper-and-steel contraption behind the counter. Finally, he began working the controls on the monstrous, hissing, mechanical beast. Like a mad scientist, he pulled a lever, scratched his chin, twisted a piece of the machine loose, pushed his hair out of his eyes, dumped grounds in the trash, coughed, rattled some dishes, bit his fingernail, turned a dial that sent out a jet of steam, cursed under his breath, scooped foam from a small stainless steel pitcher, sucked on his scalded thumb, and sprinkled something from a shaker.

With an apologetic shrug, the young man handed me a large, steaming white cup perched on a saucer. As I reached for it, he looked at it with a dissatisfied scowl and pulled the cup back from my greedy hands. He set it next to the hissing machine and squatted down behind the counter. A moment later, he popped back up like a disheveled Whack-a-Mole. He dropped a small, hard cookie onto the saucer and handed back the steaming cup of cappuccino.

"*Gratzie mille*," I said.

"Prego," the poor night clerk mumbled.

He tugged on his jacket lapel proudly, then he shot me a crooked, pleading smile. He motioned with his head toward the couch. I smiled and nodded. He winked tiredly, then lumbered silently back to the couch. Before my cappuccino was cool enough to sip, he was snoring again.

AT PRECISELY 7:30 A.m., the door to the hotel restaurant opened for breakfast. I knew this fact because I'd been circling it like a vulture for fifteen minutes. A rather surprised-looking, fifty-something waiter appeared, wearing a black suit and a nametag that read Giuseppe. He ushered me to a table covered in white linen. A placard at the center designated it for the WOW volunteers.

I took a seat and watched other patrons trickle in. Oddly, all the other guests were men. Most dressed in business suits. Breakfast was buffet style. A beautiful selection of breads, cheeses, cold cuts, fruits and cereals taunted me from a long, rectangular table in the middle of the dining room. In one corner stood a juice dispensing machine and an automatic coffee machine. While the men helped themselves to the buffet and juice, I noticed no one went near the coffee machine. Instead, they ordered their coffee from Giuseppe. I followed their lead.

"*Per favore. Uno cappuccino*, Giuseppe."

The sagging waiter puffed up like a pool float attached to an air compressor.

"Prego, Signora."

Giuseppe nodded sharply, turned on his heels and left.

"Good choice," said a blond man sporting a pair of dark-framed glasses. I gave him a quick smile and nod.

Giuseppe returned a minute later. With fanfare akin to presenting a fine bottle of champagne, he set before me a cup brimming with steamy white froth. Atop the foam, in cocoa powder, was the shape of a heart.

"*Bennissimo*, Giuseppe!"

I picked up my cup and raised a toast to the waiter. The guy in the glasses did the same, and mouthed the word *cheers*. I looked around and saw six other businessmen staring at me. A couple of them were kind of cute. *Hmmm. Maybe I really* am *a catch in Italy....*

"Hiya, beetroot!"

Tina's sharp, Jersey accent yanked me out of my Italian daydream with all the subtlety of a needle scratching through a vinyl record.

"What?"

"Sorry to say it, gal, but your face is as red as a baboon's ass. And that hairdo ain't helpin' your case."

Aww, crap! I blushed, not that anyone could tell. *So that's why the men were staring.*

"Thanks for the beauty tips," I said sourly.

Tina laughed. "Yeah. No prob. Any luggage yet?"

I shook my head.

"That's a bummer."

Val II was the next to appear. She studied my sorry state with an evil gleam in her eye.

"My goodness. Look at the state of you. Has your luggage not yet arrived?"

"No."

As each volunteer straggled to the breakfast table, I had to answer the same question over and over again.

"Has your luggage arrived yet?" Berta asked.

"No."

I guess it was one of those idiotic questions everyone felt compelled to ask. Still, I began to wonder. *Did they actually think I would have worn this outfit again if my luggage was here?*

"Hasn't your luggage arrived yet?" Frank complained, as if it was my fault.

The question grew more inane and annoying with every asking. I was about to get huffy, but then my empty stomach gurgled like a fart in a mud puddle. I got up and made a beeline for the buffet.

I chose a big, fluffy croissant, a ball of fresh mozzarella, and two delicately thin slices of prosciutto ham. Local jams and fancy-looking cakes were also on offer, but I didn't have much of a sweet tooth at breakfast time. I also wasn't tempted by the granola and corn flakes in glass jars next to huge pitchers of milk. *Corn flakes? With all these local delicacies to choose from, who in the world would pick cereal?*

We were halfway through breakfast when tall, lanky Peter finally made his appearance.

"Hey Val, did you get your luggage yet?"

"No." I sighed.

Peter sniggered. "*My* bags were the first ones off the plane."

It was official. Peter had the social skills of...*an IRS accountant.*

AT TEN AFTER EIGHT, Monica Mozzarelli arrived to take the first group of volunteers to their assigned schools. We broke breakfast with plans to meet in the lobby at 1 p.m. for lunch. I headed to the front desk to check on my missing bags. As I stood in line to speak to Antonio, a firm hand squeezed me on the shoulder. I turned to find Frank staring at me. He tapped a sausage-like finger on his wristwatch.

"We're late," he barked. "Let's get going."

"I don't think the lady should go, looking like that," interrupted Ms. Mozzarelli.

"I would have to concur," Val II said in a snotty tone. "You really should try to do something about your appearance."

I stood there, totally humiliated and mad as a hornet. My frizzy, brown hair looked like an afro caught in a hailstorm. My sunburned face and legs glowed like hot coals. My shirt was blotchy with nasty-looking coffee stains. At crotch level, a wet spot soaked through my crumpled brown skirt from my damp underwear.

I had become the incontinent bag lady from Mars.

Even Frank had to begrudgingly agree with Ms. Mozzarelli's assessment.

"Okay," he grumbled. "You're off the hook. But just for today."

"Thank you, sir," I said.

Val II shook her Botox head at me in disgust. I turned back toward the front desk. The hotel manager, Antonio, didn't need to ask why I was there.

"*Mi dispiache*, Signora Val. No luggage for you today."

The slim, elegant man in the expensive, charcoal-grey suit offered me the kind of empathetic expression usually reserved for lost kittens.

"Tomorrow, yes," he said, unconvincingly. His eyes moved down to a guest receipt on the counter. He began to study it as if it were the secret treasure map of the lost continent of Atlantis.

I pulled up my damp, big-girl panties and focused my attention on Antonio like a mooching dog watching the last bite of pork chop head for its owner's mouth. I knew if I was ever going to see my luggage again, I needed an Italian champion on my side. I smiled at the handsome man like a cat charming its prey.

"Ahem, Antonio."

The poor guy looked up from his paperwork and jumped when he realized I was still there. His startled face slowly transformed into the doomed expression of a man who'd just told his wife she didn't look *too* fat in her new dress. I stifled a snicker. Grandma Violet taught me I could catch more flies with honey than turpentine, so I laid on the Southern charm. To be honest, I also didn't want to give Val II the satisfaction of seeing me upset.

"I lost my sweater this morning," I said with a laugh. "If this keeps up, by the end of the week I'll be naked and penniless!"

Antonio studied me curiously. When he realized I wasn't angry, he let his well-guarded professionalism slip. He eyed me questioningly and said, "*No capire*...uh...I don't understand."

"Huh?"

"I don't understand why you still a smile." He tilted his head and eyed me as if I had something he might want.

"I'm on vacation, I'm in Italy, and the sun is shining," I explained, pouring on the syrup while Val II was watching. "What more do I need to be happy?"

Antonio sucked his teeth and looked at me skeptically.

"The only thing that could make me happier than staying at your wonderful hotel would be to find my luggage," I pandered. I smiled cheerfully at the suave, dark-haired man.

Antonio drew in a great breath, held it in for a second, and blew it out noisily. His head dropped down for a moment. When he looked up again, his face had taken on the resigned look of a man ready to do battle.

"Okay. I help you," he said, looking as if he already regretted his words.

AFTER FOUR HOURS OF waiting around on a couch as Antonio engaged in heated phone discussions in Italian, he finally hung up the phone and motioned for me to come up to the desk.

"I have found one of your bags. It will be delivered to the hotel tomorrow."

"Gratzie mille!" I cheered. I wanted to hug my handsome hero, but I didn't think it was local protocol.

Antonio looked at me wearily, wiped fake sweat from his brow and smiled dutifully.

"Prego, Signora."

I glanced at the clock above the front desk. It was a few minutes before 1 p.m. I thanked Antonio again and took a seat in one of the square black chairs to wait for the rest of the volunteers to pick me up for lunch. It turned out to be another long wait.

At 2:45, the volunteer group finally appeared through the lobby's glass, double-doored entryway. I stood up. When they spotted me, the looks on their faces said it all. Berta and Tina looked mortified.

"Were you *waiting* for us?" Berta asked.

"Um...yes."

"Val II said you weren't coming. Sorry," Tina apologized.

"It's okay. I'll survive."

I looked over at Val II. She was walking in the door with Frank. She shot me a smile as fake as her boobs. I decided to fake it as well. I threw back my head and laughed.

"I guess I'm the foil in an Italian comedy of errors," I giggled.

Val II sneered. But my cheerful act was more than Antonio could bear.

"How can you laugh?" he demanded of me. "You have nothing but the clothes on your body. No sweater. Not even any food. Yet you laugh. This is impossible. *I* take you to lunch. *Basta!*"

Before I could open my mouth to speak, a man who'd just walked up next to me said, "I'll take her to lunch."

Antonio flashed a dark glance at the man. Something akin to rivalry registered in the handsome manager's eyes for a second, then faded. I wondered what had caused his change of heart. Was it something to do with this other man? Or could it be that Antonio suddenly remembered his wife, who was standing right behind him? In either case, Antonio hesitated for only a split second before speaking.

"Of course, Friedrich. *You* take her to lunch."

I turned to face this man, Friedrich. He was not Italian. He was blond and fair skinned, and about six inches taller than me. His square face was unreadable. His thin-lipped mouth neither smiled nor frowned. His ice-cool, blue eyes would have made any poker professional proud. The man made me a little nervous, but hunger had yet again weakened my resolve.

I looked over at Antonio for reassurance. His handsome face softened into a quick smile and a nod. On the other hand, Val II's eyes had turned venomous.

I turned back to the stranger and said, "Okay."

He took off his dark-framed glasses and said, "Come with me."

For the second time in two days, I followed a strange man out of my comfort zone and into his car. This time, however, the car was a shiny, silver Peugeot convertible, and the man was under seventy years old. Friedrich turned the key in the ignition and we were off.

"HI, I'M VAL JOLLY," I said as I buckled myself in.

The forty-something man shot me a quick glance. "Friedrich Fremden," he offered matter-of-factly. He shifted gears and pulled out of the hotel driveway.

"I'm sorry about the way I look," I apologized.

Friedrich kept his eyes on the road. "Why?"

I opened my mouth to say something, but couldn't come up with a word.

"I think you look good," he said. "I don't know how you will be when you are all puffed up."

"Uh...thanks."

"What would you like to eat?" he asked, switching the topic like a radio dial.

"Uh...pizza? Anything, really."

Friedrich nodded. His right hand worked automatically, shifting gears. He drove without hesitation. It was obvious he was familiar with the streets and the layout of the town. He even knew when it was time to dodge the local potholes. A few minutes later, we arrived at a restaurant just in time to see a kid change the sign on the front door from *aperto* to *chiuso*. Closed.

Great. Another joke on me. I mustered a sarcastic laugh. It earned me half a smile from Friedrich.

"Why don't we go to Alberobello," he suggested.

"Sure. Why not?"

Friedrich maneuvered his little convertible out of the parking lot, shifted gears and hit the gas. A few minutes later, the bustling little city of Brindisi fell away behind us. The land opened up to sweeping swaths of green pastures dotted with giant, brown rolls of harvested hay. It reminded me of the fields outside Greenville, but there they'd grown corn and soybeans, not hay.

The breeze blew through my rat's nest tangle of hair. I untied my horrid ponytail and let my wavy brown hair fly free. We drove past gentle swells of coffee-colored earth planted with ancient olive trees. Rustic farmhouses and leafy vineyards came into view and quickly faded as we sped by. The country air smelled of rain and fresh figs. The sky was a brilliant, clear blue and the early-afternoon sun beat down brutally on my already roasted face and hands.

I fished around in my purse for some sunscreen and slathered it on my face and arms. I started to do the same for Friedrich, but when I touched his arm, he stiffened like a department store mannequin. It made me freeze, too.

"I'm sorry! Did you not want—"

"It's okay," he apologized. He fumbled for words. "It has...been...much time before someone had...touched me."

His honesty took me by surprise. As I gently smoothed the cream onto his forearms, I unexpectedly had to fight back tears. I knew just how he felt. I, too, missed the comfort of human contact. I wondered how long it had been for Friedrich.

"Where are you from?" I asked.

"Germany," he said.

"Oh! I'm from—"

"America," he blurted. "I think I am safe to say it."

I smirked. "That obvious, huh?"

"Ja," he said, then smiled and shrugged. "The volunteer groups at the hotel. Mostly Americans."

"Oh. We're not the first group at the hotel then?"

"That's a *trulli*," Friedrich said, ignoring my question. He pointed as we sped past a round, white house capped with a cone-shaped roof made of stacked, grey slate. "And *that* is Alberobello."

I turned to face forward. Straight ahead, at the top of a hill, lay a magical city made of round dollops of merengue, their tops dipped in grey. The pointy, grey roofs of stacked slate stones shone like rickety crowns against the robin's-egg, blue sky. I'd had no idea such a place existed beyond the pages of a fairytale. I caught my breath and stared.

Alberobello grew even lovelier as we drove into its center. Each small, gleaming, whitewashed house had its own hobbit-like personality. Some were adorned with strange symbols on their roofs. Others had pots of red geraniums in the windowsills. A couple of them displayed quaint, hand-painted shop signs advertising the wares of bakers and butchers. Still others nestled among the shadows of prehistoric-looking olive trees, dwarfed by their massive trunks as big-around as tables and as twisted as rope.

Friedrich shifted his convertible into an empty spot and tucked a parking pass that looked like a lottery scratch-off onto the dashboard. Like a man on a mission, he marched us quickly past the main street lined with tacky tourist shops filled with tacky tourists buying tacky tourist souvenirs.

My disillusionment over the commercialism quickly evaporated as I followed the determined German up a narrow side street. We snaked by clusters of trulli houses with cute, beckoning doorways guarded by lazy cats and huge clay pots bursting with flowering plants. As we wound our way uphill, my kitten-heeled sandals proved no match for the cobblestones.

"Could you slow down, please, Friedrich?" I pleaded.

"Turn around," he commanded.

I panicked for a second. *Did he think I was complaining? Was he was ready to put me back in the car and take me to the hotel?*

I studied his face quickly. All I could discern was a mild, scientific interest—like a botanist inspecting an interesting species of orchid. But he wasn't inspecting me. His eyes were on something over my head. I turned around. The view took my breath away.

From our vantage point on the top of the hill, the entire town of Alberobello lay before us like a gigantic, white honeycomb of houses. The effect was that of hundreds of slate-topped trullis nested safely aboard a grey raft of cobblestone streets, set adrift in a sea of silver olive trees, surrounded by purple mountains and mist.

"Bellissimo," I whispered.

Friedrich smiled fully for the first time.

"You are hungry, yes?" he asked.

"I'm famished!"

"And that means...yes?"

I'd forgotten! English was Friedrich's second language. *Or was it his third? Or fourth?*

"Si, that *definitely* means yes. I'm hungry."

"Pizza now?"

"Perfecto," I said, hoping it was a real Italian word.

Chapter Five

I woke, yawned, and looked at the clock. *Crap.* It was only 5 a.m. Still, what a difference a day can make! After the drive to Alberobello with Friedrich yesterday, he'd dropped me off at a boutique in the center of Brindisi. I'd bought a pair of white Capri pants with black floral stitching and a black top with sequin bling. It was the most sedate outfit I could find that actually fit me. When I tried it on, a man in the shop had told me I looked very Italian. I took this as a compliment, as he was a handsome man and I was doing my best to keep any and all vain fantasies alive.

Friedrich had drawn me a map with directions back to the hotel. He'd explained that it was simple—just one turn to make. But I'd insisted on the map anyway. It hadn't been worth the risk.

On my way back from the boutique to the hotel, I'd found a small shop selling toothbrushes and sundries. I'd stocked up on aloe lotion, razors, deodorant, mouthwash and toothpaste. Then I'd gone home and scrubbed my teeth and tackled the forest of hair on my legs and armpits. Afterwards, I'd stood on my balcony in the purple twilight, wearing nothing but a towel. *Scandalous!* I'd watched an incredible moon come up from beneath the sea. The warm wind had caressed my neck like a lover's breath. Or maybe it was just the sunburn....

I stretched in the bed like a cat, then smiled at my new outfit. It was laid out, waiting for me on the chair beside the bathroom door.

This morning the hotel room was full of a delicate, purple light. I got out of bed and stood on the balcony, naked, looking out at the sea. *Take that, Tammy Jeter!* I watched the violet morning sky fade to pink, its color whisked away on the cool, gentle breeze that fluttered the lacey white curtains hanging on either side of the terrace's French doors.

The sea was calmer this morning. As the sun began to crack the horizon, strange, shadowy lumps appeared in the water. As the light grew stronger, the lumps slowly took on the shapes of a dozen or so small boats, each piloted by a one-man crew. On shore, I could see a man flailing his arm up and down repeatedly. Curious, I got dressed in my new outfit *(and sexy new panties and bra, yay!)* and went down to investigate.

I snuck past the sleeping night clerk, who was passed out in a pinstriped suit on the lobby couch. One of his long legs hung over the back of the sofa. One slim brown hand touched the floor. As I passed by, he grunted, then farted. I slapped my hand over my mouth to keep from bursting out laughing. I snickered and choked and nearly strangled to death as I scurried past him to the exit door.

I managed to make it outside before I fell into a complete giggle fit. But my smile faded like a jug-eared boy's dreams when I tried to put on my sandals. After five days in the same shoes, my kitten heels had matured into full grown tigers. They gnawed cruelly at my toes and the back of my heels. I slipped them on half way and hobbled like a drunk across the cobblestone street to the rocky beach. As soon as I hit the golden sand, I flung them off like they were full of hot coals.

I picked my way over to my favorite boulder. I started to climb it when I heard a strange, intermittent, slapping noise coming from behind the rocks to my right. I scrambled over a huge white stone for a look. A man's tan, sinewy arm rose up from behind a boulder, startling me. A second later, it came down hard, like a karate chop. *Slap!*

I crept a little closer. The arm came up again. This time I could see the hand held a wad of slimy-looking stuff. I clattered over another set of rocks as the arm went down again. *Slap!* I could hear the man softly singing under his breath. I peeked around the last boulder concealing him from view. *Slap!*

The man was deeply tanned and as lean as a racing greyhound. He wore nothing but a tattered pair of light-yellow cotton shorts faded from the sun. He stooped to pick up something. When he stood up again, his six-pack abs caught my full attention. When I finally drew my eyes from his stomach to his face, he was smiling at me. I cringed. In his right hand was a squirming mass of white-and-pink flesh right out of a bad sci-fi movie.

"*Bon giorno*, Signora!" he said heartily. He waved with his free hand, then threw the glob of wriggling goo against a boulder. *Slap!*

I watched, open mouthed, as a freshly dead octopus slid down the massive rock.

The octopus fisherman held up his bucket to show me his catch. The pail was alive with writhing, greyish-white arms covered in light-pink and purple tentacles. It was impossible to say how many octopi were in the bucket. But then again, I guess it didn't matter. I smiled back at the ripped hunk in short-shorts. Having nothing better to do, I decided to stay and gawk awhile.

I took a seat on a boulder. This guy performed his task as elegantly and efficiently as a magician. Once each battered octopus was dead, the hunky fisherman quickly and efficiently removed its beak and innards in one movement, never missing a beat in the tune he sang. The gutted octopi went in one bucket, the inedible parts in another. The Adonis in skivvies was gorgeous enough to make the gross-out worth it. I pointed to the innards bucket and shrugged curiously.

"*Per domani*," he said.

I looked up the words in my trusty phrasebook. *For tomorrow.* Ha! He was saving the leftover parts for bait to catch tomorrow's octopi. What a brilliant, waste-less system! I imagined the fishermen before him had probably been doing this same thing for centuries. Man against the sea in a one-on-one, personal relationship. No commercial equipment. No greed. No excess. This man was taking only what he needed to get by for the day. And that was enough for him.

The whole scene reminded me of something I'd witnessed with Clarice outside Rome last fall. The olives had been ripening then. The Italians had tied nets under the trees to catch the fruits. They didn't shake the trees or pick the olives with machines like we did back home with the oranges. Instead, they just let them fall into the nets when they were good and ready. This harvesting method seemed more like a gift from nature than the taking of a crop. So totally different from commercial farms in the States!

I was witnessing first-hand Italy's live-and-let-live philosophy. It was reflected in everything from the attitudes of the people to the rich flavors of the food.

Oh, the food! My mouth watered as I recalled last night's dinner of impossibly red tomatoes bursting with sweet, salty juice. Plump, tender shrimp fragrant with the delicate smell of the sea. Fresh figs alive with the delicious, subtle taste of the sun and soil. *Mmmmm.*

My stomach growled so loud the yummy fisherman looked up at me in mock surprise. I smiled sheepishly and checked the time on my phone. It was 6:32 a.m.

Oh no! I still had another hour before the hotel restaurant opened. Thank goodness for the distracting hunk in a loincloth. I sat and studied the fisherman as he worked. The muscles in his long, lean legs rippled every time he took a step. When he bent over to wash his elegant, strapping arms in the sea, I nearly swooned at the sight of his cute butt.

"*Allora,* Signora, *mi chiamo Dominik,*" said the dreamy fisherman.

His strange words caught me off guard. He took my hand in his and kissed the back of it with his full, luscious lips. I stared at him, speechless.

"Me Dominik," he tried again. He pointed a thumb at his chest like he was Tarzan.

"Me Val," I stuttered, wishing I was Jane.

"*Ah. Point Amento,*" said Dominik. He pointed in the direction of a small strip of land jutting out in the sea. A small, kiosk-like restaurant was nearby. "See? A *Point Amento.*"

"Oh. Point Amento? It's pretty," I nodded and smiled.

Dominik smiled back and kissed my hand again. He pointed to his watch and shrugged.

"*Otto, bella* Signora. *Arrivederchi!*"

Dominik grabbed his buckets of octopi and innards and waded back to the small boat he'd anchored nearby. I watched his tan, sinewy muscles gleam in the morning light as he pulled the starter and waved one more time before motoring away in the Ty D Bol sea, just like the Ty D Bol guy in the commercials.

GIUSEPPE THE WAITER winked at me as I took a sip of cappuccino. Friedrich nodded at me from his table across the room. I smiled smugly and watched the other WOW volunteers line up at the automatic coffee machine. *Hmmm. Maybe I really am an "international fancy person"!*

"So, you took a little trip yesterday," Val II said snidely as she approached the table. Her injection-deadened face was hard to read, but it appeared to be frozen on disapproval. "That's pretty irresponsible, if you ask me."

"Yeah, well no one's asking," said Tina, walking up behind her.

The two began arguing in front of me as if I weren't there.

"How rude!" Val II said.

"*I'm* the rude one? Listen, lipo-lady, we know you're the one who caused Val to miss out on lunch yesterday. Stop being a witch. We're here on vacation trying to have fun here!"

"I'm only concerned for Val's welfare. I just don't think it's safe for her to go driving off with that strange man. It's not proper!"

"And fake boobs are? Listen, Red. This ain't the nineteen fifties anymore."

"I'm not *that* old!"

"Maybe not. But you *are* old."

"You know what, screw you, you...*tattooed circus girl!*"

"Yes, very classy of you," Tina said snidely.

Val II left in a huff. Tina took a seat beside me with her paper cup full of crappy coffee. She spoke to me as if her catfight with Val II had never happened.

"Okay, so spill the beans, Val. Where'd you go with Friedrich yesterday? Did you have some *fun?*" She wagged her eyebrows lasciviously.

"Yes. But first, tell me. What's your beef with Ms. Botox?"

"She treats everybody like dirt. She's a witch."

"True."

"Isn't that reason enough?"

I couldn't help but grin. "Yeah. I guess so."

"So, how was your trip with dashing Friedrich?"

"To be honest, I had a blast! Friedrich and I went to this village called Alberobello. Tina, the countryside out here is drop-dead gorgeous. I mean, the whole country looks like it was *made* for romance! And Alberobello? Amazing! The town was full of trullis, these strange little cone-topped houses."

"*Truly*, now," Tina joked. "Was it worth the trip?"

"Absolutely!"

"Maybe I'll check out those trullis myself," Berta said. "I've got a day off coming up."

She sat down beside me, took a sip of her coffee-machine brew and grimaced.

"Yuck. Nothing good ever came out of a vending machine. So what did the trullis look like, Val?"

"They kind of looked like white Hershey's Kisses. They were round at the base. Pointed at the top. The roofs were made of this greyish-colored slate, like upside-down ice-cream cones."

"Sounds sweet," cracked Berta. "Do all of your analogies involve dessert foods?"

The skinny old woman studied me coyly, as if trying to discern whether I had a fetish for Little Debbie snack cakes. I made a sneering face at her until she grinned.

"Friedrich told me that back in the Middle Ages, the roofs on the trullis used to have a rope around their top capping stones. He said that back then, taxes were collected based on the number of rooms under a roof. When word came around that the tax collector was on his way, people pulled the ropes on the capstones and the roofs collapsed."

"That's a novel way to reduce your taxes," Peter said, interrupting my story. "But I don't think I would try it back home. Sorry I'm late, gang. I engaged in a fifteen-minute nap augmentation process."

Berta eyed Peter as if he were from some strange, distant galaxy. I'd begun to wonder the same myself.

"We should check it out, kid," Berta said to Tina. She bit into a croissant. Her wrinkly face registered ecstasy.

"I'll check the bus schedule," Tina offered. "Or maybe this *Friedrich* guy can give us a lift."

Tina smiled at me suggestively. I grinned.

"Ha ha, Tina," I said. "Uh oh! Here comes trouble."

Val II came marching back in the room with Frank in tow.

"They've been talking about taking a trip to Alberto...something or other...*on their own*, Frank! I told them I think we should stick with authorized transportation!" Val II shot Tina and me another disapproving glare. "I told them we should make *proper* arrangements with Ms. Mozzarelli when she arrives."

"I think that's an excellent idea, Ms. Finnegan," Frank said. He glared as us like Val II's evil, comb-over henchman.

"We'll discuss this later, ladies," Frank said. "You. Val. Let's go. We're walking to school, so we need to get an early start."

"Okay. Just let me finish my cappuccino."

"We don't have time."

"But...."

Frank's disapproving glare got darker. "Let's go," he repeated, and started walking toward the door.

"Let him go," Tina said. "Who needs him?"

"Unfortunately, I do," I said, getting up from my chair. "Without him, I'd never find my way there and back."

"I think you'd do just fine without him," Berta said.

I looked over at the old woman. She was dressed in a pantsuit the color of lemon curd.

"Thank you, Berta. But I can get lost inside a closet."

"Can't we all," the old woman replied dryly. "Can't we all."

WE'D BARELY ROUNDED the corner of hotel, but I could already swear that Frank had diabolical plans to take over the *Scuola de Technico*.

"I have a lesson plan prepared," he explained as we walked. "I think it's time these kids learned some discipline."

"Why? What happened yesterday?" I asked.

"It's a zoo in there. The teacher doesn't even *try* to make them behave."

"Really!" My mind raced. I wondered how bad it could possibly be.

"You'll see soon enough. We're almost there. Follow me."

Frank climbed a flight of stairs and marched down a dimly lit hallway painted industrial green. He turned left and we arrived at Room 301.

"Ladies first," he said sarcastically.

I opened the door and my eyes popped out of my skull like a pug jabbed in the butt with a poker. Spaced out in rows like the most exquisite selection of gourmet chocolates imaginable, was an assortment of drop-dead gorgeous Italian men in their early twenties. I could *smell* the testosterone.

"Class, this is Signora Val," said the teacher, jarring me from my stupor. I tried to focus on just one of the future romance novel covers, but the buffet was too enticing. One luscious face after another....

A cacophony of ciaos, salutes and, to my great surprise, cat calls rang out. The over-enthusiastic welcome sent me shriveling like a hermit crab into my shell. I was flabbergasted! I raised a limp hand and waved lamely back at the pack of fledgling Fabios. The room suddenly grew stiflingly warm. I felt a trickle of sweat run down my back.

"Basta, enough!" yelled the plump, tired-looking woman in a too-tight dress. That seemed to be the local fashion. "Class, you already know Mr. Frank."

A less enthusiastic mumble of greetings emanated from the group. Frank pursed his lips, obviously ticked off. He started to say something, then stopped and stared, his mouth hung open in mid-syllable. I followed his stare.

Marching up to the front of the room was one of the gorgeous young men, a metal chair in his hands. The dark-haired Adonis flashed me a heart-melting smile and motioned with an elegant flourish for me to sit down. When I graciously accepted, the other young men actually broke out into applause.

Oh my word! I feel like Sophia Loren! Italy is turning out to be heaven on Earth for frump-a-dumps like me! Maybe one of these boys has a cute, single dad....

"Okay class. Today we continue our reading assignments," barked the weary teacher. "Marco, you start."

A daydream in tight Italian jeans and a pink polo shirt stood up. He cradled his book like a baby and smiled at me shyly. He looked down at his worn-out textbook and began to read aloud.

"I haf a beard dat sanks owsigh my windoo."

Frank and I definitely had our work cut out for us. I smiled at the sweet, handsome kid. *I guess I can find some way to suffer through it....*

AFTER LISTENING TO Frank bellyache the whole way back from class, I arrived at the Hotel Bella Vista to some good news and some bad news.

"Signora Val, your baggage has arrived," Antonio said with a smile.

"*Yes!*"

I jumped up and down with excitement as he went to fetch it. When he wheeled it out, my hopes sunk a little bit. It was my brown checked carry-on bag. I was going to have to wait a little longer for fresh clothes. But at least I finally had makeup and a good hairbrush.

"Gratzie mille." I beamed at Antonio.

"*Mi dispiache,*" he said apologetically. "It is only one a small baggage."

"That's okay," I said encouragingly. "My walking shoes are in there, Antonio. And comfortable shoes are as hard to find as good friends."

"*Va bene,*" Antonio said. His worried face melted into a smile. "*This* I know is true!"

I started to leave, then I remembered I had a question for him. "Antonio, where is Point Amento?"

"Point Amento? I never hear of it."

Antonio knitted his elegant eyebrows together and tapped an index finger on his chin. "Point Amento. Point Amento. A Point Amento." His face brightened. "Ah! *Appuntamento!* Signora Val. Appuntamento is what you in America...you call a...*date.*"

My stomach flopped.

"And otto? What does that mean?"

"It is the number eight, of course."

"Okay. Thanks, Antonio."

I wheeled my carry-on bag across the lobby toward the elevator, my mind a mishmash of conflicting thoughts. Just like with that kid in the classroom, I'd barely understood a word Dominik had said this morning. He'd kept repeating something about Point Amento. Could he have said appuntamento? I hadn't understood him, so I'd just done the polite Southern thing and smiled and nodded amicably.

Nodded amicably! Oh no! Had I unwittingly agreed to go on a date with Dominik tonight? At eight? No! It couldn't be! Maybe Dominik meant he had a date with someone else at eight. What if I showed up like a stupid, third-wheel American jerk? Or what if I didn't go? Would that be rude? What if I went and he wasn't there? What if I went and he was there! Did he want to...Oh, crap on a cracker!

I'd been raised Southern Baptist. It had been hardwired into me as a child that sex without marriage made Jesus cry. As an adult, I'd come to think that maybe Jesus didn't bother himself about such things. Still, a verse drummed into me at Sunday school always popped into my mind when I least wanted it to: *To flirt is fine. But to touch? Not divine!*

Dang it! Why did my guilt programming have to run so deep? I'm forty-one years old, for crying out loud!

I was here for romance and re-creation. If I was going to have a chance at either, I was going to have to override my old software. Considering how invisible to men I'd felt over the last few years, it had been easy to avoid bumping into the issue. But since I'd been in Italy, it kept hitting me in the face like a mean clown with a cream pie. *Could it really be possible that a woman like me was still attractive? Desirable? Sexy?*

Even though it had all been in good fun, the open admiration shown to me by the young men in the classroom this morning had unnerved me a little. The thought of actually meeting up with Dominik was about to send me into full-blown panic mode! The devil on my shoulder wanted to jump his bones. The angel on my other shoulder showed me a picture of a harlot burning in hell. It was a full-on, "bang-bang 'em or boo-hoo 'em" showdown at the O.K. Corral.

What should I do? I hadn't been out on a first date since cell phones were the size of shoeboxes. I was about to have a nervous breakdown when, in the nick of time, I thought up a brilliant plan. I smiled to myself, stepped into the tiny elevator and pushed the button for my floor.

Yes. I'll just sneak down there and hide so he can't see me! If Dominik isn't there, or if he's with someone else, I'll turn around and come back before he sees me. The hotel isn't but two or three blocks away. I can do that. Yes. That could work. But wait! What if he's actually there? Waiting for me. All by himself? What then?

A fresh bolt of panic shot through me. The elevator walls closed in, trapping me like an animal in a cage. I forced myself to breathe slowly and deeply. *Calm down, Val. You're a grown woman. You can do this. What's the worst that could happen?*

The elevator doors opened and Tina stepped in.

"Have you heard the news, Val?"

"No. What?"

"There's a psycho killer on the loose in Italy."

I SNUCK OUT OF THE lobby at precisely 7:25 p.m. I wanted to avoid having to make small talk or answer nosy questions from the other volunteers. They'd be coming down to the lobby for dinner any minute. Antonio was the only one to spot me making my clandestine getaway. He discreetly wagged one eyebrow at me as I slipped out the door.

Tina's news about the strangler had taken me off my game, if I ever had one to begin with. I glanced around wildly as I picked my way along the cobblestone street toward the tiny kiosk Dominik had pointed toward this morning. From a distance, its windows glowed like candlelight in the fading twilight. I wore my only outfit—the white capris and black sequined top. My sexy new bra dug into my sides and the underwear kept crawling up my butt. Still, with make-up and halfway decent hair, I felt presentable enough to ante up if the deal actually went down.

I crept along in the shadows like a private detective in a cheap novella. I hadn't spotted Dominik yet, but flop-sweat was already dampening my pits and palms. I wasn't sure what I hoped for more—that Dominik would be there, or that he *wouldn't*.

I found a spot to hide behind a parked car and waited. At five minutes to eight, the dreamboat fisherman with the ripped abs strolled up to the kiosk. *Alone.* Dressed in a silky white shirt and tight jeans, he looked like a slick, dating-site Romeo as he leaned against a corner of the kiosk and lit a cigarette. I took a deep breath and forced myself out into the open.

"*Ciao bella,*" Dominik said when he spotted me. His white-toothed smile seemed to glow in the dark.

"*Buona Sera,*" I replied.

Dominik took my hand and kissed it as he had earlier in the day. I could feel the electric warmth of his body as he took my arm and drew me closer to him. Without a word, he led me toward the shore-line thirty feet away. He sat on a boulder and motioned for me to sit, too. When I chose the boulder next to his, he laughed softly.

"You pretty woman," he said, in his Tarzan way. He got up and sat next to me, so close that our thighs touched. He smiled again and pointed at the moon. "Bella, no?"

I looked up at the glowing orb and felt Dominik's soft, warm lips begin to nibble on my neck. My body went limp. Dominik took my chin in his strong, rough hand and gently turned my face toward his. Before I could say anything, his mouth was on mine. I couldn't re-member *ever* being kissed like *that*. It was fantastic. And terrifying. It was *fantastically terrifying!*

"Um...are you thirsty?" I asked, interrupting Dominik's second lip-lock attempt. I was in way-way over my head and needed to catch my breath.

"Okay," he replied.

I detected a bit of disappointment in his tone, and it made me squirm with indecision.

"Si. We take drink. You want?"

I *wanted*, all right. That was the whole problem. I needed time to think. Or maybe I needed *not* to think at all. I jumped off the boulder like a frog off a hot stove. I grabbed Dominik's strong, lean arm and tugged him off his perch.

We strolled arm-in-arm to the kiosk. I watched the handsome, rugged fisherman as he stood at the counter and ordered two lemon-cellos. He carried the drinks back to our tiny table for two under the open-air porch. Dominik set my drink in front of me and eyed me seductively. Then he held his own drink to his lips.

"*Salute,*" he offered.

"Salute." I forced a fake smile of confidence.

"Smoke?" Dominik set his drink down. He fished a pack of cigarettes out of his pocket and tapped on it. It was empty. "I go. Cigarettes, si?" He tilted his lovely head toward the kiosk.

"Si," I replied, and nodded cheerfully.

I watched Dominik disappear inside the kiosk. As soon as his amazing derriere was out of sight, my gut turned to jelly. I catapulted out of my chair and ran like a headless chicken all the way back to the Hotel Bella Vista. *Dang you, Sunday school!*

I jerked open the door and flung myself inside.

Antonio took one look at me, snickered, and bit his lip. He curled his index finger at me and I took a step toward him. The elegant hotel manager drew discrete circles in the air around his face, then pointed to the washroom. Italian hand signals were a language all their own. I didn't know a single one. Clueless, I stumbled into the ladies' room.

One look in the mirror was all it took for me to nearly die of embarrassment. Between my sunburn, my smeared red lipstick and my smudged mascara, I looked like a circus clown after a psychotic meltdown. I locked the bathroom door and washed the whole tragic mess off my face. I watched the black goo swirl down the drain, along with my chance for a hot romance. I cleaned up the scene of the crime and slunk, red-faced, to the dining room to join the other volunteers for dinner.

Chapter Six

Finally, on Wednesday, a catastrophe occurred that *didn't* involve me. Peter Axion, the gangly IRS accountant, went jogging early that morning and was hit by a motor scooter. He didn't sustain any serious bodily damage, but the collision had been enough to knock whatever sense he'd had clean out of him.

Between huge mouthfuls of buttered croissants, he'd shown off his bandaged knee to each of us as we arrived at the breakfast table. Once we were all assembled, he'd picked up a little maroon-colored journal and read aloud from it.

"In Italy, one can never plan more than a day in advance, in fact, no more than an hour."

Peter paused and smiled at his own cleverness. He smacked his livery lips and continued.

"One must always have a Plan B or C, or Plan A + (B-C/2). If one does not account for contingencies, one may end up at the *Ospedale Italiano*."

Peter was an odd duck, no doubt. But that morning I could actually relate to his advice. I finally gave up on Plan A—the hope of ever getting my suitcase of clothes. I devised a Plan B.

It was time to go shopping.

AFTER CLASS, I STOPPED at a boutique that had caught my eye as Frank and I walked by on our way back to the hotel. I was ready for new clothes, *and* to end Frank's tiresome lecture on what he considered my impropriety in going on a trip with Friedrich. No wonder the man was single.

I stared at the dresses in the shop's display window. It was no secret that Italy was world-renowned for fashion. The village of Brindisi was no exception. Its main street was dotted with clothing shops. But I'd noticed something peculiar during my window shopping. The clothes and shoes displayed in the storefronts seemed to fall into two very distinct categories for two very distinct kinds of women.

The first type of clothing was for the young, the beautiful, and the sexy; lacey lingerie, short skirts and fabulous shoes. The second kind was for the old, the dried-up and the dour. I'd seen the same dull head scarfs and shapeless shift dresses on several old ladies—usually as they leaned out of windows beating rugs like they were naughty children.

Age-wise, I wasn't sure if I qualified for stilettos or orthopedic shoes. But after last night's fiasco with Dominik, I needed to choose a side and stick with it. I was in *Italy*, for crying out loud, and the guys here thought I was sexy, dang it. Now, I only needed to convince *myself* of it. I breathed in deep. *You can do this, girl.*

I stepped inside the cute boutique. It wasn't any bigger than a convenience store. With the help of a beautiful, enthusiastic sales woman about my age, I quickly settled on a short, sexy, coral-hued sundress. It featured a halter neckline and tied in the back with a smart little bow. I would have never *dared* to wear something like that in the States. But for what I had in mind here in Italy, it was perfect.

"Bellissima, signora!" encouraged the saleswoman as I eyed myself in the mirror.

A shot of happy-go-lucky confidence made my heart ping.

"I guess I'm not dead yet. I'll take it!"

The saleswoman didn't comprehend a word I'd said, but she understood attitude when she saw it. She shot me a thumbs up and the universal, "You go, girl!" face. Then she gave me a really sweet little round of applause. I felt like a million euros!

After handing her my credit card, I had her snip the tag off my new dress. I wore it right out of the store and straight into the beauty salon next door. After a few minutes of pantomiming and pointing at pictures in books, I managed to get my hair shampooed and styled just like I did back home. I looked at myself in the mirror.

"How do I look?" I asked the fashionable, thirty-something stylist.

She shrugged. "Okay."

I looked at her cute, carefree hairdo. It was fun and flirty, something between a pixie cut and a shag. Like all good hairdressers, she read my mind. She led me back to the shampoo chair to start again.

ON MY WAY OUT OF THE salon, appreciative glances from two nice-looking men made me think dirty thoughts as I clicked down the sidewalk in my cute little dress and matching coral heels. New clothes. New hairdo. I was ready for action. Now if I could only garner enough courage to pull the trigger....

It was fascinating and frustrating at the same time. Compared to Americans, Italian men were master flirts. To be fair, they probably couldn't help themselves. Like good old Lipton tea, they'd been steeped in a culture of adoration since birth. From what I'd seen, they'd grown up surrounded by acceptance and *amore*. Expressing appreciation and admiration was the normal thing to do. The fact that Italian women were smoldering, natural beauties probably didn't hurt matters, either.

Though I was certainly no beauty pageant winner, at least in Italy I operated on a level playing field. Here, I didn't have to compete with the scores of fake women like Val II. These airbrushed, Botox-injected, lipo-suctioned, breast-augmented, made-up fairytale women were practically worshiped in the States. Here, they were disdained. Despite the fact that I'd already seen forty come and go in the rearview mirror, I couldn't recall ever feeling as beautiful as I did the moment I stepped out of that salon.

IT'S AMAZING WHAT A difference a great outfit and a new hairdo can make. When I got back to the Hotel Bella Vista, nobody in the WOW group even recognized me! I decided to make the most of it. I sat in a black leather chair and pretended to read a newspaper while I spied on the other volunteers.

Berta marched across the lobby in her yellow pantsuit, her nose in a travel book. I snickered to myself as she disappeared out the door. Peter limped by on his bandaged knee, heading toward the pool. Frank and Val II appeared at the glass entry doors together. Frank went to the bar and ordered a beer. The Botox queen stepped inside the rickety elevator. I glanced over to the front desk and winked at Antonio. He'd been sneaking furtive glances at me the whole while.

He wiggled his eyebrows at me seductively. All of a sudden, his face went limp. His eyebrows scrunched together and his mouth flew open.

"Ahhh! Signora Val! Bella! Bellissima!" he practically shouted.

I winked at him again and grinned.

He winked back and ran the side of his thumb down his cheek. That was one hand signal that needed no interpretation. I wasn't accustomed to receiving attention like that. I giggled like an idiot. Then I stood up and twirled around to show off my new outfit.

"Fantanstico!" Antonio said. "And I have a good news. We have a located your other baggage."

Of course. Right after I bought new clothes, grumbled the old woman I thought I'd left in a box back home. *Shut up, old Val!*

The new me thought the timing was pretty spot-on. The delay had been the catalyst for a wonderfully self-indulgent afternoon—something I'd done *far* too seldom in my past life.

My past life. It felt good to think of it that way. *Yes. Stay in the dad-burned box, old Val.*

"That's wonderful, Antonio! Where is it?"

"Oh, Signora, your bag is not *here*. It is at the *aeroporto* in Bari," he said, as if I should have known. "Mi dispiache, but you must a go through the customs before they will release it."

"Why would they let one of my bags be delivered here without going through customs, but not the other one?"

Antonio pursed his lips and shook his head softly. "Signora Val, it is best not to think about such a things."

"Okay, Antonio. You're right. Call me a taxi, per favore."

IN ITALY, IT WAS ABSOLUTELY true that decent legs and a short dress could get a woman darn near anything she pleased. I climbed into the passenger seat next to the cabbie and asked him to step on it. He took a look at my gams and hit the pedal hard. I gritted my teeth into a makeshift smile and held on for dear life as we hurtled down the highway at 160 kilometers an hour the entire way to the airport.

Horns honked and middle fingers jabbed at us from steamy car windows. That cab driver wove his way through traffic like a Turkish rug maker, putting Vittorio to shame. When he slammed on the brakes in front of the airport entrance, I jumped out of the cab in my coral halter dress and stilettos and raced up to the customs counter, my paperwork in my hot little hand.

That's when my wild ride came to a screeching halt. That same sullen-faced clerk from Saturday was at the window again. She frowned at my forms and pointed for me to take a seat against the wall. I could almost hear the brakes squealing. I walked over to the row of empty chairs, but I couldn't sit down. The kamikaze ride there had pumped me full of adrenaline like a hound on a coon hunt.

It must have been a slow day, or maybe I was being rewarded for following the Sunday-school rules last night with Dominik. I hadn't been waiting more than a minute when that the sour-faced clerk wheeled out a blue suitcase with my green luggage tag on the handle.

"Signora, this your baggage?"

"Si, Signora. It is."

"*Benvenuto a Italia.*"

"Gratzie." *Yes. Welcome to Italy, indeed.*

The cabbie's face registered surprised relief as I scurried toward him, dragging my case. He threw my bag in the trunk and hustled me into the taxi as if the paparazzi were hot on our heels. Before I knew it, I was back at the hotel. The one-way trip that had taken an hour and a half when I'd arrived a week ago with Vittorio had been accomplished by this speed demon, round trip, in just under two. I wasn't even late for dinner.

I wheeled my precious suitcase into the dining room as if it contained the entire Jeff Foxworthy Golden Anniversary DVD collection. The other volunteers had told me they would throw a party to celebrate when my bags finally arrived. But they didn't even offer up a toast with the free wine that came with our dinner.

Oh well. *Tutto va bene.* It was all good. I had my luggage!

AFTER SUPPER, I ROLLED my bag into the lobby and ran, quite literally, into Friedrich. I'd been looking back, admiring my long-lost suitcase, and had walked head-on into him. The German stopped and eyed me curiously.

"Val?" Friedrich asked. "That is you, ja? I did not know you."

"Yeah, I got my hair done."

"You are all puffed up now! And your baggage arrived. Goot. Berry goot."

"Yeah. Now you won't have to see me in my awful brown skirt ever again."

"It was not *so* bad. Let us take a drink together. To celebrate!"

"Sure. Why not."

"Why *not*? You don't want?"

"Oh, *no*." I tried to explain. "Why *not* means...oh, forget it. I mean, *yes*, I *do* want."

Friedrich studied me curiously, like I was a lab rat with an interesting tumor.

"Follow me."

He led me across the lobby to the coffee counter that, by night, transformed into a pretty decent-looking cocktail bar. The blue haze that emanated from the ceiling spotlights was almost invisible during the day, but at night it created a completely different, club-like atmosphere. Giuseppe, the breakfast waiter, was behind the bar dressed in his typical penguin suit. He raised a seductive eyebrow at me.

"Buona sera, Giuseppe," I said.

Surprise registered on his face for a millisecond, then his stoic, professional veneer closed over his features again.

"You look a very nice, Signora Val," Giuseppe said without making eye contact.

"Gratzie," I giggled.

Friedrich turned and spoke to Giuseppe in what sounded like perfect, beautiful Italian. Whatever the two men discussed, it seemed to involve a lot more words than required for a simple drink order. When their conversation ended, Friedrich glanced at me, then back to Giuseppe. We both watched as the waiter placed two small shot glasses on the counter and poured a foul-looking, brown liquid into them.

"This is an Amaro, a digestive," Friedrich explained. He handed me a glass. "Drink it slowly."

I held the glass to my nose and sniffed. It smelled like medicine. I took a sip. It tasted like Aunt Patsy's homemade kerosene pickles. *Yuck!*

"This must be an acquired taste."

"Yes, perhaps it is," said Friedrich. "You don't have to drink if you don't want."

"Thanks." I set the glass on the counter. "I'll give it another try in a minute."

My comment seemed to amuse Friedrich. He smiled and patted a pack of cigarettes in his shirt pocket. "Shall we go outside?"

"Sure."

I picked up my drink and followed the German out of the lobby's side exit door into the purple twilight. We found seats by the unlit pool and exchanged small talk until the sky grew so dark all I could make out was the small, red glow from his lit cigarette.

"Are you married?" he asked.

"Not anymore."

"So you are divorced. Me as well. Do you have kinder...uh...kids?"

"No. You?"

"No. What are you doing here, on this trip?"

"I don't know. Exploring, I guess."

"What are you exploring?"

Maybe it was the Amaro, but something had me all mixed up like kale in a NutriBullet. For the first time in forever, I felt a familiar attraction—a chemistry—between myself and a man. I glanced at the big blue suitcase that contained everything I'd brought with me. I strained my eyes to see the man across from me who held nothing but mystery.

Part of me wanted to go to my room and get into my luggage. Part of me wanted to go to his room and get into his pants.

Sadly, sensibility won out. "It's late, Friedrich. I need to go."

I stood and wheeled my suitcase behind me. As I took the last step toward the hotel entryway, Friedrich's hand reached from behind me and opened the door.

"Would you like to go to Matera with me on your day off?" he asked.

I smirked. "As long as I don't have to drink an Amaro afterward."

The corner of Friedrich's lip curled upward and he gave me a quick nod.

Our date was on.

Chapter Seven

Ironically, teaching class with by-the-book Frank turned out to hold some interesting lessons for me as well. Frank wanted—no, Frank *needed* everything to follow a certain set of rules. It had taken me nearly forty years, but I'd finally wised up enough to figure out that life just didn't work that way. Frank was in his sixties. Intelligent. Educated, too. I would have thought he'd have been smart enough to see he was fighting a hopeless battle. I guess my Uncle Jack was right: *Old dogs can't learn new tricks if they're not willing to let go of the same old bones they keep pickin'.*

Italy was not America. And Italian schools were most certainly *not* like those in the States. Frank was ruled by his watch. Italians wore them merely as fashion statements. In Room 301, our teacher began class only when she was good and darn ready. Students came and went as they pleased throughout the day. No permission was requested or required. It wasn't uncommon for our English lessons to be interrupted by students from other classes. They'd pop by to make announcements, talk to friends, or sell tickets for an upcoming football (soccer) game.

Whenever any of our young, hunky students got hungry, they would whip out a homemade sandwich wrapped in aluminum foil and chomp away. At any given time during the class, a random young man would get up and leave, then return a few minutes later carrying a white paper bag full of warm panini. Class would grind to a halt as the sandwiches were divvied up and passed around the room like an impromptu picnic.

Side conversations during our lessons proved as impossible to thwart as a hive of killer bees. The buzz would start slowly, with one handsome darling whispering to another. Before long, three or four young men would be talking earnestly amongst each other. Another would join in by yelling something across the room. Soon, the noise would grow to such a din that Frank and I could hardly hear ourselves speaking. Eventually, the long-suffering teacher would reach her limit. She'd slap a plastic ruler on her desk and yell, "*Basta*." The room would go quiet for about a minute. Then the whole process would start over again.

The relaxed environment and constant distractions drove Frank bonkers. I'd be the first to confess, I enjoyed a good portion of satisfaction watching him struggle in vain to keep his no-nonsense composure. The first tell-tale sign Frank was losing it would be the squinting of his eyes. Next his jaw would tighten. Finally, his face would grow as red as a Roma tomato.

To be fair, I was pretty sure I wasn't the only one who derived secret pleasure from watching Frank's grandiose plans disintegrate and his blustering self-importance backfire in his face. In fact, I was quite certain a few of the boys made a contest of setting him off. Why else would they wink at me when Frank, vying for attention, tapped his chalk so hard on the blackboard that it broke to pieces? Frank's egomaniacal attempts to seize power and control didn't mean squat to our budding, tech-school cuties. In more ways than one, they just didn't speak Frank's language.

In fact, they appeared quite incapable of either rivalry or power struggles. Even when we divided them into groups to compete against each other in games, these good-natured young men helped each other when someone was struggling, regardless of which team they were playing on.

When someone did well, he was bombarded by a round of hoots, hand-slaps and hugs. If someone couldn't see the blackboard, he was invited to come and sit on the lap of another student with a better view. And when a game was over and Frank announced the winning team, *every single one of them* hollered out cheers of victory and patted each other on the back. After all the cutthroat capitalism I'd endured in the business world, it was truly an inspiring spectacle to behold.

Frank kind of summed up everything I saw wrong with men and the US in general. I guess that's why I'd found it so funny to watch him struggle in vain in an environment that didn't cater to his sort. I'd had to bite my lip so often to keep from laughing that my bottom teeth had made a semi-permanent indentation on the inside of my lower lip.

Today I watched a red-faced, frustrated Frank try to teach a young stud in tight yellow pants and a smiley-face shirt how to pronounce the word *bird* correctly.

"Beard," said the Adonis in Gucci loafers.

"It's BUUUURD, not beard," Frank corrected impatiently. He pulled on his own chin and jutted it forward above his leathery, turkey neck. "BUUURD."

"Burt," replied the brown-eyed cutie. He laughed and pulled on his own firm, stubbly chin.

A vein began to throb on Frank's age-spotted forehead. I looked away to keep from snickering. When I did, my eyes landed on a calendar taped to the classroom wall. It must have been hanging there the whole time, but I'd never noticed it before. Above the numbered squares outlining the month, a voluptuous, brunette bombshell in a bathing suit too small to cover a Dollar Store IOU eyed me alluringly from atop the shiny chrome motorcycle she straddled.

Signorina Maggio (Miss May) was the kind of cheesecake not found in any bakery. I grinned. We were definitely not in the Bible Belt anymore.

AFTER CLASS ON THURSDAY, all six of us WOW volunteers loaded up in a van we'd hired and headed to Ostuni. Geographically, Italy was, quite appropriately, shaped like a thigh-high stiletto boot. Ostuni was located more or less where the heel connected at the back. If that boot had been made in Ostuni, it would have been creamy white, because everything in the ancient town was fashioned out of vanilla-colored rock. Dubbed the *white city* by the locals, Ostuni's houses, churches, and even its streets were constructed of the same smooth, eggshell-hued stone. As we drove through the town in the glare of the midday sun, the effect was almost blinding.

The van stopped and we all donned our sunglasses and tumbled out into the street. We followed the driver like ducklings through the bright, white haze toward the arched doorway of a local trattoria. Despite the heat outside, the interior of the restaurant was as dark and cool as a cavern.

I marveled at the contrast, and at the genius of the architects who'd constructed this place of solid rock four or five centuries ago with nothing more than picks and knives. I wondered if any of the people seated at the tables around us were progeny of those clever forefathers. In Europe, it seemed, anything was possible.

We were seated at a rustic, wooden table for six. I looked around at what the locals were eating. When the waiter asked for my order, I pointed at the plates with the best-looking meals. The waiter smiled and scribbled on his notepad.

"I'll have what she's having," said Berta.

The waiter gave the old woman a blank stare.

"Doo-ay," I said, and held up a thumb and index finger.

The waiter looked over at me and nodded. "Prego." He made a check mark on his pad.

"Make it three, Val," Tina said.

I held up three fingers. "Trey."

"And wine. Don't forget the wine!" Berta added.

"Red or white?"

"Red!" the two women said simultaneously.

"Per favore, *vino rosso*. Trey."

The waiter wrote in his pad, then turned to Peter.

"Val, how do you say 'hamburger' in Italian?" he asked me.

"I have no idea, Peter."

Peter's face scrunched up like he was sucking on a sourball. "How about spaghetti and meatballs?"

"Uh...spaghetti, I guess. Bolognese?"

"I'll have spaghetti Baloney, then," Peter informed the waiter. "And a Budweiser."

The waiter sighed and scribbled, then turned to Frank. "Signor, prego."

"Oh no. Ladies first," Frank corrected the waiter. "What would you like, Val?"

I was about to say I already ordered, but then I remembered Val II's name wasn't really Val II. It was just Val, like mine.

"Oh, I don't know Frank," Val II said. She leaned in until her fake boobs brushed Frank's arm. "What are *you* having?"

Geez. Really?

"Order something already," yelled Tina. "We're starving over here!"

Frank shot Tina a nasty look, then smiled patronizingly at the waiter.

"Well, the lady here and I will both have the 'pesky dell gee orno.'"

Tina and Berta both kicked me under the table. To be honest, I was kind of glad they did. The pain in my shins kept me from laughing out loud.

"*Scusi mi?*" asked the confused waiter.

Frank's face grew redder than usual. "I said we'll both have the pesky dell gee orno."

The waiter looked over at me pleadingly. I guess he thought, out of this bunch, I was his best hope.

"Signora, *aiutare?*"

I didn't know what the waiter said, but any fool could understand what he meant.

"Frank, what is it you want? Show me on the menu."

"It's not on the menu," Frank groused. "It's on the board right there!"

Frank stabbed an angry finger at a chalkboard placard perched on an easel. Written in blue chalk were the words; *Pesce del giorno.*

"See?" Frank argued. "Pesky dell gee orno."

The waiter finally got it and burst out laughing.

"Doo-ay," I said.

Between giggling fits, the waiter marked in his notepad.

"There goes *your* tip," Frank barked at the waiter as he disappeared into the kitchen.

"He doesn't understand you, Frank," I said. "Besides, here in Europe they pay wait staff a living wage. They don't have to live on tips like they do back home."

"That kind of defeats the purpose of good service, doesn't it?" Val II said snippily. Frank patted her hand in agreement.

"No. It defeats the ability of people to work for slave wages. And their lives don't depend on the moods and whims of the people they have to cater to."

"Oh, what do *you* know about it?" Frank said angrily.

"Plenty. I waited my way through college, Frank. What about you?"

"I'll have you know that—"

"All right everybody. Simmer down!" Berta interrupted. "If you two want to argue the point, do it on your own time. I'm too old for this crap." Berta glanced over our heads and smiled. "Besides, the wine is on its way."

The waiter brought a huge pitcher of red wine. He poured everyone a glass except Peter. He handed the lanky, liver-lipped accountant a can of beer. Peter looked pleased as punch.

"All right!" he exclaimed. "You know what? And this is a fact. Here in Italy, Budweiser is imported beer."

"Look at you, mister international man about town," Tina said derisively.

As usual, subtlety was wasted on Peter. "Why thank you, Tina." He held up his can of Bud. "Cheers, everybody."

We all raised our glasses and toasted. A few minutes later, the waiter set our plates before us. Peter got his spaghetti, Frank and Val II their fish in cream sauce. Berta, Tina and I got a colorful plate of *insalata caprese* and a bowl of fresh cherries. The salad's soft, milky mozzarella, juicy red tomatoes, and fragrant green basil blended together to deliver the perfect taste of Italy.

"I think this is the best thing I've ever had in my mouth," Berta said.

"You sure about that?" Tina taunted. Then she took a bite and nearly moaned. "Oh my gawd! This is delicious!"

"Told ya," Berta said smugly.

I took a bite of a large, plump, burgundy-hued cherry. It was so fresh and crisp it crunched like an apple. The sweet, dark juice flooded my mouth.

"Oh, wow! Try the cherries, girls!"

Tina popped one in her open maw. "They're like an orgasm in your mouth!"

Berta grabbed one and bit into it. "I never tasted an orgasm as good as this. Mmmmm! Fantasic!"

"Excuse me, *ladies*," Frank said. "Could you keep it down? We're trying to eat like civilized people over here."

Berta, Tina and I glanced into each other's eyes and burst out laughing. Frank's face turned as dark red as one of our delicious cherries. Val II could have burned a hole in a boulder with her stare. Peter was oblivious, reading the ingredients on his can of Bud.

AFTER FINISHING OUR simple feast, Tina, Berta and I went for a short walk around the town center of Ostuni. Peter had wanted to tag along, but Tina had given him the heave-ho, saying it was a girls-only afternoon. Berta was keen on checking out the famous Mother Church where it was said the bones of Saint Nicholas (Santa Claus!) were buried. I thought, *What the heck. It would make a good Christmas story to tell my cousins' kids.* Then I realized if I told them Saint Nick was buried there, I'd be informing them Santa Clause was dead. *On second thought, maybe not such a good idea.*

As we made our way in the direction of the church, we stopped at a few tourist shops to check out Ostuni's other claim to fame—whistling birds made of clay. Tina haggled with an old shopkeeper in a tired blue headscarf and faded sack dress. As their debate grew more animated, Berta and I meandered toward the adjoining shops to browse amongst fancy lace tablecloths, colorful pottery and garish, orange-and-green Fuji Film stands.

"Who needs all this crap?" I asked. I showed Berta a plastic finger puppet of the pope.

"Guess you gotta make religion entertaining nowadays. Get 'em while their young."

Her comment struck a nerve.

"That sounds pretty jaded. I'm a Southern Baptist survivor. You?"

"Got you beat, kid. Ex nun."

"No way!"

"Yeah. But don't let the cat out of the bag, okay?"

"Sure. But I'm curious. Why not?"

"I guess I'm just not in the habit of caring about it anymore."

"Was that a joke?"

"Was it funny?"

"Meh."

Berta shrugged. "Oh well."

We both gave up shopping and sat on a bench in the middle of the square to people-watch. A minute or so later, Tina walked up holding a crudely made clay bird. She put her lips to its butt and blew. An anemic whistling noise wafted out.

"Well that's some quality crap-manship right there," Berta said.

Tina hiked up a corner of her lip. "Yeah. I guess they don't make them like they used to."

"You can say that again, kid," Berta replied. "Ready to go find that church?"

"Nah, I'm not into it. But I think it's right over there."

Tina pointed to a spot over our heads. Berta and I turned around and saw a thick, rectangular church spire rising at least fifty feet above the other white stone buildings surrounding it.

"Yeah, that's it," said Berta, slapping on her sunglasses. "I recognize it from my travel book."

"I'm gonna go get a gelato," Tina said. "I'll catch you guys back at the van."

"Be careful," I said. "The Italian strangler. He could be anywhere."

Tina snorted with laughter. "Oh Val. You're such a putz. I just made that up to get a rise out of you."

"Not cool. You really scared me."

"Come on. Relax. Nothing bad's gonna happen."

Tina went her way and Berta and I headed in the direction of the church. As we drew nearer, we could make out more details on the chunky spire. It had a triangular-shaped top covered in terracotta tiles. Two statues of praying saints flanked its upper corners.

"Recognize either of them?" I asked Berta.

She snorted out a laugh. "I think—"

"Guys! Wait!" someone yelled.

We turned and saw Tina running down the narrow alley toward us.

"You...won't...believe it!" she said between gasps for breath.

"What?" Berta asked.

"I...just...saw...."

"Who? The strangler?" I asked.

"No. Red and...Frank...beside the...gelato shop...making out!"

"Who's Red?" asked Berta.

"Val. The other one, I mean," said Tina. "Val II. Here. Look!"

Tina handed me her cell phone. There, in full technicolor, was a shot of Frank and Val II up against an alley wall, lips locked, Frank's hand fondling an expensive bag of silicone.

Chapter Eight

I squirmed impatiently through breakfast like a kid waiting on the ice cream truck. I tried to hide it, but an unfamiliar nervousness made my stomach flop like a pancake on a trampoline. It was Friday, my day off, and I had plans to spend the day with Friedrich.

"Hey, kid. What's up?"

Berta sat down next to me, a paper cup of vending machine coffee in her hand. "Any sign of the love turds this morning?"

"No, thank goodness. But Berta, I'm dying to ask. How did you go from being a nun to a psychologist? That's a big switch."

Berta shrugged the shoulders of her lime-green shirt.

"If you think about it, it's not that big a leap. As a sister, I had people spilling their guts to me all the time. They expected me to have all the answers. I didn't. But I wanted to. So I traded in the convent for college. Got my degree. Then I sat in an office and listened to people tell me the same kind of problems. I still didn't have the answers. But I *did* have a plaque on the wall and a bill to slap in their hand afterward."

"Do you think it's possible for people to change? Fundamentally?"

"Well, I've looked at human nature from both sides of the fence. I'd have to say yes, it's possible. But it's not probable. In my experience, people tend to stay who they are, Val."

AFTER BREAKFAST, I went back to my room to get ready for my trip with Friedrich. I fidgeted with my face and hair in the bathroom mirror. I tried to convince myself my nervousness was all about Matera, but I wasn't fooling anyone. I felt as awkward and unprepared as a first-grader in hand-me-downs. What was I going to say to this strange German man? I was lousy at playing mind games, and I'd been told more than once by Clarice that I had the flirting skills of a maladjusted gerbil. After the Tuesday-night fiasco with Dominik, I was more convinced than ever that I was playing with fire. I didn't have a clue how to talk to a man on a date.

Hold it right there, Val. This isn't a date. It's just a day trip with a man who volunteered to be your tour guide for a few hours.

"*Basta!*" I said aloud to my reflection. I tried to mimic the classroom teacher's scowl. If I'd had a hold of a ruler, I'd have slapped my hand with it.

I closed the door to my room and headed to the lobby to meet Friedrich. On the ride down in the pint-sized elevator, my stomach flopped like a bad contestant in a pancake cook-off. I got out and saw Friedrich waiting for me. He greeted me across the lobby with that familiar head nod of his.

"Goot morning, Val,"

"Good morning, Friedrich."

"I checked. It is a nice day today. As they say, 'When angels travel, the weather is always good.'"

I wasn't sure what to read into the remark, so I just smiled and nodded. Friedrich ushered me out the door and toward his car pulled up just outside. Friedrich's shiny, silver Peugeot was parked alongside a dingy white minivan. The van driver turned the ignition and a belch of white smoke enveloped me. I waved it away and noticed that the van was packed with my fellow WOW volunteers.

Through the van window, I saw Berta wave at me. Val II's mouth formed a deep frown, and she shook her head disapprovingly from side to side. Frank sat beside her, a blue vein throbbed on his forehead. Peter sat up front with the driver, and was busy adjusting the radio knobs.

I felt a bit scandalous as I climbed into Friedrich's convertible. Tina rolled down a window on the beat-up old van.

"Have fun, Val! Don't do anything I wouldn't do!"

I smirked. Friedrich turned the ignition. As we rolled away, I turned and slowly waved at them like the Queen of England acknowledging her subjects. I caught a glimpse of Val II burning up in the backseat. I snickered. I felt...*deliciously naughty*. And *that* in itself felt *darn good*. After we'd cleared the van, Friedrich stepped on the gas and we peeled out of the driveway with a squeal of rubber.

"Goot. You have on goot walking shoes," Friedrich said, nodding his approval. "I was afraid, you being American, that you would wear high heels."

"At my age, I'd rather be comfortable than glamorous."

Friedrich smiled. "So, how old are you?"

"Forty-one." I wasn't taken aback in the slightest by his question. In Europe, age didn't seem to be a diabolical, shameful secret a woman had to keep from everyone—especially herself.

"So...you are older than me. I thought you were younger." Friedrich's tone was matter-of-fact, not disappointed.

"How much younger?" I asked playfully, fishing for a compliment.

"At least ten years less."

"Oh! So, how old are *you*?"

"Forty," he said. "I am born in *Mertz*. A fish."

It took me a moment to realize that he meant March, and that he was a Pisces.

"Oh, my birthday is in April. I'm an Aires."

"Oh, ja. A ram." Friedrich's lips formed a half smile. "So you are almost a year older than me."

"Yes, and since I am the oldest, that means you must do what I say," I joked.

Friedrich's right eyebrow rose slightly. "Zo, what would you have me to do?"

Was he flirting with me?

"Take me to Matera, of course!"

"Right away, madam." Friedrich mashed the gas pedal and shifted into a higher gear.

Powder-puff clouds lolled lazily in the blue sky as we whizzed past undulating hills striped with vineyards and olive orchards. Fig trees with bright green fruits as big as pears hung over curves in the road. Ripe cherries filled the air with a sweet, earthy aroma. Italy was doing its best to convince me it was one big picture-postcard.

Friedrich played a CD of his favorite Italian opera as we chatted. I learned that his job had taken him all over the world. He'd lived in Boston, Finland, Indonesia and Egypt, to name a few places. For the last two years, he'd called the Hotel Bella Vista home, and had fallen in love with the warm weather and easy-paced life of Italy.

"I am not the typical German blockhead," he explained. "I am open to new ideas and new ways of doing things."

He sounded as if he were trying to convince himself as much as me, and his hard face contradicted his words. His gaze was often distant, as if his thoughts were somewhere else. Awkward silence forced me to think of something to say.

"Is this a date?" I blurted. I immediately wanted to kick myself.

"This is *not* a date." Friedrich answered. His voice had a hard, warning tone.

"I only meant...." I attempted to backpedal, but Friedrich saved me the trouble.

"Val," he said in a softer tone, "you are only here for one more week. There is no time for dating. There is only time for us to enjoy each other's company."

His honest words caused the nervousness I'd been feeling to evaporate. He was right. This was a time to enjoy the moment. I breathed in and felt my whole body relax.

"That sounds like an excellent plan." I turned and grinned at him.

Friedrich studied my face intently for a moment. Satisfied, he gave me one quick nod, then faced the road ahead.

WHEN WE ARRIVED AT the narrow, gravel road leading up to Matera, its entry was blocked by a policeman standing guard in front of a barricade. Higher up the hillside we could see a scattering of trailers and trucks and a few men milling about.

The policeman and Friedrich spoke for a few minutes. He then translated to me that a movie was being filmed at the site, so we couldn't enter. Friedrich spoke with the policeman again. I had no idea what Friedrich said, but by the time the conversation was finished, the policeman's face expression had hardened. He moved the barricade for us and let us through.

Friedrich maneuvered the Peugeot slowly past the film crew to the top of a flat mesa. From there, we picked our way on foot through rocks and boulders to the mouth of a gaping ravine. Across an expansive, rock-strewn valley, jutting out from the opposing mountain face, was a primitive village carved right out of the mountainside.

The craggy, light-colored stone was dotted with dark holes that, upon closer inspection, turned out to be the pane-less windows and gaping doorways of abandoned dwellings. The buildings had been excavated from solid rock, one atop the other, and climbed like stone steps up the side of the ravine. The effect was spooky and raw, and reminded me of exposed catacombs. As we drew nearer, the primitive openings stared blankly back at us like a jumbled stack of huge grey skulls. The wind howled over the scene and seemed to carry with it the haunting voices of the people who once dwelled there.

A shiver went up my spine as we stood staring at the silent, pensive city.

"The movie, *The Passion of the Christ*, was filmed at Matera a few years ago," said Friedrich. "I watched the movie and it destroyed me."

"What do you mean?"

"It took me to a dark place," he said. "I have come back here many times since, to sort through my thoughts. This place makes me question my beliefs."

"What *are* your beliefs?"

"We live. We suffer. We die. Only God knows the meaning for it."

I stood silent, unable to speak or to take my eyes off the mournful place.

"Finally, you are without words," Friedrich said.

He was right. But my mind was not without thoughts. *Ancient, mournful Matera. How many loves have you known and lost?*

"Are you ready?" Friedrich asked.

I nodded. He drove us to the other side of the ravine and into Matera itself. We parked, then trekked on foot, following narrow stone walkways through the wistful ghost town of solid rock. We walked past wells full of stagnant water. We tread on paths that meandered along the side of the mountain. We crossed over the flat rooftops of hidden houses carved into the rock underfoot.

The cave-like dwellings ranged from small, one-room hovels to grand, multi-room apartments laid out similarly to more modern homes. Despite the scorching sun, inside each room was surprisingly cool. When I placed my hand on an interior wall of solid-rock, it was cold to the touch.

Matera had appeared sullen and grey from the opposite side of the ravine. But in its midst, I found it was not as dreary as I'd feared. Even though the spirits of the dead seemed to whisper mournfully around the place, new life sprang up from everywhere.

Bright green moss and lichens of pink and yellow dotted the stone walls like mosaic tiles. Orange-red poppies, small white daisies and purple stalks of sage scrambled for footing among the cracks in the rock walls and steps. Overhead, swallows dove bat-like into narrow openings in the rocks, carrying insects for their young. A few stray cats sat on the sunny rooftops and drooled with anticipation of a meal on the wing.

Toward the end of the walk, to my great surprise, I discovered that not all of the structures were abandoned after all. Some of the houses and shops were still being inhabited by artists and shepherds. Friedrich and I walked by several buildings in which men sat at crude wooden tables, creating miniature models of Matera from plaster and stone. Sitting beside many of these craftsmen were young apprentices, learning the trade.

It turned out that Matera was *not* a dead city. Still, my overall impression of the place remained wistful, serious and sad. I felt relieved when Friedrich finally turned to me and said, "Let's go."

Chapter Nine

I awoke Saturday morning with the tattered cobwebs of Matera still clinging to my brain. Just like a masterful piece of art, Matera had changed my mood. I was in a deep funk. The startling contrast between Matera's cold, sullen rock and the hardscrabble hopefulness of its new inhabitants had me comparing my own life experiences. Italy versus Florida. More specifically, American men versus Italian ones.

It wasn't looking good for the Americans.

At breakfast, Peter, the pasty tax collector, continued his miscalculations on the best way to get into Tina's tight, tattered pants. It was painful to observe, like watching a guy strap on rollerblades and head down a mountain. Everyone but the dummy on wheels knew there was zero chance it would end well.

"Did anyone ever tell you how dangerous you are?" Peter asked Tina. He stuffed a giant wad of croissant into his mouth, then grinned at her, exposing the mashed beige goo oozing from between his long, yellowish horse teeth.

Tina turned my way and rolled her eyes. She tugged at the bottom of her shoulder-length black hair and pulled it across her face, trying to create a screen between her and the offending scene. Oblivious, Peter poked Tina's shoulder with a greasy finger. She let out a big sigh and turned to face the clueless cretin.

"Well? Did they?" Peter asked.

"Oh, were you talking to *me*?" Tina's voice contained not a whisper of interest.

"You betcha!"

Peter appeared ridiculously confident for a man of his dubious looks and charm. Tina let out the loudest sigh I'd ever heard.

"No, I guess not, Peter. No one ever has told me I'm dangerous."

"Well, you are!" Peter wagged his eyebrows obscenely.

Tina shot me a WTF look. "Why?" she asked, her face already cringing in anticipation of his forthcoming reply.

"Because you have a dynamite smile!"

Peter laughed loudly, then sat back in his chair and folded his gangly arms across his chest, impressed with his own cleverness. Tina stood abruptly. The legs of her chair screeched across the terrazzo floor. She rolled her eyes at me again and headed toward the exit door.

Peter's eyes followed Tina across the room while his mouth chewed on the croissant like a cow on a cud. His eyebrows knitted together in confusion, then went slack, as if he'd arrived at a solution to the problem at hand. A sly smile flashed onto his lips and he pinched his chin. He rubbed his hands together quickly, stood up and took off in Tina's direction. As he left, a trail of croissant crumbs fell from his clothes like flakes of brown snow.

Typical American male, I thought. Tina had to be at least a decade younger than Peter. And on the looks scale, she was at least a nine. Peter was pushing a five, and that was with extra credit for having a job and all of his original body parts. American men seemed to think they deserved the best, no matter how little they offered in return.

As Peter disappeared out the door, Giuseppe arrived in his crisp suit carrying a warm smile and a steaming-hot cappuccino. I returned the smile and thanked him. I made a note on my mental scorecard: *Americans zero. Italians one.*

Despite the caffeine rush, my Matera-inspired funk deepened. I thought about my first husband. I'd married Ricky so that God would grant me permission to have sex. Why he'd married me, I still couldn't say. A few months after our honeymoon, I'd caught him in bed with a red-headed girl who worked the candy counter at the movie theater he'd managed. At the age of nineteen, I'd been dumped for a younger woman. I'd been devastated at the time, but looking back on it now, I was grateful for the favor. Ricky had shown me his true colors before I'd gotten in too deep. The divorce had taken a year. Longer than the marriage had lasted.

I took a deep breath and let it out. As bad as that time had been, it had brought me a lot of clarity. I'd made the decision that I would never be dependent solely on someone else ever again. I went to college. I waited tables and paid my own way through school. I got a degree in Communications. Despite the fact that I was the only person in my family to ever earn a college degree, my single-handed feat went uncelebrated. Actually, I think it was seen as more of an embarrassment by my family than an accomplishment.

After college, I'd gotten a job writing copy for an advertising agency. That's where I'd met Jimmy. He'd been fun and approachable and made me laugh. He wasn't handsome, and was eleven years older than me. He'd also been a bit of a cheapskate, and therefore never wooed me in a traditional sense.

But he'd taken the time to be my friend first, and that was a novelty for me. I'd married him because, after five years of dating, he'd been the nicest man I'd met in a very long lineup of deadbeats and jerks. Romance never was Jimmy's style, and he didn't change that on account of me. After fifteen years of a nice, boring, and nearly sex-free partnership, I'd ached to the bone for something more. Intimacy. Passion. *The real deal.*

"Are you ready?"

I peeked out of my grey cloud of memories. Frank was standing in front of me, tapping on his watch.

"It's time to go."

"Frank, why don't we try something new today," I suggested as we walked through the lobby.

"What do you mean?" Frank groused. He kicked a stone off the sidewalk into the cobbled street.

"While the students are reading their English assignments, I could write down the words they are having trouble with most, and we could go over them afterward."

"What's wrong with what we have been doing? I think my idea of having them make sentences with English words is better."

"It's a good lesson," I said. "I just think we could use some variety. To break things up a little."

"Are you saying it's *boring*?"

I watched his neck turn pink. "I was just thinking—"

"Do me a favor, Val. Don't think. We're doing it the way we've *been* doing it."

"But I—"

"Don't you get it? This discussion is over." Frank shook his head at me like I'd been crazy to even consider questioning his ideas. "Case closed."

TODAY, JUST AS WE HAD done every day, Frank and I stood in front of the classroom and had our gorgeous students make up sentences using three English words pulled, literally, out of a hat. One pair of young men had pulled the words music, math and candy from the black fedora. Their sentence made me blush.

"Miss Val is as sweet as candy, and she likes music but we hate math."

Frank ground his teeth. I grinned from ear to ear. The conspiratorial wink from a cute student in the back row, combined with the generous helping of eye candy from the classroom of delectable darlings in front of me, shifted my mood from bad to badass. And the gifts just kept coming. Right after class, a hunk of beefcake put his arm around me and thanked me for my help. Frank almost blew a gasket! Then another young charmer asked if I was single. When I'd answered in the affirmative, he said he wanted to marry me. He had to have been half my age! Even though he'd been joking, it felt good to be...*flirt worthy*.

I was finally convinced. In Italy, I was a viable, sexy woman. A goddess! Everywhere I went, the men wanted to talk to me. Viva la difference! Italy had turned out to be the greatest ego boost ever! Score? *Americans*—who cares? *Italians*—four million...and counting!

MY STOMACH WAS FLOPPING again. In a few hours, Friedrich was taking me to the seaside village of Pulignano. It was Saturday night. Friedrich promised that Pulignano had more of a night life than Brindisi. After the great day I'd just had, I was ready for a little partying!

I had an hour to kill before dinner, so I stood on my balcony and watched Brindisi's nightly mating ritual begin to unfold. It wasn't much of a show, but maybe that was part of the little town's charm.

Young people in cars and motorbikes began to cruise slowly up and down the street between the hotel and the sea. Apparently, this little corner of town was the place to see and be seen. All along the seawall, groups of young men did their best James Dean impressions. Clusters of young women paraded by in front of them, gossiping amongst each other, pretending not to notice the boys noticing them. Horns honked. Kids shouted greetings to each other. Music blared from car stereos.

The whole scene had a safe, sweet innocence about it, like something out of the 1950s. I was watching the antics of a boy and his trick-performing pooch when someone knocked on my door. I opened it to find Tina standing there, her thin arms crossed over a black t-shirt that read: *98% Princess, 2% Witch. Don't Push It.*

"Hey, here's your Italian book back. Thanks for the loaner."

She pushed by me into my room and tossed the book on the side table. My book looked as if it had been raped and murdered. I picked up my poor, victimized book and studied its ragged corners and crumpled pages. I was such a nerd I wouldn't even mark my books with a highlighter pen. Tina had dog-eared pages, underlined passages in blue ink and used it for a coffee coaster.

"Sorry for the damages," Tina offered with a shrug. "I've been trying to teach Jonny some stuff."

"Jonny? As in the hot little Italian running the pool café?"

"That's the one," she said and smiled coyly. "C'mon. Don't tell me you haven't been working the room yourself, Val."

The good girl inside me gulped involuntarily. "What do you mean?"

Tina grabbed the book from my hand and flipped it over to the back cover. "This guy," she said, pointing at a photo of the author, Rick Steves. "Looks a bit like *your* Friedrich, don't you think?"

I snatched the book back from her. I studied the photo for a moment. At the angle the photo was taken, Friedrich was almost a dead ringer for Steves.

"You're right about the way he looks, Tina. But you're wrong about the other. There's nothing going on between me and Friedrich."

"Not *yet....maybe.*"

I laughed. The sarcastic tone in Tina's voice was the perfect match for the jaded mystique this girl worked so hard to cultivate. She was way too young to be truly world weary. Still, her suggestion of a fling with Friedrich sent my stomach fluttering. I needed a diversion. Suddenly, a wickedly wonderful idea popped into my mind. I looked Tina in the eye and raised an eyebrow.

"Are you up for some shenanigans?"

Tina didn't reply. The crooked grin that crept across her face was all the answer I'd needed.

"GET READY," I WARNED Tina from our lookout post behind the cracked door of the hotel's internet room. "Berta, hush!"

Berta had been pecking away on a computer and talking to herself. In the wrong place at the wrong time, she'd become an unwitting accomplice to my plan, albeit a willing one. The three of us peeked out from behind a crack in the door. Like clockwork, Friedrich arrived at the lobby bar for a beer before dinner.

"Go...*go!*" I whispered to Tina. I pushed her out into the open lobby, toward the cocktail bar.

"All right, already. Hands off the merchandise!" Tina took a deep breath, shook her head confidently, grabbed my tattered phrasebook and strolled out the door like an actress making her Broadway debut. Tina sauntered up to the unsuspecting German.

"Excuse me, do you speak English?" she asked. Somehow the tough Jersey girl managed to look innocent despite her scruffy jeans and scrappy appearance.

"Yes," answered Friedrich. He eyed Tina with no particular interest.

Exactly according to plan, Tina glanced left and right, then whispered to Friedrich. "Tell me. Are you Rick Steves?"

"My name is Friedrich Fremden. I don't know who is this Rick Steves."

Tina turned the abused book over and showed Friedrich the author's photo. "This looks like you. Come on. You can tell me. Are you really him?"

Friedrich eyed the photo. "No. That is not me."

Berta and I watched from behind the cracked door, snickering like prankster schoolgirls. When Friedrich unexpectedly glanced our way, we ducked our heads and held our breath. A second later, we peeked out again. Tina had regained his attention.

"Come on," she insisted. "Isn't Friedrich Fremden just a code name?"

"I am sorry to disappoint you, but I am not this man." Friedrich's face registered a tinge of annoyance.

"Don't lie. I *know* this is you."

Friedrich took a big gulp of beer. He looked uncomfortable and shifted on his feet. Berta and I held our hands over our giggling mouths as we watched him squirm.

"Just sign my book." Tina shoved the ragged tome toward him. "One autograph and I'm outta here. I won't tell a soul."

"I am *not* signing, because I am *not* him," Friedrich insisted. His face flushed with frustration.

Out of ideas, Tina shrugged and looked over at me for guidance. Friedrich followed her eyes. Being an engineer, Friedrich did the math in an instant. The gig was up. Berta and I burst from the doorway, laughing.

"Ha ha! Did we fool you?" I asked.

Friedrich shot me a pursed-lip smile and said nothing. I wasn't sure if that was a good sign or a bad one.

UNCERTAIN OF FRIEDRICH'S mood after our prank, I'd felt awkward at the thought of being alone with him. I'd asked his permission for Tina and Berta to accompany us to Pulignano. He'd nodded his approval.

After dinner tonight, we all piled into his tiny Peugeot. Like a chauffeur not quite certain he had permission to join the party, Friedrich maintained his distance as he drove Berta, Tina and me, laughing and screaming like a carload of college grads, to Pulignano.

The place surpassed every fantasy I'd ever had about a quaint, seaside village. Small, stately and dignified, Pulignano looked like a fairytale castle perched on the cliffs overlooking the Adriatic Sea. The town was alive with hundreds of people milling about, there to see and be seen. The girls looked fancy in glittering tops, short skirts and impossible stilettos. Boys with furtive eyes ambled about, taking in every detail.

We walked through a stone archway to a bridge that led to white cliffs plunging down to a fake-blue sea. The closest thing I could compare such a spectacle to was at Disney World.

"I hate to say it, but this place reminds me of that ride, Pirates of the Caribbean," I said as we gawked at the sights and sounds.

"You could be on to something, Val," Berta agreed.

"Replace the pirates with Italian studs," Tina said.

"Oh! And their swords with glasses of wine," said Berta.

"And their pantaloons with chinos tight in all the right places," I added, "and you've got Pulignano!"

Friedrich shook his head at our analogy, and led us to a bar abuzz with friendly chatter. Friedrich ordered a bottle of wine, and all four of us sipped it and took in the show. Thousands of candles shone from the tops of stone walls and café tables. Their warm, yellow glow reflected in the eyes of people passing by. An elegant couple strolling arm in arm along the cobblestones caught Friedrich's attention.

"The men hold the women like that to keep them from falling off their shoes," he said. "I wonder how much pressure per square millimeter a stiletto heel must bear."

No one else seemed concerned about such details. I guess that's one difference between Germans and Italians.

Chapter Ten

D*ing dong. DING DONG. Ding Dong!*
   I woke to the relentless chiming of church bells. They seemed to call to each other from every corner of the city, ringing out a song as old as the city itself. *Wake up! Wake up! Get out of bed, you lazy head. Come to me! Come to me!*

I checked the clock. It was 7 a.m. One late night out and one too many glasses of wine had been just what I'd needed to finally get in sync with Italy's time zone. Despite the little demon thumping inside my head, I sat up in bed and smiled. The lovely sights of Pulignano lingered in my mind like a sweet fantasy. I wanted to savor them as long as they lasted. I closed my eyes and vignettes from last night's trip came into view, set to the soundtrack of the insistent chorus of church bells.

Besides Pulignano, the only thing on my mind this morning had been getting my hands on a cappuccino. I was officially addicted. I slipped into a cute little floral dress and white sandals, then fluffed up my new casual hairdo with my hands. I peeked in the bathroom mirror. For a quick coffee run, that would do. I slipped out the door.

The breakfast area was empty except for my beautiful, Italian cappuccino god. With just an exchange of nods, Giuseppe fetched me my Italian drug of choice. Cappuccino in hand, I crept quietly back up to my room to enjoy it in peace.

I lay in bed and sipped my delicious cup of warm, frothy inspiration and declared Sunday my official day of rest. I stayed tucked away in my room until I was absolutely certain that the van carrying the other WOW volunteers to Lecce had gone. Beautiful silence filled the hotel, and I savored every last drop of it along with my perfect cappuccino. Ah! I was finally giving in to *il dolce far niente*—the sweetness of doing nothing.

MY SUNBURN HAD FADED without peeling, except for a small spot on my nose. With my face back to normal and clothes in my closet, I was all set to play the role of Italian goddess at large. I changed out of my floral dress and clothed myself all in white; white Capri pants, white halter top, white cotton over-blouse, white headband, white sandals. I felt as giddy as a new-born foal.

I took a peek at my reflection in the mirror. *Rock on with your bad self!* I grabbed a book and my big Italian sunglasses and pretended I was a filthy-rich movie star. "*I must remain incognito*," I told myself. I stuck my head out the door and peeked left and right down the hallway. *Empty.* I snuck down the back stairwell to the pool area. I hid behind the door as one of my adoring fans passed by. With no other stalkers in sight, I claimed my stake on a beach lounger near the edge of the pool. I looked around for paparazzi. The coast was clear. I pushed my sunglasses up on my nose and dove into my book.

I WAS AWOKEN BY THE sound of a man's voice. Through squinted eyes, I could only make out his dark silhouette. His torso blotted out the bright orange sun behind him like a total eclipse.

"Your feet are in goot conditions," said the black image surrounded by fiery rays from the sun.

"Huh?" I said, still half asleep.

"Your feet are in goot conditions," he repeated.

My eyes began to focus enough to make out more detail. The silhouette belonged to Friedrich. He leaned over me and whispered in my ear.

"You look like a frog on vacation."

To my horror, I realized he was right. I was sprawled out in the lounger with one leg straight down, the other one wide open, bent at the knee, like the number four. My prior delusions of movie-star glamour evaporated in the glare. I struggled to sit up into a more lady-like position. Then I realized it didn't matter. Compared to Friedrich, I looked like Audrey Hepburn in *Breakfast at Tiffany's.*

Like a good German, Friedrich wore black socks, Birkenstocks, a red Speedo and a white Gilligan hat. His nearly hairless chest and potbelly glowed white like the octopi I'd seen Dominik slapping against the rocks. *Where was that romance novel cliché when I needed it?* I drew my legs together and touched my hand to my chin to cover the drool creeping down the corner of my mouth.

"What did you say...something about my feet?" I pointed a finger at my toes. As soon as Friedrich diverted his eyes, I wiped the drool away with my headband.

"I said your feet are in goot conditions," he repeated patiently. He looked at my feet way longer than he needed to.

"Well, *that's* an original compliment."

"Ya. You can tell a great portion about a person from their feet," Friedrich explained. "Someone can have a beautiful face or hairs. Or wear beautiful clothes. But if they do not take care of their feet, they do not respect themselves."

"I never thought about it like that." I sat up in the lounger. "How interesting."

"You take care of what is *important*. The true foundation of your body," Friedrich continued. "I can see that you do not focus on the superficial. That is a good sign. That makes me happy."

"Wow, I didn't know you *cared*," I joked. I always joked when I was nervous. And I always wanted to kick myself afterward. But, as usual, I was unstoppable.

While I argued with myself, Friedrich sat down on the edge of my lounger. He took my right foot in his hand and a bolt of electricity shot up through my inner thigh. Stunned, I sat and watched as, one by one, he massaged my toes, then toyed with the silver ring on my middle toe. It was all I could do not to moan.

"A toe ring," he said, almost under his breath. "I've never touched one before."

I lay there like an idiot, rendered speechless from his completely unexpected and incredibly intimate touch. Fortunately, he was facing away from me and couldn't see the mixture of terror and ecstasy on my face. Unfortunately, someone else could.

"Hello, Rick!" Tina called out.

Friedrich cringed, then smiled. Tina sauntered up wearing a dingy-grey bikini top and dark-green boy shorts. A gecko tattoo peeked out above her left hipbone. She shot me an I-told-you-so smirk. "Hello, Val. I see you didn't make it to Lecce this morning."

"No. You either. Is Jonny working today?"

Tina glanced in the direction of the poolside cabana café. "Right over there. At ten. I'm going for a coffee. Ciao for the moment, you two." Tina shot me a wink and padded off.

As Tina left, Friedrich sat up and leaned over me again. I could smell his delicate cologne.

"You owe me," he whispered. A devilish look flashed in his eyes. "Have dinner with Rick Steves tonight?"

I accepted with a simple nod, then leaned back to savor the warm glow of the sun on my face, and the unfamiliar heat that burned deep inside of me.

THE WOMAN IN A BOX in Clarice's garage began beating on my door, big time. She wanted to know what in the hell I thought I was doing, going out with Friedrich. It hadn't been a year since I left my husband. The ink was barely dry on my divorce papers, for crying out loud! And now I had the audacity to have dinner with a strange man in a strange country. *What was I thinking? Maybe Val II was right...maybe I was taking a big risk.*

My confidence eroded and washed down the drain as I showered and dressed for the evening. *Who was I to dare think I still had a shot at romance?*

I thought about Dominik, and wondered what that poor fisherman's face must have looked like when he came back from buying cigarettes to find nothing but a Road Runner dust trail heading back to my hotel. I cringed. That night I'd proven what a total chicken I really was. *Better just forget the whole thing, Val.*

I wrote a note to Friedrich, calling the whole thing off. I planned to slip it under the door to his room, number 222, then do an encore performance of my disappearing act. I reached for my doorknob and heard voices coming down the hall. I recognized them immediately. They belonged to Frank and Val II.

"I can't wait to get home and have some *real* food," Frank said.

"You and me, both, Frank. They just don't make it here like they do at The Olive Garden."

I envisioned the two jerks strolling down the hall, arm in arm, their faces twisted with that smug, morally superior expression of the wantonly ignorant.

Screw that. I'd rather be wrong than be like them. Before I could change my mind, I threw the note in the trash and bolted to the lobby to meet Friedrich.

THE GERMAN GREETED me with a nod and a small curl of a smile. Thankfully, he'd taken a fashion note from the Italians tonight and wore tan chinos and a white, cotton dress-shirt with sleeves rolled up casually to his elbows. I'd put my cute little floral dress back on, along with a pair of glittery silver sandals with chunky heels. We spoke very little, just nervous small talk, as Friedrich led the way toward one of his favorite haunts. It turned out to be a typical, open-air bistro overlooking a small, inlet harbor.

We took our seats at a table for two next to a stone seawall. I noticed a small flotilla of painted wooden boats floating like colorful fishing bobbers in the calm sea below. I wondered if one of the beautiful red-and-blue skiffs belonged to Dominik. The thought made me cringe.

"Are you okay?" asked Friedrich.

"Oh. Yes," I faltered. "I, uh, I was just admiring all the craftsmanship put into these little boats. They're only used for catching a few fish and octopi, but they're painted and decorated with such care."

"You are observant. In Italy, nothing is designed purely for function. Beauty must also play its part."

"I like that philosophy. It makes for a life not just lived, but *savored*. I'd like to adopt that for my own life."

Friedrich smiled blankly. Perhaps he didn't understand some of my English words.

"A glass of wine for you?" he asked. Dusk was falling and his Nordic skin glowed pinkish-gold from the fading sunset.

"Of course."

"Oh. And dinner is on me, Friedrich. I owe you so much for all the time you've spent driving me around."

"You owe me nothing." Friedrich said. "But I accept your gift with thanks. You are not like other women."

When Friedrich didn't put up a fuss about my offer to pay, a conflicting blend of magnanimity and skepticism washed over me. Was he being gracious? Or cheap? Did he think of me as a potential lover? Or just a friend?

Will I ever shut my brain off? Or will I continue to analyze everything to death? Shut up and enjoy the moment!

The waiter approached. Friedrich nodded at me. "Red or white, Val?"

I smiled and shrugged. "After all this time living here, you should know which wine is good. Order what you think I would like."

"The *Primitivo rosso*, then," he instructed the waiter.

"Primitivo?" I asked.

"Ja. It is the oldest wine grapes of the Puglia region," explained Friedrich. "It is the city of Manduria where they grow the grapes and make the wine. The Primitivo grape makes a dark, earthy bouquet. It has a sweet ending, as you say. With a hint of *himbeerin*. Uh, what you call *raspberries*. It is actually a very traditional wine. Simply made, yet surprisingly complex. Very similar to the woman sitting in front of me."

If some man back in the States had delivered Friedrich's last lines, I would have rolled my eyes and dismissed him as a fake, womanizing dirtbag. But there was a blunt honesty about Friedrich that made me believe in his sincerity. I blushed a little at his compliment, and hoped the fading sunset would hide my indiscretion. I'd never thought about myself that way before. *Earthy? Maybe. Sweet? Hmmm. Raspberries? Yes. Definitely raspberries.*

"Now *that's* some pretty smooth talking," I said before I could stop myself.

I regretted my stupid comment as soon as I heard it come out of my mouth. Typical me. Whenever a man I liked paid me a compliment, I had to spoil the moment. It was as mandatory as it was involuntary. *Why do I do this to myself? Why?*

"What does this mean, this smooth talking?"

All right! I've been granted a do-over! I decided to cover my blunder with a white lie.

"It means elegant...to speak *elegantly*," I improvised.

"Ah. Then I accept your compliment." Friedrich's half-smile made another appearance and decided to stay awhile. It softened the hardness of his taught, square jawline. The candlelight played in his blue eyes, and as the waiter poured the wine, I realized Friedrich's eyes were the same color as the sea.

"A toast," he said, and raised his glass.

"A toast." I started to take a sip of wine.

"Stop!" Friedrich commanded. He stood abruptly, knocking the table forward a few inches. "Don't drink it!"

"Why? Is it poisoned or something?"

"No. Two reasons," he explained, sitting down again. "First, we must toast *to* something. Second, you must look in my eyes before you take the first drink."

"Okay." I shrugged my shoulders and raised my glass in anticipation.

"A toast to friendship." Friedrich's eyes focused intently on mine as he said the words. For emphasis, he pointed an index finger to his eye.

"To friendship," I echoed. A sliver of disappointment deflated me ever so slightly. I looked into Friedrich's sea-blue eyes and took a sip.

The wine was just as he'd described. Rich, complex, with a slightly sweet berry finish. I savored it for a moment, and watched

Friedrich do the same. When he looked at me again, I asked the obligatory question.

"Why do I have to look into your eyes when we toast?"

"If not, seven years bad sex," Friedrich said matter-of-factly, as if it were common knowledge.

Something in his professorial manner cracked me up. I started giggling and nearly spewed my mouthful of wine. I couldn't stop myself. Friedrich studied me curiously at first, but when I snorted as I gasped for air, he gave in and attempted a hesitant laugh. He looked as stiff and rusty as a wrench left out in the rain. But the more he tried, the easier it got for him. After a while, all I had to do was point a finger at my eye and he'd crack up, making me laugh right along with him.

We kept this up until the first course, the *antipasti*, arrived. The somber waiter set down a rustic, clay bowl piled high with small, green and black olives. A basket of warm, crusty bread accompanied them, along with a bottle of golden-green olive oil and a plate of milky mozzarella. I guess there was no German protocol for food like there was for wine, because Friedrich dug right into the feast. I followed suit.

The *primo piatto* came next. A plate of succulent, balsamic shrimp and calamari insalata. Next came the *secondo piatto*—the main course. Mine was fresh, Adriatic mussels smothered in cream with a side of thick, homemade linguini. Friedrich ordered a delicious-looking, roast duck carbonara. As we dined, the crowd grew thick and the sky grew dark. We took turns coming up with things to toast to, always careful to look into each other's eyes.

We toasted to old friends, new adventures, *la dolce vita*, and the beauty that surrounded us. I don't remember all of them, but the last one will stay etched in my memory forever. Friedrich took my hand and looked softly into my eyes. He raised his glass with the last sip of wine.

"To this moment in time," he half-whispered. "May it never be forgotten."

I batted back unexpected tears and raised my glass. "Never forgotten," I managed to choke out.

After dinner, Friedrich and I strolled to the *piazza*, a small park at the heart of the city. Unlike Dominik, Friedrich didn't touch me or even try to hold my hand. In the soft lamplight, we watched young lovers neck, and children of all ages play gleefully up and down the square, as carefree as birds on the wing. Parents and grandparents sat vigil on benches nearby, one eye on the kids, one eye on the passersby as they gossiped amongst themselves. In this land of the truly living, not even the pitch-black sky could convince an Italian it was time to call it a day.

Friedrich and I strolled along together, silently watching the world go by. Lost in my own thoughts, I suddenly realized we were walking over familiar ground. We were back at the Hotel Bella Vista. Antonio acknowledged us with a nod as we entered the empty lobby. We squeezed into the tiny elevator and rode it to my floor, our faces mere inches apart.

"Thank you for such a wonderful evening," I said, afraid Friedrich could smell the garlic on my breath.

"You are welcome."

The elevator door opened. I smiled. "Well, goodnight then."

I turned to step out of the elevator. I felt Friedrich's hand touched my cheek. I looked back to face him and he kissed me—a light peck on the lips. From the look on his face, I think he was as stunned by his action as I was.

"Thanks," I fumbled. My eyes as wide as jar lids. Friedrich gave a perfunctory, tight-lipped nod.

I stepped out of the elevator. I heard the door closing behind me, but I didn't look back. I fumbled for my room key, but my mind had turned to mush. My hands jerked like I had ahold of a jackhammer as I struggled to get the blasted key inside the lock. Finally, the door opened and I tumbled into my room. A jolt of electricity shot through me. I felt something begin to unfold—no—*reawaken* inside me. I burst into tears. I wasn't sure what for.

I kicked off my shoes and sat on the bed. My head spun like a top. Suddenly, I heard a strange thump from the room next door. I sniffled, dried my tears on the backs of my hands, and listened in the quiet. I heard the thump again, followed by a moan. Then another thump. Another moan.

I broke out into a grin. Then I started snickering. Unlike chicken-liver me, someone next door had said yes to amore—and was getting the ride of their lives.

Chapter Eleven

My cappuccino grew cold as I sat lost in my thoughts, replaying last night with Friedrich over and over in my head. The sunset. The wine. The walk home. The elevator kiss.... *Was it a real kiss, or just an afterthought?*

"You're up early."

Berta's voice burst my daydream bubble and teleported me back from laugher and soft candlelight to breakfast clatter and fluorescent lighting. I blinked up at the woman taking a seat across from me at the table.

"Actually, this is my normal time," I replied. "*You're* the one up early today. I'm glad to have the company for a change."

"When you're my age, you don't *have* to get up early. So far, that's the only advantage I've found about old age."

Berta flashed a smile, revealing a row of pearly whites too perfect to be anything but dentures. Well into her seventies, Berta wore the neat costume of a dignified senior citizen; fashionably color-coordinated polyester pants, wrinkle-resistant patterned top, knit jacket, and white slip-on sneakers. But for me, her cover was blown as soon as she opened her mouth. Berta was as conservative as Lady Gaga.

"I'm on at 8:30 today," she said sullenly, staring dully at her vending machine coffee. "That's freaking early, if you ask me. How about you?"

"Class at 8:20. Frank should be down any minute."

"Now *that* guy's a piece of work."

"I guess you should know, being a psychologist."

Berta laughed. "Major control issues. You don't need to be a psychologist to see *that one* coming. Looks like you drew the crap end of the stick with the partner assignments, kid."

"Yeah. But at least I'm not married to the guy. What does Botox Broad see in him?"

"A wallet, most likely. It's amazing what some people will put up with for a meal ticket."

"I know, right? I'd rather starve than sell my soul to a dirtbag, no matter how thick his wallet might be."

Berta studied me for a moment. "You know, I like your attitude, kid. You seem hell-bent on making the best of things. Like with your luggage. Kudos on how you handled that fiasco. I think I would've have blown a gasket over that one."

"Thanks. It's a new thing I'm trying out. Going with the flow. Maybe you've heard of it?"

Berta laughed. "Could be."

"To be honest, Berta, I messed up the first half of my life pretty darn badly. I'm trying not to waste the second half, too. That's why I'm here. I'm on kind of a...mission. I'm trying to figure out what I want to do with my life."

"Divorced the sucker, huh?" Berta smiled wryly and showed me the left side of her upper dentures.

"You're *good*."

"Nah. Some people call it a mid-life crisis, but I think it's more like a wake-up call. You hit forty and you realize you don't have so much time to piss around anymore. Your shoved-away dreams gang up on you and kick you in the proverbial ass. You're left with two choices. Either get off your butt and get going, or fall back into the familiar and sleepwalk yourself into an early grave—if you're lucky."

"My word! Are you some kind of mind reader?"

"Hardly. Hate to break it to you, kid, but you're a typical, text-book case. But unlike most folks, you chose to get going. Good choice."

"What do you mean, good choice? Do you think everyone should get divorced when they turn forty?"

"Naw. Everyone should wake up and smell the coffee, kid. They should take stock. Figure out if they're on the right track or not. Then make the tough choices, if need be."

Berta took a sip of her vending machine coffee and made a sour face. I waved a thumb and index finger at Giuseppe. He acknowledged me with a quick nod.

"So my situation is not so unusual." I felt less special and brave, somehow.

"Not at all," laughed Berta. "After I left the convent, I got married. We both tried, but it just didn't take. We split up twenty years ago, and I've never looked back. I wasn't sure what I wanted back then, but I knew one thing for dang sure. I didn't want *him*."

"*Exactly!*"

I felt a growing camaraderie with the crusty old sage disguised as some kid's great grandmother.

"That's *exactly* how I felt about Jimmy, *my* ex. But where do I go from here? If I read another candy-coated book telling me everything will be all right if I just *believe in miracles and rainbows and unicorns*, I'm going to projectile vomit!"

Berta nearly choked on a sip of coffee. I suddenly felt awkward. *Had she just written just such a book?*

"What a bunch of flapdoodle!"

I sighed with relief. "I don't mean to sound like an ingrate, but if all anyone had to do was *believe*, wouldn't everyone have what they wanted? And what does that make people like me who are still trying to figure it all out? Unbelievers? Lazy slobs? Idiots? Infidels?"

"Not at all, kid. Actually, just the opposite, believe it or not. After all my years sorting out the jerks from the angels, *I* should know. I call people like you *truth seekers*. Your kind isn't after a quick-fix, feel-good pile of horse hockey like so many people are. I can tell by your moxie that you're a fighter, not a victim. You're willing to do the dirty work to find your own truth."

"How do you *know* all this?" I asked, incredulous.

"Because you and me, kid, are cut from the same bolt of cloth. Like it or lump it, for people like you and me, nothing but our own truth will do."

Giuseppe arrived with the cappuccinos and placed one on the table in front of me, the other in front of Berta. The old woman looked down at hers, then up at me. A perfect, pearly-white smile of delight spread across her wise face.

"Thanks for the advice." I raised my cup to her.

"Cheapest session I ever gave." She shook her head in mock lament. We clinked our cappuccinos together and took a sip.

"Ahhh, now *that's* a cup of joe!" said Berta. "I tell you what, kid. This alone could make me want to live in Italy the rest of my days. I could hang a sign out, 'Will Psychoanalyze for Cappuccino.'"

"That's a thought. But I don't think the Italians are as neurotic as the Americans. Clients could be pretty scarce."

The old woman shrugged her shoulders nonchalantly. "Oh well, there's always blow jobs."

I nearly dropped my cup. Berta grinned and tilted her gray-haired head to the right. "Speaking of BJ's...."

I looked in the direction of her nod and saw Frank walking into the dining room.

"You are so bad!"

"Yeah, I know," she said proudly. "With age comes privilege. Follow your own drummer, kid. It works for me. It'll work for you, too."

I reached across the table and took Berta's thin, delicate hand and squeezed it. "You rock, Berta."

"Yeah, I kinda do, don't I? You too, kid."

"I better go before BJ blows his top."

"Eeww."

A visual came to mind that made me grimace. "You are so *so* bad!"

Berta grinned, and I headed toward Frank. I could hear him crabbing at Giuseppe about the hot weather, as if it was the poor waiter's fault.

"LOOK WHO'S *not* coming to dinner," said Val II to Frank.

I'd tried to sneak past the dining room unnoticed, but was nabbed by the disapproving duo. They'd obviously dressed to impress each other tonight. They both reeked of what Grandma Violet called, "too much cologne and not enough good intentions."

"You're right. I do have other plans tonight."

"I'm sure you *do*," Val II hissed. She and Frank scrutinized me from head to toe, their sour mouths puckered as if they'd both been weaned on the same mildewed pickle.

"I heard the *two of you* went to a fancy restaurant last night," I said, ignoring their glares. I'd wanted to drive home the point that we were *all* free to opt out of the group meals in the evening. The fact that they were being hypocritical was totally lost on them, naturally. "You missed a great minestrone soup."

"The food was a lot better *there* than this dump," Frank said

"Yes! We had a *wonderful* time last night," Val II added. Given the straining tendons in her neck, I wasn't sure she'd *ever* had a good time.

"Well, I'm glad that we're *all* able to enjoy the delights of Italy."

"Some of us more than others," Val II said with a sneer.

I'd never been accused of so much and been guilty of so little. I scoured my mind for a couple of snappy comebacks, but settled on silent dignity. Besides, I didn't owe those jerks a dang thing, not even an explanation.

"Enjoy your meal." *I hope you choke on it.* I pivoted on my heels and clicked across the lobby toward the stairwell. I wanted to put some distance between me and those two turkey vultures before their combined negative energy vortexes sucked me under. I needed to stay positive. I was on my way to room 222.

EARLIER THAT AFTERNOON, I'd gone to swim a few laps in the pool and run into Friedrich out on the deck having a smoke.

"Hallo Val. I've been thinking about Matera."

"Me too. That place is a punch to the gut. Pretty powerful."

"Ya. It is. You understand now, why it haunts me."

"I think so, yes."

"Would you like to see *The Passion of the Christ,* then? The movie filmed at Matera?"

"Is it playing at a theater?"

"No. I have the DVD. We could watch it...in my room."

"Oh..."

"I could also offer you dinner," he added. "But I have to warn you first. I would be cooking. And the only place to watch TV is on my bed."

On his bed? What did he mean by that? Before I could think it through, I heard myself say, "Okay."

I STOOD IN FRONT OF room 222, debating whether to knock. *Had I made the right choice? Why had I decided to wear my sexy purple*

underwear? Clarice had given me the lacey, purple thong as a gag gift, "in case of emergency." I guess this qualified. I'd never worn a thong before. The unfamiliar feel of it between my butt cheeks made me squirm like a wormy puppy.

"How does anybody stand to wear these things?" I asked myself under my breath. I tugged on the back of my pants trying to free the rude scrap of material from my crack. Suddenly, the door opened.

"Oh. I thought I heard someone out here," Friedrich said. "Come in."

I cringed and stepped awkwardly inside. Friedrich shut the door, then kissed me lightly on the lips, exactly like the night before. Like his poker face, the kiss's intent was hard to decipher. Friedrich walked over to a small, wooden table and poured two glasses of wine. As he did, I couldn't help but think that maybe our kiss last night had meant nothing at all. It was just a normal, German greeting.

Hello kiss. Goodbye kiss. See ya later, alligator kiss. Shut up, Val. Stop thinking! Just relax and enjoy the moment, for crying out loud!

I distracted myself by nosing around his apartment. His room was on the corner of the building, and was only slightly bigger than my "deluxe digs," as Tina had described them. One open space served as the dining, living, and cooking area. Like me, he had a terrace and a private bathroom. The only differences were his tiny kitchenette and an extra, separate room for the bedroom.

Looking around the place, it was obvious Friedrich had been here a while. Family pictures lined the top of a bookshelf used as makeshift storage and as a dumping ground for mail and magazines. I walked to the terrace. A small metal table and two folding chairs had been set up among a jungle of potted plants. I glanced around the rest of the living room. It contained the typical, boring bachelor-pad stuff. Except for one corner. It was stacked high with an odd assortment of electronic equipment. Green and red lights blinked like fireflies from the boxes, and at least one was giving off a weird buzzing sound.

"What's all that?" I asked as he handed me a glass of wine.

"I'll explain you in a minute, but first, a toast."

I dutifully looked into the German's blue eyes and held up my glass.

"*Prost*. That is a traditional German toast."

"What does it mean?"

"In your language? Cheers, I suppose."

"Well then, prost!"

We took our first sips of wine, eyes locked.

"Do you like to funk?" asked Friedrich, his eyes still locked on mine.

I nearly inhaled my wine. "Excuse me?"

"Are you interested in funking?"

I felt my legs go weak. "Ummm...I...."

Friedrich eyed me curiously. "Don't tell me you never did it before."

"It's been a while."

"Do you still remember how?"

"Um. Well. I think so. Yeah."

"You can play with mine, if you want. Here, let me show you."

Friedrich reached toward me and my knees plum near buckled out from under me. I braced for impact, but his hand went past me and grabbed hold of a chair behind me. He pulled it toward the corner of the room and motioned for me to sit. He leaned over me from behind the chair and put a hand on my shoulder. His other arm reached forward. I closed my eyes in anticipation....

"Here is the power switch. I can tune it to American radio stations, if you want."

"What?" My eyes flew open. Friedrich's hand was twirling a knob on something that looked like a stereo.

"What do you call funk in America? Oh ya. Ham radio. All of this equipment is my ham radio station."

Relief and disappointment washed over me like a bucket of ice water down my back.

"Oh. I see." I laughed nervously. "Friedrich, how about we do this later?" I bolted out of the chair. "What's for dinner?"

"*Spätzle* and lentils, my favorite German food."

"What's a spätzle?" I asked.

"It is a fancy name for noodles." Friedrich walked to the kitchenette and picked up a ball of light-yellow dough. He held it up for me to see. "Watch." Friedrich rubbed the dough ball across what looked like a cheese grater. Stringy dollops of dough fell into a bowl. "That's a spätzle. "Lentils are—"

"Beans," I said, cutting him off. "*That* I know. No meat?"

"Did you want some meat?" He looked taken aback.

"Oh! No," I faltered. "I just thought that Germans typically ate a lot of meat...sausages and stuff."

"Ah. But remember, I am *not* the typical German."

"Oh, yeah. I forgot." I smiled.

Friedrich waved away my faux pas like a gnat in the wind. He finished making the spätzle and dropped it into a waiting pot of boiling water. I watched as he carried out his culinary tasks with the comfort and ease of a man used to doing his own cooking. Before I could finish my wine, he had filled two plates from the well-worn pots on his two-burner stove and carried them to the terrace. I followed him outside.

The steamy piles of noodles and lentils slowly disappeared along with the sun as we dined and chatted the evening away.

"I use the ham radio to talk to people all over the world," said Friedrich. "You should try it. You will like it."

"How did you learn it?"

"From my father. He loved to talk on it. Some of that equipment is his."

"Oh! Do you and he talk on the radio together?"

"No. He died of a heart attack. I was halfway around the world at the time. I couldn't get to his funeral. I still regret it."

"How long ago did he die?"

"Hmmm. It has been seventeen years now."

That's a long time to hold onto regrets. "How about your mom?"

"She's turning eighty in December. My sister is putting together a party for her. That's a big deal for Olga. She and my mother don't get along very well."

"Too different?"

"No. Too much alike."

"Oh. Do you have any other brothers or sisters?"

"Not any more. My other sister Birgit died of breast cancer two years ago."

I was beginning to understand the source of the sadness that appeared so often in Friedrich's solemn blue eyes. But he wasn't the only one to have to live with the loss of loved ones. My own father had died nearly a decade ago. And both Grandma Violet and Grandpa Hue were long dead and buried.

"Shall we go to bed?" Friedrich asked abruptly.

I nearly inhaled my sip of wine. I nodded, too choked to speak.

"I will start the movie."

He stood up and disappeared into the bedroom, leaving me alone on the terrace. I swallowed the lump in my throat, picked up the empty plates and went inside. I set the plates in the kitchen.

"Come!" Friedrich called from his bedroom. I walked to the doorframe. "Lie down," he instructed.

I scooted onto the right side of the bed and propped my head up on a pillow. I could smell the earthy musk of him in the white cotton bedsheets. He slid a DVD into the player and lay down on the other side of the bed, leaving a good foot of space between us. He smiled at me for a brief second, then turned his attention to the TV.

The Passion of the Christ turned out to be the most violent and bloody movie I'd ever seen. I closed my eyes repeatedly to escape horrific images I knew would otherwise haunt me forever. I understood why Friedrich said he'd felt "destroyed" by it. Between squinty grimaces and hiding my face in my hands, at some point I realized Friedrich had turned over on his side. He lay facing the wall, asleep.

I turned the sound down on the DVD player and listened to Friedrich as he snored lightly. It had been a long time since I'd heard the sound of another person breathing beside me. After witnessing the horrors played out in the movie, the sound of his snoring comforted me. I lay there until I felt my own calmness return. I climbed carefully out of bed and snuck quietly out of the room. As the door to his apartment closed with a click, I realized I'd had nothing to agonize about. He just wanted to be friends. I vowed to stop over-analyzing things, and to never wear thong underwear again. *Ever!*

Chapter Twelve

Just when I was getting to know Berta, she up and disappeared.

It was dinner time, and, as usual, the running joke amongst my fellow volunteers was what the "mystery meat" would be disguised as tonight. The mystery meat was a flat, thin, brown slice of animal hide about the same size, shape and tenderness as the heel of an Italian loafer. In fact, it could very well have been that some poor guy was limping lopsided around Italy as we tried in vain to carve up his shoe.

The leathery hunk of animal flesh first appeared on the dinner menu a week ago, disguised as "prime rib." Those who had ordered it (Frank and Val II) had complained so loudly about it that we'd all been made well aware of the culprit's existence *and* its inedibility.

Every night since then, the villainous cut of meat had attempted to pass itself off on unsuspecting diners under the guise of "veal picatta," then "pork medallion," and my personal favorite "beef *tender*loin." No matter what the chef decided to call it for the night, the beastly hunk of sinew and gristle always kept the same form and shape. It was indestructible.

The only person to have actually managed to wound the formidable hunk of flesh was Frank. That first night he'd sawed a sliver off the side of it and chewed it until his jaw hurt. Finally, he'd given up and, in a real touch of class, had passed the masticated mess around in a napkin for our dining pleasure.

Last night, the mystery meat was disguised as *"carne assado,"* grilled meat. Tina had been the unfortunate soul to order it. When it arrived, we'd all recognized it right away and burst out laughing. Tina had laughed along with us, then speared the thing with her knife and held it up like the booby prize in a gift exchange.

"Maybe they should have called it *carnage* assado," she'd quipped.

Accident-prone Peter had fallen out of his chair laughing at her joke. He'd leaned back in his chair and placed both hands on a stitch in his side when his chair had gone out from under him. But working for the IRS must have given Peter a hide as thick as a rhinoceros. To his credit, he'd simply gotten up, dusted himself off, and dug his fork back into his linguini marinara. He uttered not even a whimper about his knee, which was still bandaged from his run-in with a scooter a few days back.

After ten nights of mystery-theater dining under our belts, tonight we were all abuzz with anticipation. Would it be Tina in the blue dress with the sirloin?

"Tina, you were the last one to have it," Peter said. "What do *you* think it'll be called tonight?"

Tina rolled her eyes. "Who knows?"

"It's weird," I said. "The rest of the food here is so good. How can they keep getting the meat so wrong?"

"I have a theory," Tina offered. "I bet it's the same exact piece of meat. Think about it. It's always the same shape and size. I say whoever gets it next should tag it. Put some kind of mark on it or something, so we can identify it if it comes back around."

"It couldn't be the same piece of meat!" objected Val II. "The hotel would be under some kind of code violation. Right Frank?"

"Right, Val," Frank said supportively. "Besides, I cut a piece off of it once. And a couple of times two or three of us had it at the same time."

"Yeah, but nobody else has been able to make a dent in it but you," Tina argued. "It could be that they are, let's say, *recycling* the intact ones."

"It would be a viable way to reduce overhead," Peter said.

"That's revolting!" Val II cried. "They'd better not be doing that!"

"You'd be surprised at what some people will do to save money," Peter added. His tone assured us that we didn't want to know the gory details. "I say let's do what Tina suggested. Let's tag it. We could put a toothpick in the center."

"Have you got a drill to make the hole?" Frank laughed loudly at his own joke.

"If it comes back to me with a toothpick, I'll sue this place," said Val II, her Botox-paralyzed face twisted in indignation.

As we spoke, Giuseppe tiptoed around us like a thief in the night and laid tonight's menus on our plates.

"Why don't we just vote on it," Frank said.

He stood and banged his handle of his dinner knife on the table for us to come to order. The look on the attorney's red face made my mind flash to a scene from *Lord of the Flies*.

"Those *for* tagging, raise your hands," he barked.

Slowly, hands went up: mine, Tina's and Peter's.

"That's three for," Peter reported.

"Those *against*?" Frank raised his hand and looked down at Val II.

She smiled up at Frank sheepishly and raised her hand.

"That's two against," Peter said.

"Wait. There's six of us," I said. "Where's Berta?"

Everyone looked around, as if they expected to find the old woman squatting between the chairs or under the table.

"I don't know where *Berta* is," said Tina. "But I think I just found tonight's mystery meat." She held up her menu and pointed at an entree. "It's *gotta* be the "Sucking Pig.""

NO ONE HAD NOTICED Berta missing before dinnertime. The last time I'd seen her was this morning. She'd gotten up early again and joined me at breakfast to deliver her second-cheapest therapy session ever. The bill had come to *two* cappuccinos. I remembered that she was dressed like Kermit the frog.

"Nice sweater," I'd said cheerfully to Berta when she'd sat down to join me at the breakfast table. She'd looked down at her bright green sweater as if she'd never seen it before.

"This?" she'd croaked as she'd pulled on the sweater at a spot above her right breast. "Kid, don't patronize me. You wouldn't be caught dead in this polyester frog outfit. I know it. You know it."

"It's not *that* bad," I'd backpedaled. "Besides, if you don't like it, why wear it?"

"Keeps the creeps away." She'd drawn her boney face closer to mine. "Val, if I wanted to get laid, I wouldn't choose *this* outfit. But I don't speak much Italian, see?"

"No. I don't see."

"Look. Here, I want to look like somebody's dear old granny. That way, everybody treats me nice. Cheaper cab fare here. A free cup of coffee there. These clothes...this sweater...they're just...*props*. They help me get what I want. Nothing more, nothing less."

"Oh," I'd replied, dumbfounded. "Is everything you do so...*calculated?*"

"Let's just suffice it to say I don't do too many things *unconsciously* anymore. At my age, I want to be *awake* every minute I'm *awake*, if you know what I mean."

I'd nodded. "Yeah. I get it. Want a cappuccino?"

"Sure. What's it gonna cost me?"

"Just a few minutes of your precious time, Madame."

"Better hurry. That may be all I've got left."

I'd laughed out loud.

"Come on, Berta, you've got more life left in you than most people I know. Besides, the half-life on that sweater's got to be at least another hundred years. You might as well get your money's worth."

Berta had stared at me for a second, then thrown back her head and laughed her butt off. When her grey-haired noggin had finally come forward again, she'd wiped tears from her twinkling eyes.

"Okay, you got me, kid. That laugh alone was worth five minutes of free advice. Shoot."

I'd smiled at the geriatric frog and grabbed the chance she offered.

"Okay. Yesterday you told me that everyone makes their own choices in life. To paraphrase you, 'We either chase our dreams or dig our graves.'"

"Nice. Mind if I steal that line?"

"Consider it yours. So. I *get* that. But what I *don't* get is why Frank and Val II are so darn *disapproving* of me. Of *everyone*, really."

Berta had scrunched her mouth sideways, but said nothing.

"It's weird," I'd continued, searching for the right words, "but it's almost as if they believe that there's only so much happiness to go around, and...and—"

"And you took it all."

"*Yes! Exactly!*" I said. "How do you keep doing that?"

Berta laughed. "Seen it a million times. It's all part of the same thing we talked about yesterday. It's the classic victim-versus-champion mentality. A victim doesn't take responsibility for her life. That way, she can't be held accountable for its sorry state."

"I don't understand."

"You don't understand because you're *not a victim,* Val. You're a champion. You pull yourself up by your bootstraps. You make the best of a given situation. Like with your luggage. That's how I knew what kind of person you are. A victim would have wallowed in self-pity and blamed the world for her rotten luck. You came out punching with an arsenal of jokes and laughs. A formidable sense of humor is the hallmark of a champion, kid. Believe me. You're a champion."

"Thanks, Berta. I appreciate that. But answer me this. Why in the world would those two think *my* happiness was stealing from *their* happiness?"

"Because it's easier for them to say you took their happiness than to admit to themselves that they threw theirs away."

"Wow. That's pretty profound, Berta."

She'd flashed me a smile and waggled her eyebrows. "Not bad for an old lady in a frog suit."

WE WERE ALMOST THROUGH dinner. Berta still hadn't shown up. No one had ordered the "Sucking Pig," so our toothpick experiment remained theoretical for the moment.

"Did you see Berta today?" Tina asked me as our desserts arrived.

"I saw her at breakfast. She told me she was off today, but I haven't seen her since."

"Did she mention any plans to go anywhere?" Frank asked.

"Not that I can recall."

"*Think,* Val," Frank demanded impatiently, as if I'd been too lazy in my first attempt. "Did she say anything that may have implied a trip, illness, anything like that?"

"No."

"I rang her room but no one answered," Peter said, returning to the table. "I also checked the front desk. There was no note."

"Isn't there a rule about going off without proper notification?" Val II asked.

"We should get the key and check inside her room," Frank said.

"I'll go with you," Val II said.

She and Frank got up and left the dining room. As I watched them disappear, Tina leaned over and whispered in my ear.

"I don't think it's any of their business to go in Berta's room. I'd be pissed if they did that to me."

I felt the same way. But I'd already learned my lesson about trying to talk reason into Frank. He and Val II were definitely in charge of this rescue mission. I ate my cannoli and kept my mouth shut. A few minutes passed, and the dictator and his minion mistress returned.

"Her purse was there," reported Frank. "But no money. And no passport."

"Maybe she just went out for a walk," I suggested.

"Or maybe she got kidnapped. Or raped! Or that strangler guy got her!" Val II said.

"I don't think that's a very helpful thing to say," I said.

"Helpful?" Val II said angrily. "You just sat on your butt while Frank and I went to check on her welfare. *You're* the unhelpful one."

It was all I could do to keep my redneck roots from twisting around that Botox witch's throat and giving her a good throttling. But if Berta really was lost, I couldn't help her from inside an Italian jail cell.

Chapter Thirteen

I didn't sleep much last night. A cold wind swept in across the sea and blew the terrace's lace curtains around like an angry ghost. I kept thinking of Berta out there somewhere, all alone. When I woke up at 5:13 this morning, I decided to check on her. I went to the balcony to get the pair of panties I'd washed out, but like Berta and Scarlett O'Hara, they were gone with the wind.

It was early, so I snuck out in my nightgown, and padded down the staircase to Berta's room to check on her. I knocked on her door, but no one answered. I turned around to see Frank backing out of room 235 in his boxer shorts and t-shirt. He closed the door with a click.

"You're up early," I said.

He jumped like a spooked tomcat.

"I was...going to check on Berta."

"I just did. She's not answering."

"Hmmm."

Frank stood motionless, staring at me. His comb-over was flying at half mast.

"Okay. See you at breakfast," I said, and scooted back to my room.

BERTA DIDN'T SHOW AT breakfast. On my way back from class, I stopped at the front desk to pick up my room key. As usual, Antonio was on duty.

"Any word from Berta Goodman?" I asked.

"No."

"What should we do?"

"Wait a few more hours."

The normally poker-faced Italian looked worried. That made me worry even more.

Across the lobby, I saw Peter and Tina over by the Internet room. He had her cornered between his outstretched arms, her back pinned against the wall. Curious, I took a seat with my back to them and eavesdropped on their conversation.

"I found your little present last night," I heard Peter say.

"What are you talking about?"

"Come on. You don't have to play shy with me."

"Honestly, Peter. I don't have a clue what you're talking about."

"These."

I turned around to take a peek. Peter tugged at something is his pocket. My eyes followed his gangly hand down toward his crotch.

Slowly, Peter pulled a small, flimsy object from his pocket. It was almost the same shade of purple as Tina's ticked-off face. Peter held up the scrap of material between two sets of pinched thumbs and index fingers. It was the pair of panties I'd lost to the wind last night. *Oh, crap on a cracker!* I looked away quickly. I could feel my face heat up like a gas stove.

"Are you all right, Miss Val?" Antonio asked, eyeing me curiously.

"Oh. Uh. Yes," I stammered. "Uhh...just the heat. Hot. You know?"

The handsome hotel manager nodded at me. "I tell you a little secret. Do like I do." He pulled up his pant leg enough to reveal a slim, naked ankle peeking out of his exquisite Italian loafers. "No socks."

"I'll keep that in mind."

I avoided making eye contact with Tina and Peter as I hurried along to the elevator. I stepped inside the lift and sighed with relief as the grumpy doors jerked their way toward closing. Just as I thought the coast was clear, four fingers appeared between the last few open inches between the doors. They forced the elevator open. Friedrich side-stepped his way inside.

"Hallo, Val." He studied my red face. "Hot today, ya?"

"Yes."

"Are you all right?"

Friedrich studied my face again. It was maddening how he seemed to calmly and clinically see right through my skin and into my soul. I, on the other hand, couldn't read him at all. Once or twice I thought I'd seen desire register in his eyes, but most of the time I couldn't get past his internal wall of stoicism.

"I'm fine, thanks."

I hadn't spoken with Friedrich once since I'd snuck out of his room after the movie. I would be leaving in three days and would never see him again. He was just a friendly face on my journey. There was no point in allowing any feelings I had for him to grow.

"Would you like to have dinner with me tonight?"

My heart jumped at his unanticipated invitation. The debate I thought I'd just put to rest came rushing back to life. *Did Friedrich like me just as a friend? Or was there more to it?*

"I hope you are not thinking to say no." Friedrich's mouth crinkled with concern. "After the other night, I would not blame you."

I looked into the German's sea-blue eyes. They were apologetic and inviting. I smiled, and his lips formed that charming little curl of a smile.

"Do you promise not to snore through dinner this time?"

"I promise."

The tiny elevator ground to a halt. I started to get out, but Friedrich placed his hand gently on my neck and kissed me hard on the mouth, leaving no trace of doubt—or anything else—in my mind.

I SPENT THE AFTERNOON with Tina, walking around Brindisi trying to find Berta. We didn't have a picture of her, and neither of us could speak Italian. The few shopkeepers we found that could speak English said they hadn't seen her. We went back to the hotel empty handed and heavy hearted.

"What do you think happened to her?" I asked Tina as we walked into the lobby. "You were just kidding about the strangler guy, right?

"Yes. It was just a bad joke. I wanted to get Val II riled up. Now she's gone nuts over it."

"So where could Berta be?"

"Who knows? Maybe in a hospital. She'd old, you know."

"Oh my gosh! Why didn't I think of that?

Antonio was at the front desk.

"Antonio, could you call the hospitals? Berta might have gotten ill while she was out and been taken to one."

"Yes," agreed Antonio. He knitted his eyebrows together and tapped an index finger on his chin. "If she had taken a lover, she would be back by now. I make the calls."

"Thank you."

Tina and I walked to the elevator. She pushed the button and looked at me.

"No offense, but Berta with a *lover*? Yuck!"

"Wait a few decades and the idea will grow on you."

"Yeah. Like a wart."

I STOOD IN FRONT OF the bathroom mirror and adjusted the black lacey underwire bra. I'd had it on less than a minute and it was already digging into the soft flesh under my arm. The clock on my nightstand read 6:30 p.m. In half an hour, I was supposed to meet Friedrich in the lobby for a *real* date. I buttoned my peachy silk blouse and tried to recall what it was like to have sex with a man I wasn't married to. *Geez. Tina probably wasn't even born at the time!*

I thought about Tina and her slim, tan body. She couldn't be any older than twenty-three. I'd been twenty-four when I'd married Jimmy. I remembered how insecure I'd felt about my body even then. Oh, what I would have done to have those thighs back now! I thought about the cruel irony of it all. I was so self-doubting when I was young and firm and beautiful. Now that I'd gained a bit of confidence and self-worth, Mother Nature had come along and replaced my thighs with cottage cheese.

I turned and studied the backs of my legs in the mirror. *Screw you, Mother Nature.* For the last two years, no matter what I did, that dreaded curse of hers had crept its way slowly up the backs of my thighs, and had just recently made a gambit for my butt cheeks. Funny, I hadn't had sex in over two years. Which had come first? The cellulite or the celibacy?

Even though my sex life had died, my vanity had remained alive and kicking. I'd hidden my married life as a nun from all my friends, including Clarice. It had just been too painful and embarrassing to mention.

I slipped on a white denim skirt and a pair of sexy sandals. Even though I didn't look as good as I'd hoped, I tried to take comfort in the idea that at least as I'd grown wider, I'd also grown wiser. I knew I was never going to look any better than I did right now, so I might as well make the best of it. Besides, even if Friedrich did see my crater-pocked full moon, I would be leaving in a few days. I'd never see him again. As long as he didn't secretly film us and put it on the internet, no one else would ever know.

"Ready?" I asked my image in the mirror. I took in a big breath and blew it out. "Ready." I took a step toward the door....

I FOUND FRIEDRICH WAITING for me in the lobby, dressed in chinos, a blue dress shirt and a smart sport jacket. We walked, arm-in-arm, to a romantic patio café draped in purple wisteria blooms. By candlelight, we talked and drank a bottle of rich, red wine. My pasta dinner was the best I'd ever eaten. The light shone in Friedrich's eyes. My romance novel cliché had finally gotten back on track.

After dinner, Friedrich held my hand firmly as we slowly picked our way along the narrow, cobblestone streets that led back toward the hotel. As the peachy walls of the Hotel Bella Vista came into view, Friedrich stopped suddenly. He took me by both hands and spoke with a brutal honesty that left me blindsided.

"Val. Seeing you last night. It cut me like a knife. The thought of you leaving makes it hurt to see you. I...I can't stop thinking about you."

"I...I don't know what to say, Friedrich."

"There is nothing to say. I only wanted that you know this."

I nodded. Friedrich dropped one of my hands and began walking toward the hotel again, gently tugging me along. When we reached the lobby, I was surprised to see the bar was closed. The sleepy night clerk who made my early-morning cappuccinos was just coming on duty. He smiled at me as we passed by. I looked at the clock. It was half past eleven. *Where had the time gone? Weren't we just sitting down to dinner a minute ago?*

Our footsteps rang hollow as we crossed the empty lobby toward the elevator. When we reached the lift, Friedrich pushed the button, then took my hand again.

"I had a wonderful time with you tonight, Val. I really don't want the evening to end. You will be gone soon. Won't you come to my room and have a drink? I promise you don't have to do anything you don't want to do."

I felt my body go limp. My heart began to pound in my chest so hard I wondered if Friedrich could hear it.

"Okay...just one drink. But first...I need to...go back...to my room and...put away my umbrella."

As we rode the elevator to the third floor, Friedrich kissed me tenderly. His sea-blue eyes were softer than I'd seen them before. They seemed to see right through my fears. The elevator lurched to a stop on my floor.

"Take your time," Friedrich said as I stepped out into the hallway. He didn't mention the fact that I didn't have an umbrella.

"See you soon," he said as the doors began to close. He smiled in a resolute way that let me know he would honor whichever choice I made.

I watched Friedrich disappear behind the elevator doors. I took a step toward my room and my knees nearly went out from under me. I stumbled to my door, opened it and flopped onto the bed. My head spun like a garden whirligig. I was torn between desire and discretion. Between romance and reality. The attraction between Friedrich and me was undeniable. So was my airplane ticket to Rome on Saturday morning.

Friedrich's passionate kiss in the elevator had removed all my doubts about his intentions. Things were about to get real—if I wanted them to. My pulse thumped in my ears. The clock read 11:41. It was fight or flight time, and the chicken-livered jury inside my head was still frantically deliberating my fate.

When I'd announced my travel plans to Clarice, she'd told me to enjoy my freedom. *Now's your chance. Find a lover! Be free!* But I just wasn't made that way. Try as I might, I just couldn't turn off my heart and let my body take over. I was an all-or-nothing kind of gal. Or, at least I *had* been. Maybe it was time to change that. It wasn't as if that strategy had worked out so great for me. Why should I hold onto it?

"What do you want?" I asked myself aloud.

I sat on the bed and chewed my nails. *I could just go for a drink. I don't have to sleep with him. I mean, I really would like to spend more time with him. It might be nice to just kiss and cuddle a little bit. It's been so long....*

I stood up.

Come on! Who are you fooling, Val? If you go there, you're going to have sex with him. Plain and simple.

I sat back down on the bed.

It's not against the law. I'm single, for crying out loud! And like he said, I don't have to do anything I don't want to.

I stood up.

But you can't! You're not that kind of girl! What do you really know about him, anyway? He could be that psycho killer!

I sat back down.

I might be missing the chance to find my love of a lifetime. Do I really want to blow it now?

I stood up.

It's been so long since you've had sex, you probably don't remember how. You could be all dried up down there!

I sat back down.

Shut up, stupid brain! What do I want? What do I want?

A punching bag full of unfulfilled desires swung around and hit me in the gut. I collapsed from the below-the-belt punch and folded myself up on the bed in a fetal position. My heart pounded like a sledgehammer.

So, is this it, then? You're giving up? Another dream down the drain because you're too afraid to admit to your own feelings?

Leave me alone!

When are you going to stop doing what you think other people want you to do, and start doing what you *want to do?*

What? Does that even make sense? I must be drunk. I should stay here. My judgment is impaired.

I'm not buying that excuse. Not today. Now tell me. What do you want to do, Val?

I want to make love with Friedrich!

That instant, a beautiful serenity flowed over my body like warm honey. Every trace of fear washed away. I sat up in bed and calmly put on my shoes. I walked to the elevator, then rode it to the second floor. I walked down the hall to Friedrich's apartment. At exactly midnight, I tapped lightly at the door numbered 222. It opened immediately. Friedrich smiled at me tenderly, and gathered me into his arms.

Chapter Fourteen

Friedrich's hands felt like hot silk as they slid around my waist, over my back, along my legs. His warm, gentle touch reawakened my half-frozen body, which had begun to thaw the moment I'd finally admitted my desire for him. With tenderness and talent, Friedrich helped me return to the place lovers know.

As I lay in his arms, it finally made sense why poets made such a fuss about the act of lovemaking. I'd had sex plenty of times, but I'd never felt fully consumed like this. For the first time, it wasn't just my *body* that had disintegrated into bliss, but my *soul* as well. I felt strange and new and completely satisfied.

The soft light of the crescent moon shone into Friedrich's room. I could see his strong hand holding mine next to my heart. We were lying on our sides, spooning. My naked back was against his naked stomach. I could smell his musk and the scent of sex in the air. I was completely calm. Nothing else in the entire universe mattered. Complete contentment cocooned us. In the shelter of his warm embrace, I began to doze off.

Suddenly, a long-ago thought jabbed my sleepy brain like a boney finger. I wriggled out of Friedrich's arms and sat up.

"What time is it?" I asked.

"Are you okay?" Friedrich mumbled, half asleep.

"Yes. What time is it?"

Friedrich looked over at his clock radio. "It's one a.m. Why?"

"That means it's...the first of June."

"Ya."

"I just remembered something. I had an astrological chart done back in Florida. The woman told me I would be relieved of a heavy burden on the first day of June."

Friedrich eyed me curiously through one sleepy eye. "And what burden was that?" he asked.

"She didn't say. And I didn't know...until now."

"And what do you know now?" Friedrich sat up and wrapped his warm arms around me.

"I think it was the heavy burden of sadness I'd been feeling. I thought I would never enjoy making love again."

Tears welled in my eyes.

"Val, on this I promise you. You don't have to worry about that anymore."

We laughed softly in the dark together, then moved back into our spooning position. Soon, I heard the rhythmic rasp of Friedrich gently snoring. I quietly slipped from his arms, dressed, and crept back to my room.

It was nearly two a.m. I had class to teach in the morning. Still, as I lay in my bed alone, I couldn't sleep. Without a naked Friedrich for evidence, I could barely convince myself that what had happened *had* actually, really happened. But it had. Friedrich and I had made love. And my body had responded with a passion I thought was dead and buried decades ago.

My ecstatic soul kept poking me awake, repeating the same mantra over and over:

I'm alive! I'm alive! I'm alive!

Chapter Fifteen

The piercing glare of the morning sun on my face woke me from my fitful slumber. I bolted upright and looked at the clock. It was already 7:30 a.m.! My body felt like a bag of wet cement as I dragged it out of bed, showered and dressed. The only thing that kept me from falling back asleep was my mind. It spun like a looped movie reel, replaying last night over and over and over again.

I caught my breath every time I thought about it. My body shivered from tip to toe. *Last night!* I dragged a brush through my crazily matted hair. I worked on the snarls at the back of my head and wondered when I would see Friedrich again.

I DIDN'T HAVE TO WAIT long. When I stepped into the dining room for a quick cappuccino before class, I saw him sitting alone at his normal breakfast table. I'd asked Friedrich to keep our affair a secret between the two of us. I hoped he would keep his promise. As I passed his table, I tried to play it cool, but I couldn't help it. I smirked. I felt sexy, mysterious and voluptuous, like an international spy in an old, black-and-white movie.

"Good morning, Freidrich," I said, perhaps a bit too nonchalantly.

"Good morning," he replied casually.

Friedrich was keeping our secret. I smiled and breathed a grateful sigh of relief and walked over to the noisy group at the volunteer table.

"Well, I was just about to call out the cavalry," said Frank. "I don't need another person to have to worry about."

I studied Frank's grouchy, arrogant mug and wondered what Val II saw in him. *Oh yeah, not my problem.* I shrugged and sat next to Tina.

"Sorry. I overslept."

"Looks like the early bird didn't get the worm *this* morning," sniped Val II.

Tina poked me in the ribs and whispered. "Maybe because you got the worm last night, huh?" She studied me with her too-young-to-be-so-jaded face.

A wave of heat warmed my innards. I could feel it shoot up my neck. I forced my best poker face.

"Such a dirty mind for such a pretty girl."

Tina grinned slyly, then stared at me as she chewed on my comment, unsure whether to swallow it or not. I turned my attention back to Frank.

"Any word on Berta yet?"

"Well, I didn't want to bring this up at breakfast, but Antonio said there was an unclaimed body in the morgue that fit her description."

"Oh no!" I cried. "Someone needs to go find out if it's her!"

"Obviously," Frank said. "Who wants to do it? Any volunteers?"

"I will," offered Peter. "I'm off today." He took a giant bite of croissant. "And I know where the hospital is." He poked his bandaged knee up above the table for our viewing pleasure.

"All right then," said Frank. "I've informed Ms. Mozzarelli. She'll be here soon. You can go together."

"Hey, I just remembered," Peter said. "There's a great pizza place next to the hospital. Anybody want me to pick one up for them while I'm there?"

The thought of Peter looking at dead bodies one minute, eating pizza the next turned my stomach. But his strong constitution did seem to make him the right one for the job. Who else could be so callous and uncaring?

"Do they have pepperoni and mushroom?" asked Val II.

FRANK WAS SILENT AND sullen all the way to class. I couldn't have been more grateful. To keep from being a nervous wreck, I'd put thoughts of Berta on hold until Peter came back with his news. No use worrying. It wouldn't help anything. Besides, my mind was preoccupied with another thought. *I, Val Jolly, had actually had sex last night.*

I wondered if anyone else could tell I'd fallen off the celibacy wagon. On my way to class, I thought I detected a look of recognition in the eyes of an old woman sweeping a doorway. I was almost *certain* our weary classroom teacher was on to me. After class, I was positive a handsome young man in the bakery window had gotten wind of my lewd and lascivious deed. Even the tomcat I petted outside the hotel winked at me as if he was well aware of my naughty, nocturnal shenanigans.

"Keep it under your hat, cat."

I scratched the kitty behind his ears and smiled at my own silly imaginings. *No one looks different from having sex. Do they?*

I took a step toward the hotel entry door and was almost run over by a dilapidated old car. I was about to give the driver a piece of my mind when I realized it was Vittorio, the cabbie who'd picked me up at the airport.

"Vittorio! How are you?"

The threadbare old man's eyes registered not a hint of recognition.

"I need a cab to the airport in two days."

The old man's face cracked into a snaggle-toothed smile. "Ah, bella signora! Prego!"

Vittorio handed me an appointment card. As I filled in the time I needed to be picked up, one of the businessmen from the hotel climbed into the cab. Vittorio snatched the card from my hand, gave a quick nod, and peeled out of the driveway faster than my Uncle Jack on a beer run with five minutes to go before Earl's Liquor Store closed.

I watched the black cab leave. A white van pulled up. Ms. Mozzarelli was at the wheel, looking tired and put upon. Peter climbed out of the passenger seat carrying two pizza boxes.

"Well?" I asked, nervously eyeing the pizza.

"Oh. Did you want a pizza? I only got enough—"

"No, Peter! Was it her?"

"Berta, you mean?" he asked.

"Yes, of course!"

"Geez. You don't have to get all huffy! Calm down. It wasn't her."

I frowned. "Are you absolutely sure?"

"Val, the stiff on the slab was wearing a blue dress, pearls and a headscarf."

"Oh." I sighed with relief.

Definitely not our Berta. She wouldn't be caught dead in a headscarf.

"PURPLE. INTERESTING," Friedrich said.

We'd met after dinner at the lobby bar. For some reason, I was at a loss for words. What could I say to the man who, mere hours ago, had seen me in all my naked lack of glory? I was desperation for something funny to say, to lighten the awkwardness I'd felt. So I told Friedrich about Tina and Peter, and their misunderstanding involving my wind-swept purple panties.

"Do you know what, in Germany, the color purple means?" Friedrich raised one eyebrow as he awaited my answer.

"No."

"A frustrated woman."

I laughed involuntarily, then blushed.

"This is one color you no longer need, ya?"

I punched Friedrich on the shoulder and leaned in to kiss him. He jerked back, and I suddenly remembered our affair was a secret. I jerked back, too, then looked around to see if anyone had noticed. It didn't appear so. I took another sip of the horrible brown drink Friedrich called a "digestive." I resigned myself to the fact that I would never acquire a taste for Amaro. I set the nasty aperitif back on the bar.

"Well, I guess I'll say goodnight," I said to Friedrich.

I left him standing alone at the bar and made a show of saying goodnight to the other WOW volunteers. At dinner, we'd all agreed it was time to call the police about Berta. Frank and Val II were over by the front desk, talking with an officer while Antonio interpreted. I'd wanted to help out, but Frank had shut me down, insisting on taking charge of the situation. Whether that was a good thing or not, I didn't know. I'd already told Frank everything I knew about Berta's disappearance, which was zilch.

On the ride up in the elevator, worry grabbed me by the shoulders and shook me down like a schoolyard bully. Friedrich and I had made secret plans for tonight. He was supposed to come to my room fifteen minutes after I left the lobby. As soon as I'd stepped into the elevator, I'd begun to second-guess the sanity of the scheme.

This man is a stranger! What if that's what happened to Berta? Had she met a man and he'd done...who knows what to her?

I mean really, what was I doing? I'd be leaving in a few days. Was it really worth the risk to my heart? To my *life?* A gentle tap sounded on my door. I opened it to find Friedrich there, holding a red rose. I hated red roses. Grandma Violet's coffin had been covered in them. My misgivings reared up like a bucking horse.

"I don't want to go chasing any more dead ends, Friedrich."

He stepped inside and closed the door behind him.

"Val, don't you know by now? They're all dead ends."

Chapter Sixteen

It was Friday, and still no word on Berta.

I would be leaving tomorrow. My class duties had ended yesterday. After our last lesson, the handsome young men had showered me with passionate hugs and kisses on the cheek. I'd also been given a small, silver-colored box containing four exquisite, hand-made chocolates. They'd looked more like works of art than food. But their beauty hadn't been enough to save them. I'd taken a picture of them with my phone and devoured them all on the walk back to the hotel. Frank had been given neither kisses nor candy, and I hadn't shared mine. I was done trying to impress the boorish blowhard.

I met up with Tina for our final breakfast together. Vittorio was picking me up at 7 a.m. to catch a flight from Bari to Rome.

"Did you hear the latest on Berta?" she asked as she sat down across from me.

"No! What?"

"The police went up to inspect her room, and all her stuff was gone. The closets were empty. The only thing they found in there was an empty purse and a used bar of soap."

"So...are you saying that maybe Berta just up and left?"

"Probably so."

"Why on earth didn't Frank and Val II tell us that Berta's luggage was gone?"

"I know, right?" Tina rolled her eyes. "Those two are idiots! They're so wrapped up in themselves they probably didn't even think to check."

"I've been worried sick for days! At least now there's a good chance Berta just left, and isn't dead somewhere."

"Come on, Val. You didn't seem *that* worried. I mean, not enough to keep you out of the sack with Friedrich."

My face suddenly burned like hot coals.

"What are you talking about?"

"Ah ha! I knew it! That red face says it all!"

"Hush!"

"Why? What's the big deal?"

"I don't know. I...I've just never done anything like this before."

"Come on. Don't tell me you're a forty-one year old virgin. Not buying it."

"No. I've never had a...*casual affair* before."

"What? You're kidding!"

"No, I'm not."

"Well, I've never had married sex before, so we're even."

I laughed softly. "Thanks for not judging me."

"Judging you? For what? I've been screwing Jonny the pool guy for over a week."

"Really?"

"Sure. So tell me, Val. How do they compare?"

"What?"

"Married sex and unmarried sex. Which is better?"

I smiled slyly. "I think I need a bit more research before I can give my final answer."

"Hmmm. Does that mean you're staying?"

"Oh. No. Are you?"

"I don't know yet. But there's nobody back in Jersey missing me."

"I'll miss you."

"Thanks. I'll miss you, too."

WITH BERTA'S LUGGAGE gone and no body floating in the sea, the police refused to pursue the case until further evidence became available. I tried to picture Berta in her green pantsuit off on some new adventure. I only wondered why she hadn't bothered to say goodbye.

I went back to my room and got ready for my trip to the beach with Friedrich. It was my last day in Brindisi, and it was a stunner. The sky was the color of sapphires, unmarred by even a trace of clouds. Friedrich had instructed me to bring along a camera and plenty of sunscreen. The plan was to drive along the coast and find a cove where we could sunbathe a bit and take a swim.

I slipped into my floral sundress and sandals. I pulled my lavender, two-piece suit from a drawer and giggled. *Purple! I guess I won't be needing this anymore.* I tossed it on a chair and decided to leave it behind tomorrow. I found my white one-piece and tucked it into a cute straw tote I'd bought at an open-air market yesterday. Then I added a book, a bottle of wine, and a half-gallon container of industrial-strength sunblock.

I'd told Friedrich I would wait for him in the lobby after breakfast. When I stepped out of the elevator, he was already waiting for me, dressed in a white cotton shirt and knee-length khakis. The white Gilligan hat was back, perched on his head like a wilted pizza crust. The Birkenstocks also made a reappearance, minus the black socks, thank goodness. Through the lobby's glass doors I could see his little silver convertible glimmering in the sun.

"You look goot," he said as I handed him my straw tote.

"Thank you. You, too!"

Our affair was still a secret, as far as I knew, so I waited until we were safely off the hotel grounds before I leaned over and kissed Friedrich on the cheek.

"What was that for?"

"Do I need a reason?"

Friedrich cocked his blond head and gave me a half a smile. "No."

He shifted gears and soon the fresh, salty air off the Adriatic filled my senses. For a Friday, the beaches were surprisingly packed with kids who barely looked old enough to be out of high-school. Both sides of the road were lined with cars parked haphazardly in the sand and grass. A couple of times we thought we'd found a free space, only to discover a motorcycle or scooter tucked inside.

We drove on for another twenty minutes or so, until the vehicles finally began to thin out. Friedrich parked the Peugeot in the sand next to a stack of white boulders, each one bigger than his car. We grabbed our beach bags and picked our way around the huge stones. On the other side shone the crazy-blue Ty-D-Bol sea.

We found a spot in the sand and lay down our towels. I fussed with mine, putting my shoes on the corners to hold it down against the breeze coming off the water. Satisfied, I looked up to see Friedrich bent over in front of me, his naked butt in my face. He was fishing something out of his bag. He stood up with his red speedo in his hand. He casually stepped into it.

I looked up and down the beach. There was no changing room. There wasn't even a bathroom. There were probably fifty people milling about. I saw a young woman slipping on a bathing-suit top. I suddenly realized Friedrich was watching me. I gulped and let out a determined breath.

"Well, just let me slip into this," I said. I pulled my suit out of my bag and sat on the towel. I changed out of my sundress and into my suit in three seconds flat.

"Care for a swim?" Friedrich asked.

I could use some cooling off after that totally embarrassing moment.

"Sure!"

As we walked to the sea, I noticed the crowd was pretty young. "These kids look like teenagers. Shouldn't they be in school?"

"Oh, you didn't hear. They are on strike today."

"The students? On strike? Why?"

"You see how nice the weather is today?

"Yes, but—"

"What more reason does an Italian need?"

I stood in silence for a moment, a monkey wrench thrown into my American mindset. Then something inside me relaxed, and I grinned from ear to ear.

What better reason indeed? Here's to la dolce vita!

THE REST OF THE DAY with Friedrich went by like an old family video. Nothing spectacularly interesting happened during it, still, it was a memory I wanted to hold on to because I knew it wouldn't last. I think we both were haunted by the lingering thought that tomorrow was goodbye. We'd returned to the hotel and made urgent, desperate love, the sand and the smell of the sea still clinging to our bodies.

That evening, we'd returned to Friedrich's favorite little bistro. The same place he'd introduced me to Primitivo Rosso, the wine he said reminded him of me. We'd strolled to the town square and listened to a children's choir. Then I'd spent the late evening in his room, wrapped in his arms. He tried to discuss the future with me, but I'd silenced him with a finger to his lips.

"Let's just let it be what it was, Friedrich. The perfect affair."

Chapter Seventeen

F riedrich had offered to drive me to the airport this morning, but I'd begged him not to. I couldn't bear another minute of good-byes. I packed my belongings and snuck out of my room. I rode down the jerky little elevator for the last time, sandwiched between my suitcase and my carry-on. When I stepped into the lobby, Friedrich was nowhere in sight. He'd kept his promise.

I couldn't tell for sure if I was relieved or disappointed. The young night clerk saw me and, without a word, dragged himself off the couch to start fixing my cappuccino. Just as he finished, Antonio arrived through the glass entry door.

"Ah. Leaving us so early," he said.

"Si. Gratzia mille for everything."

Antonio's mouth alternated back and forth between a smile and a frown as I handed him my keys for the last time.

"You need a cab, Signora Val?"

"No, Vittorio should be here any minute."

"Arrivederci, signora Val. *Buon viaggio.*"

Antonio nodded at me, then turned and busied himself with pa-perwork. I took a seat on the black sofa, sipped my last cappuccino and waited for Vittorio to arrive.

I'D JUST RETURNED MY cup to the coffee bar when a hotel maid came bustling out of the elevator, waving something in her hand.

"Signora Jolly! You have forgetted this!" She scurried up to me and handed me the purple bathing suit I'd hoped to leave behind.

"Oh. Thank you. Gratzie," I fumbled.

As the maid walked away, I sighed. *I hope this isn't a portent of frustrations to come.*

I shrugged the thought away, bent over and unzipped the side pocket on my big blue suitcase. I started to tuck the suit inside when I spied something red in the pocket. I pulled it out. It was a pair of Friedrich's sexy underwear. I stared at the underpants for a moment and smiled. It dawned on me that I'd never had a lover before. Not like *this*.

I saw Vittorio's cab pull up. I looked up and jumped like a frog in a frying pan. A pair of judging eyes glared at me from a face that looked as if the whole world smelled like a sewer. *Aww, crap!*

"You're leaving already. Good," Val II said sourly. "You know, an educated man like Friedrich is too good for a flabby-assed little hick like you."

If I didn't have a plane to catch, I'd have shown her just what this flabby-assed little hick was capable of.

"Oh really? Then why did he take me on all those rides?"

"A cheap ride for cheap ride, my dear. And now you're gone. Frank and I, we have a relationship. We're *dating*. We decided to stay in Italy another week. He's taking me on a tour of the Amalfi Coast. You got a tour of what? A pizza parlor and a cheap hotel room?"

The woman had gone and gotten on my last nerve, but I wasn't about to give her the satisfaction. I smiled cheerfully.

"Well, I think you and Frank make the perfect pair."

Val II's face went from sour to smug. "We do, don't we."

"Absolutely. You kiss *his butt* for his money, and every time he locks onto your freakish, butt-blubber lips, he's kissing fat that came out of *your ass.*"

Val II's Botox face went crimson. I smiled brightly, then turned and headed out the door.

I STUMBLED OFF THE airport bus and stared up at the gleaming white whale that was to be my home for the next week. The King Kavanaugh was the pride of the Kingman Cruise Line. According to the brochure, the ship had been refurbished just last year. Its itinerary would take me, my best friend Clarice Whittle, and 4,800 other passengers and crew up and down the western coast of France and Italy.

I snapped a picture of the ship, then followed the steady stream of folks pulling suitcases toward the port building. I took my place in line. It moved quickly, and soon I stood before a young Asian woman. She reviewed and approved my documents, and handed me a plastic card.

"It's your shipboard room key and credit card," explained the way-too-enthusiastic check-in clerk. "Use it for everything on the ship, instead of cash."

I slid the credit-card/key thingy into my purse. I watched with a tinge of separation anxiety as my luggage went one way and I went the other. The clerk said the luggage had to go through security scans, but I knew the main reason was to confiscate contraband booze being snuck on board. I convinced myself there was no way my luggage could get lost twice, and made my way onboard.

I was supposed to meet Clarice at the airport in Rome, but she'd emailed me saying her flight was delayed a few hours and to go on to the ship without her. She would catch a later shuttle bus. With no luggage to weigh me down and a few hours before we sailed, I set off to explore the ship and try to get my bearings. Given my sense of direction, it could take me three days just to find our cabin.

I rode an elevator up to the top of the ship and looked around at the port. Compared to Rome, Civitavecchia was ugly and uninteresting. I went down a floor and followed an orange carpet and a din of voices to the Circus Buffet. A cute young girl in a blue, nautical uniform instructed me to put my hand under a disinfectant dispenser. A glob of clear goo plopped into my palm. The girl smiled brightly and rubbed her hands together. I aped her performance, and was allowed admittance.

I stepped into the restaurant and nearly had a panic attack. Hundreds of people were running about like they were on fire, carrying plates heaped with cupcakes, cookies, cakes and pies. The orange and yellow upholstery and balloon-print carpets added to the carnival atmosphere, but there was no clowning around going on. For the gluttons inside, this was serious business. I found a little spot out of the fray next to a fountain spewing liquid chocolate.

"Are you gonna get some or get outta the way?"

I turned to find a woman who was even bigger than my mom's next-door neighbor, Tiny McMullen. She must have weighed over four-hundred pounds. Her striped moo-moo was so big it looked like it was made from a stolen sideshow tent.

"Oh. Excuse me. I didn't realize I was in your way. Nice dress!"

The obese lady eyed me suspiciously from the small crevice in the fat above and below her eye sockets.

"Move it!"

It took me five steps, to get around her, but I squeezed by and hightailed it out of that feeding frenzy of freaks before I ended up on the menu as meatloaf. Once I was beyond reach of anybody's knife and fork, I slowed down and looked at the art hanging on the walls. It was a lineup of clown faces. A plaque next to each one said prints could be bought at the Circus Circle Boutique on level three for just $129.00 each. Shoot. I'd pay that much *not* to have them in my house.

I walked along a mall of small shops and pubs until the hallway gave out at a pair of doors with a sign over them that read: Kingman Theater. I pulled on the shiny, gold double-doors, but they were locked. I went to find the cabin and wait for Clarice.

After ten minutes of bumbling around on the port side of the ship, I finally figured out that odd numbers were on the stern side. I found it 737 and slid my key thingy in the door. A green light came on and the door unlocked. I stepped inside. The cabin was tiny, but functional. Over the years, I'd kind of lost my taste for a lot of needless space and useless things to take care of. The room had two twin beds, a desk, a TV, a nightstand a closet and a washroom. It would do just fine.

I sat on the corner of one of the beds and clicked on the TV. A shiny white couple straight out of an infomercial were talking about how excited they were that I was on board. If I was going to believe that, I needed a drink first. I looked in the mini fridge built into the desk. It was stocked with sodas and miniature alcohol bottles. I made myself a Tanqueray and tonic, grabbed a notebook that said, "Let's Get Acquainted!" and sat back on the bed. The first page in the book was a minibar price list. I did the math. My drink had cost me $17.35.

"What the hell!"

"Hey! That's no way to greet an old friend!"

Clarice pushed her way into the room.

"Clarice! You made it!"

"I did—just barely! Val, aren't you a sight for sore eyes!"

Suddenly, the ship's horn sounded. An announcement came over the intercom in the hallway.

"Ladies and Gentlemen, the captain welcomes you aboard the King Kavanaugh. Join us up on the deck for a sail-away party!"

"You look beat, Clarice. You want to stay in and rest?"

"Hell no! Let's go party!"

"Well all right then!"

We made our way to the elevators. The crowd waiting to get on was ridiculous.

"What about the stairs?" Clarice suggested.

We walked to the staircase. It was practically deserted. We trudged up five flights to the top floor. As we got to the open deck, a young Indian man handed us each a flute of champagne.

A deafening horn blast nearly caused us both to drop our glasses. We'd barely recovered when the ship jerked unceremoniously, sending us tumbling into each other. A voice came over the loudspeakers:

"Welcome aboard! First port of call; Monte Carlo, Monaco!"

"Woo hoo!," Clarice exclaimed.

I sighed and silently said goodbye to Italy and my sad German lover with the sea-blue eyes.

"Are you okay?" asked Clarice.

I turned toward her and plastered on a smile. "Yeah, sure. Why?"

"It just...you have tears in your eyes."

"Oh, that? I'm just so glad to see you, girl!"

Chapter Eighteen

On Sunday morning, reality crashed over me like a tidal wave. I awoke and bolted upright in bed, drenched in sweat. I'd dreamt of Val II. She'd been in my face, pointing her finger at me and shaking her head. The giddiness I'd felt over my affair with Friedrich mutated into full-blown panic. *Oh my lord! I'd had sex with a stranger! What did I really know about Friedrich Fremden? Nothing, really. I could have an STD! No, no, no! Why had I been so stupid? Why?*

At forty-one, I'd already made a lifetime's worth of mistakes. Was my affair with Friedrich merely the latest chink in my unbroken chain of bad judgement calls?

A little over a year ago, I'd had it all. A successful career. Plenty of money in the bank. A beautiful house in a great neighborhood. A marriage that had endured more than fifteen years. And a gnawing, ravenous emptiness that had clawed me awake every morning at 3 a.m. to remind me what a sham my life really was.

I'd graduated from college. I'd worked hard. I'd married a nice guy. I was healthy. I'd kept in good shape. I'd even volunteered at the local elementary school, for crying out loud! So, why in the world had I felt so...*hollow*? Was something wrong with me? Did I want too much? Was I simply ungrateful?

I looked over at Clarice, sleeping like a newborn pup in the twin bed next to mine. I'd confessed all of this to her back then. I'd been surprised to discover that she, too, had been waking up at 3 a.m., her mind racing like the long shot at the Kentucky Derby. At the time, we'd laughed uneasily about it, then chalked it up to our busy lives. We'd even joked about starting a 3 a.m. knitting circle. That had been the end of the discussion for her. But for me, the relentless, unwanted nocturnal intruder hadn't been a joke.

Those deep-rooted longings that had struggled so fiercely to rise to the surface had scared the living hell out of me. I'd stuffed them back down inside with both fists. In an effort to get a decent night's sleep I'd cut out caffeine. I'd changed my diet. I'd stopped drinking liquids after 7 p.m. I'd taken warm, candlelit baths. I'd read boring books. But nothing had worked. Finally, one day, when I'd been feeling about half-past dead, I'd hauled my zombie-like body to a doctor and gotten sleep medication. I'd known exactly which brand I'd wanted, because I had seen about twenty-thousand ads for it on late-late-night TV.

Those ads had not only educated me, they'd proven to me that I wasn't alone. I'd wondered how many fellow desperados were out there, wandering the back country of their minds each night, chasing forgotten dreams, like sheep, off a cliff to their inevitable deaths. That night I took a pill and let the luminous green moth in the commercial carry me in its wings to the never-never land of chemically induced unconsciousness....

A knock on the cabin door startled me out of my sad-sack memories.

"Room service, Ma'am!" the male voice behind the door said. It sounded strangely contorted, as if English wasn't his first language.

I jumped out of bed and cracked open the door. A small, delicate-looking young man with skin the color of coffee and cream smiled at me broadly.

"Good morning, ma'am!"

"Oh! Good morning! Could you come back later? My friend Clarice is still sleeping."

"Certainly, ma'am." He reached in and grabbed a sign hanging on the inner door knob. With the patience of a saint, he said, "Just hang this on the *outside* of the door any time you don't want to be disturbed."

"Thank you, I will."

He demonstrated how to hang the sign on the doorknob.

"Like this, see?"

"Yes, I think I have it. Thanks again."

I wondered how many times each cruise he had to teach that lesson. If it was me, I'd have been in the loony bin by now. And here I was boo-hooing about my past. About problems most people on the planet would be *delighted* to have.

What the hell are you doing, Val? Stop this crap immediately! You're on vacation, for crying out loud! Get dressed and get your butt out of this freaking cabin!

I dressed quickly, left a note for Clarice, and scurried out of the room. I followed the ship's deck-plan signs, one-by-one, to the promenade level. I figured a good walk or two around the exercise track on the open-air deck would clear my head before breakfast.

The fitness room was deserted. As I rounded the track to the other side of the ship, a dramatic scene came into view. I recognized it from a travel book. It was the first of five cliff-side villages that made up the Cinque Terre. But the picture in the book hadn't done it justice. In real life, it took my breath away.

Narrow, three-story buildings scaled the mountainside like an open zipper. The candy-colored, stucco-clad structures formed two zig-zagging rows along a huge crevice in the stone. They appeared to defy gravity. They clung miraculously to the rocks like dirt-dauber nests, from the very top of the cliffs all the way to the sea.

I tried my best to focus on the beauty right in front me, but just like insults from mothers in law, the memories of my past kept finding their way to the top of my mind.

Why had I left my husband? Maybe the better question to ask was why I had married Jimmy in the first place. Jimmy had been nearly the opposite of unreliable Ricky. He'd also been a lot older than me. Even though he'd lacked ambition, he'd been faithful, *and loyal.* He'd had a great sense of humor. And he'd treated me with respect. As an *equal,* even.

My family was unpredictable, irrational and dysfunctional. And those were their *good* qualities. Looking back on it, I guess I was seduced by the peaceful, normal fairytale Jimmy had offered. A man of little drama and no dreams of his own, Jimmy had agreed without hesitation when I'd told him of my desire to ditch my corporate job and form my own advertising company. As a result, I'd been able to make a really good living for us.

So why had Jimmy and I fallen apart? No huge event stood out in my mind. There'd been no affairs. No lies. No gambling. No physical abuse. Instead, there'd just been a slow, steady *unraveling* of our connection to each other. Over the years, we'd talked less and less, and done fewer things together. At some point I woke up to realize we'd become nothing more than housemates living separate lives on paths that seldom crossed any more.

Like a comfortable sweater, our relationship had been too easy to put on and too easy to toss in a drawer. After too much wear and not enough care, it had lost its shape. It had become stained and frayed. It no longer fit. For a while, we'd tried to mend it—putting patches over the unsightly spots. But in the end, the effort had made us both exhausted. Finally, we'd admitted it was simply beyond repair....

A flash of light roused me from my melancholy daydreams. I caught the last misty glimpses of the second village as it stair-stepped down the side of a grey cliff. At its base, a small clutch of buildings surrounded a harbor full of colorful wooden fishing boats. I watched it slowly disappear from view. *Let it go, Val. How can you expect to find love again if you won't leave the past behind?*

"Have you checked out the breakfast buffet yet?"

The tinny, male voice startled me. I turned away from the scenic view to find a plump, greasy-looking bald man in his fifties standing beside me. He wiped beads of perspiration from his red, furrowed brow with a paper napkin.

"I'm sorry. What did you say?"

"Have you been to the breakfast buffet? It's awesome!"

Sweat ran down the man's crimson neck, despite the cool breeze coming off the sea. He wore a short-sleeved, brown-and-yellow striped polo shirt and beige shorts. The morning sun glared mercilessly off his white socks and tennis shoes. I smiled wryly to myself. He looked just like a middle-aged Charlie Brown.

"Did you just get off a treadmill or something?" I asked, trying to ascertain the source of his perspiration.

"No way! I just ate fifty strips of bacon. My new record!"

"Oh. Well...congratulations."

I hid my disgust behind a cheerful smile. The fat man grinned proudly, revealing evidence of his recent pig-out on pork. As he reached to wipe his brow again, I turned and walked away. It may have been rude, but I didn't care. I was grateful that I wasn't a swine—and that I wasn't married to one, either.

WITH THE SHIP SET TO dock in Monaco tomorrow morning and Clarice still in the sack, there was nothing for me to do on board except eat and watch the beautiful Italian coastline pass by. I sat in a deck chair and tried not to think as flat, rocky cliffs topped with green pastures rolled lazily by, punctuated by the occasional, picturesque cove, massive boulder island, or tiny village of stucco houses perched atop the cliffs.

At eleven, I went to the cabin to check on Clarice. She was still in bed, but she was awake.

"There you are," she said, and yawned.

"Did you sleep all right?"

"Like a drunken sailor."

"Good old jet lag. Better than a sleeping pill. Are you hungry?"

"I'm starving."

"Get dressed and we'll head up to the buffet. It's seafood day."

"Sounds yummy! I'll make it quick."

Quick in Clarice terms meant under an hour, if I was lucky. Unlike me, she was a girlie girl who wouldn't be caught dead going out to pick the newspaper off the driveway without her full war paint on and her hair just so.

"Okay. I'll just watch cruise info on TV. See if there's an excursion we want to go on."

AT LUNCHTIME, I PROVED myself a total hypocrite by totally pigging out at the seafood buffet. But to be fair, Clarice matched me shrimp for shrimp.

"I ate enough to be arrested in some countries," joked Clarice. "Stop me before I eat again!"

I snickered and looked at my gorgeous blonde friend with the button nose and sparkling green eyes.

"If I don't pace myself, by the end of the week I'll be looking like a Macy's Thanksgiving Day Parade float," I grumbled. "Look, ma. It's Bloatie."

"Well, if we *do* get fat, it might not be a total loss. We need to buy new clothes, anyway. I didn't get the memo that the ship's dress code was Oscar de la Geriatric."

I laughed. "We're in Monaco tomorrow. Maybe we can find a boutique and buy us a nice pair of polyester stretch pants."

"Perfect."

"Gosh, I've missed you, Clarice."

"Thanks, but I don't believe it. I hardly heard a word from you for the last two weeks. What have you been up to? Or should I say, *who* have you been up to?"

My traitorous face grew hot. "Nobody."

"Come on! I know that look. Who do you think you're talking to, Little Miss Red Riding Wood?"

"You know, for such a high-society gal, you've got a real gutter mouth."

"I know! Isn't it great!?"

I laughed and wished I owned my stuff the way Clarice did. "Yeah. It is."

"So? What's his name? How big was he? Was he circumcised? I want all the gory details!"

"Kiss and tell? Never!"

Clarice pouted. Something she knew I couldn't resist.

"Geez, Clarice. I never knew sex could be so...*fanfreakingtastic!*"

Clarice looked to the right and giggled. A handsome young waiter stood at our table, a stack of dirty plates in his hand, his eyes as big around as teacups. I looked at Clarice and we burst into roars of laughter. Even the waiter snickered as he picked up our plates and added them to the heap.

"I've never had, you know, *casual sex* before, Clarice." I looked around to make sure the coast was clear. "Please don't tell anyone! I'm afraid they might think—"

"Forget about what anybody thinks. There's getting screwed, Val, and then there's getting *screwed*. You? You had sex with a guy you barely know. That's getting screwed. Pay a hundred bucks for an extended warranty on a Mr. Coffee machine? Now *that's* getting *screwed*."

I cringed. "I get your point. But I just don't know where to go from here. I feel...*lost*."

"Where are you?"

"Huh?"

"Where are you? Right now."

"Here? In Italy, you mean?"

"Exactly. You know where you are. So you're not lost."

"Clarice, I didn't mean *geographically*."

"I know that! Don't be a dingbat, Val! You're not *lost*. You're not lost because life isn't about *finding* yourself. It's about *reinventing* yourself. What do you want to be *now*? *That's* the *real* question."

"Oh." I looked down. "I don't know. I never thought about it that way."

"Well, give it a shot. And hurry. You've got about three minutes before the button on my jeans pops off and puts somebody's eye out."

THAT OLD TRUISM REALLY *was* true. There's no such thing as a free lunch.

I'd eaten half my weight in lobster tails and shrimp and my waistline had paid the price. By the time our assigned dinner hour rolled around, I could hardly fasten the rhinestone belt that was supposed to wrap around my blue dress. After all the rigmarole with lost luggage in Italy, I didn't want to have to ditch my clothes now because I couldn't get my fat butt into them.

I decided to skip dinner and spend my remaining calories wisely—on a Tanqueray and tonic. I sipped it as I watched Clarice put away a ribeye steak the size of her plate. Not only was she beautiful. Clarice had the metabolism of a teenage boy. If she wasn't such a wonderful person, I'd have seriously considered throwing her overboard.

"So what's on the agenda for tonight?" she asked between mouthfuls of steak.

"Not much. I haven't spotted a guy yet that's young enough to date my mother."

"Promise me that's the last time you'll mention your mother on the cruise."

I remembered why I forgave Clarice for being so perfect. She *truly was* best friend material. My mother was a piece of work, and no matter what I said or when I needed to vent about her, Clarice was there, by my side, one hundred percent in my corner.

"I promise."

I unfolded the *King Kavanaugh Daily*, a newsletter touting the day's events and happenings. I'd found it tucked in a cubbyhole by our door this morning.

"Let's see. This evening's on-board entertainment is...in the Kingman Theater... a comedian named Vinny Cannoli."

"I hope for his sake that's a stage name."

"It has to be. Let's check it out, Clarice. You love comedians."

"I do! Almost as much as I love eating."

Clarice put the last bite of steak in her mouth.

"I love you Clarice. But don't push it."

We both giggled. I swirled my Tanqueray and tonic and drank the last drop.

"Ready?"

"Ready."

WE TOOK A SEAT AT THE high-top stools at the back of the red-velvet-everything Kingman Theater. From our perch, Clarice and I scanned the audience.

"You and I might be the only ones here not wearing orthopedic shoes," Clarice said.

"The horrors!"

I jokingly tucked my feet under my stool to hide my sparkly, silver stilettos of shame. The lights went down and a curtain opened up on the stage. When the comedian walked out, I nearly choked. He was as thin as gold plating, and as old as dinosaur dung. Dressed in a faded tuxedo, a top hat and a pair of black-and-white spats, he was ghostly pale. The effect was eerie, as if he'd teleported in from a time before color was invented. I elbowed Clarice and whispered.

"I'm worried that maybe he just escaped from a steamer trunk."

"I know, right? The only thing missing from his repertoire is a metal walker and an IV drip of embalming fluid."

We giggled and watched Vinny the ancient cannoli hobble up to the microphone and smile. He tugged on his left sleeve a couple of times until his bowtie began to spin like a whirligig. The crowd broke out in cheers and hoots of laughter. He tipped his hat and bowed.

"Ladies and Germs, I just flew in from Vegas, and boy are my arms tired!"

His opening line sent the floating geriatric center into howls and applause. I had to admit, it was so bad it was actually kind of good. I chuckled despite myself. But the novelty wore off fast, and Clarice and I decided to leave the inevitably tragic comedy on a high note.

"Let's go check out the dessert buffet," Clarice said.

"Are you kidding? Where do you put it all?"

"Oh, here and there," Clarice quipped.

"Thanks, but I'll pass. Go ahead, though. I'll meet you back at the room."

"Okie dokie."

Clarice disappeared up the staircase. I floundered around the ship until I found the Internet Café. Inside, I found five bored teenagers trapped like rats aboard the *SS Depends*. I chose a cubicle next to a young girl with long dark hair who looked as if her world had recently come to an end.

"Excuse me," I asked. "Do you know how this works?"

"Sure," she said sullenly. She grabbed my ship card from my hand, swiped it, and punched a few buttons on the computer. "Service provider?"

"Uh. G-mail."

"Finally. I don't think I could take another AOL'er."

"What's your name?"

"Charlotte."

"Thanks, Charlotte."

The girl flashed me a courtesy smile and returned to her computer. I fished around in my purse and found the last of my stash of cinnamon fireballs. I placed the candy by Charlotte's mousepad. She looked up at me curiously.

"For services rendered," I said.

Charlotte shot me a quick grin. "Thanks," she mouthed, then went back to her screen.

I logged on and checked my emails. There were a few spam ads and a notice it was time to renew my homeowner's policy. *Not likely.* There was no email from Friedrich. I guess he had taken me at my word. He was going to let our time together be what it was—a perfect moment shared by two. After a lot of muddy mind-wrestling today, I'd decided to label the whole thing as an affair to remember, instead of a mistake to forget.

I logged off the computer and headed back to the cabin. When I opened the door, I found it had been cleaned and straightened up, just like at a fancy hotel. My bed had been neatly folded down for the night. Perched atop my pillow was a single, foil-wrapped chocolate, and something else. I picked up the strange object and turned it over in my hands. The twisted lump of cloth was Friedrich's sexy underwear, folded like origami into the shape of a frog. My face turned as red as my lover's dirty underpants. When I'd unpacked yesterday, I'd discretely tucked them under my pillow. I'd forgotten and left them in the bed....

The cabin door flew open and Clarice stepped in, holding an ice cream sundae.

"I'm glad you're here. I didn't want to eat alone," she said. "Hey, what's up with you? Why's your face red?"

I tried to hide the underpants behind me. Clarice grinned and put her sundae on the desk. "Whatcha got there, Val-pal?"

I showed her. "Just a frog, see?"

She snatched it from my hands and pulled the underwear free from its contortions. "Ha! Frog my ass! Do these belong to Friedrich?"

"Give me those back!

Clarice held the underwear to her crotch and began thrusting her hips.

"Ride 'em, cowboy!"

"Stop it, you crazy woman!"

Clarice danced around with the underpants.

"So tell me, Val. How did you like his 'German engineering'?"

I grinned despite myself.

"A hell of a lot more than the old Ford I traded in."

Chapter Nineteen

After tucking away eggs benedict, asparagus and two cappuccinos this morning, Clarice and I'd been contemplating the after-breakfast dessert cart when I realized something.

"I need to get my fat butt off this boat, Clarice, before it grows to unsavory proportions."

Clarice looked at me, then at a slice of Key Lime pie, then back to me. "You're right. Let's go check out Monaco."

We got up and headed for the gangway. Clarice looked gorgeous in a green sundress that matched her eyes. I was wearing my favorite outfit—a cute white skirt, a blue-and white striped top and a white straw fedora. Despite a full tummy, I felt flirty and fabulous. We took our places in line to go through ship security and out into the jet-setting land of Monte Carlo, Monaco.

"Excuse me, do you have any more brochures?"

I turned around in line to find a kindly little old lady looking up at me expectantly.

"I'm sorry?"

"Do you have any more brochures with the map of Monaco? I can't seem to find mine."

"I only have the one they gave me."

"Oh. I'm sorry. I thought you worked here."

Clarice turned around and raised her eyebrows at me.

"No. Sorry."

Clarice went through security ahead of me. I stepped forward to take my turn at the card scanner and discovered that the Asian woman at the machine was dressed nearly identical to me.

"Ship card and ID, please." She smirked ever so slightly as she ran my card through the scanner. A green light came on and the machine pinged.

"Enjoy your day...Ms. Jolly. Nice outfit."

Feeling a tad less fabulous, I walked the plank off the ship with Clarice.

"Was that rude, or was it just me?"

Clarice laughed. "I don't know. I didn't see her face."

"Well I did, and...uh...oh my word! Look!"

Clarice turned and we both stared, slack-jawed, at a sparkling, golden city in front of us. It appeared to have dropped straight from heaven onto the shores of the Ligurian Sea. To the right, an immaculate, white-sand beach was abuzz with beautiful sunbathers and fabulous yachts. In the center of the city, glass skyscrapers reached like crystals into the blue sky. And to the left, buff-colored cliffs served as perches for ancient buildings that looked like storybook castles.

"Where do we start?" Clarice asked.

I pulled out my copy of the *King Kavanaugh Daily*.

"Let's see. It says here that 'the tiny principality of Monaco is no bigger than a city. Nevertheless, it has everything a nation needs—including royalty. It's run by Prince Albert, head of the Princely House of Grimaldi. With the old-world allure of riches and monarchs, Monaco attracts international jet-setters from around the globe.'"

Clarice grinned. "We can *so* pull off being international jetsetters, Val. Let's pretend we belong here!"

I smirked. "Works for me."

WE FOLLOWED THE LINE of tourists down the narrow streets of Monaco, gawking at fancy shops with shirts that cost more than my car. We toured some gardens full of huge bougainvillea and roses and castle ruins. We even climbed to the highest point in the city for a look down at the sea.

"I'm beat!" Clarice said as we took in the panoramic view. "Let's find a place to have a drink."

I studied the *King Kavanaugh Daily*.

"How about trying out the Casino de Monte-Carlo? It says a James Bond movie was filmed there."

"*Casino Royale,* with Daniel Craig?"

"No. *Goldeneye.* Filmed in 1995 with Pierce Brosnan."

"That'll work too."

"I'm not sure how to get there from here."

"Hand me that."

Clarice grabbed the newsletter from my hand.

"Good grief, girl. I can see it from here."

Clarice pointed down to a building on the left.

"Follow me."

Clarice led us right to the casino. We walked inside and found a couple of barstools. We ordered two TNTs. I left Clarice ogling the posh surroundings while I went to find the toilets. When I returned, she was talking to her own 007—a young, drop-dead-gorgeous, deeply tanned man of mystery. I sat down next to Clarice, but neither one of them noticed. The handsome hunk wore a white dinner jacket over a black shirt unbuttoned down to his chest. His smoldering brown eyes almost made me forget my own name. I felt like an invisible fly on the wall as I eavesdropped on their conversation.

"You are a very lovely woman."

His voice was even sexier than him. *How was that possible?*

"I am Marcello."

I swallowed hard against the disbelief. I'd never seen Clarice so transfixed. I was, too, and he wasn't even talking to me.

"I'm Clarice. Nice to meet you."

"Ah. American. You are here on a ship, yes?" His dark brown eyes never left Clarice's.

"Yes. And you?"

"Italian. I live here, of course. Which ship?"

"The King Kavanaugh."

Something registered on his features that I couldn't discern.

"What a pity," he said. "When do you sail?"

"Tomorrow at noon."

"Ah! Then we have the night." Marcello checked the gold watch on his elegant wrist. "I must go. Meet me here again, tonight, Clarice? I will show you some of the beautiful places of Monaco. Beautiful, secret places."

The promise in his eyes turned Clarice into a Borg. Resistance was futile.

"Uh...okay...what time?"

Marcello's eyes brightened, if that was possible. "Eight o'clock?"

He took her hand and kissed it with debonair swagger. Lust shot through me like a bad burrito. I suddenly felt like a voyeur. I could only imagine what Clarice was feeling.

"Okay," she mumbled, like a woman in a trance.

"Until then, my beautiful Clarice."

Marcello shot her a sexy smile that nearly finished *me* off. We watched him disappear into the crowd. Clarice spoke, her voice a mere whisper.

"Did that really just happen?"

"I was right here. It really did."

We walked in semi-stunned silence back toward the ship. Clarice was so deep in thought she might as well have been floating on the moon. We stepped up to the ship's gangplank to have our cards swiped. The same Asian woman took my card again and ran it through the scanner.

"Welcome aboard, Ms. Jolly."

I stepped aside and waited as the woman scanned Clarice's card.

"Welcome aboard, Ms. Whittle." Then the smart-ass woman looked me in the eye and smirked. "Nice outfit."

I glanced at her nametag. Sung-Li. It sounded like a perfect name for a Bond nemesis.

CLARICE HAD GONE OUT of her cotton-picking mind. For the last three hours, she'd been running around in a panic. Every stitch of clothing, every shoe and every purse she'd brought with her were flung all over the room. It looked like a yard sale had exploded in our cabin. By 6:30, I'd had enough. I'd wished her good luck and went to find some dinner.

I was standing in line at The King's Court fine dining restaurant when someone tapped me on my shoulder.

"Do you know where the employee lounge is?"

I whirled around, a bit peeved. "Look, I don't work on the ship, okay?"

"Don't get your drawers in a wad, kid. Oh! Val! How's it going?"

I gasped with surprise. There stood a skinny old woman in a lime green pantsuit.

"Berta! You're alive! What happened to you? Where did you go?"

"Yeah, I'm still alive. Sorry for the quick exit back in Brindisi. I had to get out of town quick."

"Why?"

"Well, let's just say Giuseppe started serving me more than cappuccinos."

"What?!"

"Don't looked so surprised, kid. It's rude."

"I...I'm sorry. So, okay. You had an affair. That happens here a lot, apparently. But why did you have to leave all of a sudden? You didn't even say goodbye!"

"Yeah, I know. Sorry, kid. It was an emergency exit."

"What do you mean?"

"Well, Giuseppe never mentioned that he had a wife—or that she worked as a maid at the hotel. I came back from class one afternoon and found a turd in my purse, along with a two-word note. I looked it up on the internet. You don't even want to know the translation. Suffice it to say, it was time for me to leave. *Immediately.*"

"That's insane!"

"Yeah, well, that's what happened. I'm too old for crap like that. I tried to wash my purse out, but I couldn't get over the idea of it, you know?"

"Uh...yeah. I get it. But you didn't even leave a note, Berta. I've been worried about you."

"I *did* leave you a note. I slipped it under your door. Said I was taking off, and that you should watch your back. Lipo-lady was spreading nasty rumors about you."

"I never got it."

"Huh. Room two-thirty-five, right?"

"No. I was in room *three*-thirty-five."

"Oh. Crap. Old-timer's brain. Sorry, kid. I wonder who was in two-thirty-five."

"I have a pretty good idea. I saw Frank sneaking out of it one morning in his underwear. So it was either his room or Val II's—the lipo-lady's."

"Well, that explains why you never got the note. Botox Witch strikes again."

"Yeah. Hopefully, she'll get hers someday."

"Time wounds all heels, as they say."

"One can only hope. Berta, you asked about the employee lounge. Are you working on the ship?"

"Yeah. After you told me about your cruise, it sounded like a good time. I googled it and got myself a last-minute gig...giving cultural lectures. They told me the person that was supposed to do the job came down with Norovirus or something like that. I got a free cabin and all the booze I can drink. Not a bad way to see the world, heh?"

"Wow! Not at all! The drinks alone are worth, like, ten-thousand dollars."

"Yeah. Fifteen bucks a pop adds up fast. Only bad thing is, *I* gotta watch my manners. Unlike you, kid."

"Oh. Sorry about that. It's just that...this outfit...well, people have been bugging me all day, thinking I work on the ship."

"Guilty as charged. What are you up to now?"

"Uh...dinner?" I pointed a finger at the restaurant sign.

Berta laughed, flashing her manufactured pearly whites.

"Yeah. Hey, I tell you what. The people at my dinner table are a complete snore. Want to sneak off and join me at the Asian Grille tonight?"

"Sure, that would be great. My friend Clarice ditched me for a guy she met in Monaco."

"Her loss, my gain. Give me thirty minutes. Meet you there?"

"I might never find the place on my own. How about I stop by your cabin first. What's your number?"

Berta glanced left and right, then whispered, "Three-three-two."

I watched the mysterious old woman disappear behind the elevator doors. I went to the staircase and started trudging my way up, hoping the effort would take an inch off my thighs.

"HIYA, KID. YOU LOOK different," Berta said as she cracked opened the door to her cabin and slipped into the hallway. The slim, silver-haired old woman was dressed in lemon-yellow polyester pants and a white top with yellow pockets. "What happened to you?"

"For crying out loud, Berta, am I such an open book?"

"You forget, kid. I've had a library card since 1938."

I smiled wryly. Berta motioned to the right and I followed her down the hall.

"I just got an email from Friedrich. I'm not sure how to respond."

"What did he want?"

"He wants to meet me in Naples."

Berta pushed the elevator button and sighed. "Why?"

"He says his heart aches for me."

"Yeah? And what about *your* heart. It doesn't look too achy to me."

"Are you saying I shouldn't meet him?"

"I'm saying follow your heart, kid."

As we rode the elevator up, I thought about Berta's advice. Clarice had a lover. Berta had one, too. Why shouldn't I?

"I think I *will* meet Friedrich."

"Oh."

How could one little syllable say so much—and nothing at all?

The elevator opened and I was taken aback by the brisk pace Berta maintained as she scurried along the ship. By the time we got to the Asian Grille, any thoughts I'd had of helping a doddering old woman find her way around had vanished. A waiter led us to a table for two.

"Let's be naughty and have some wine," Berta said as we looked over the menu.

"Sure, why not. I'm in the mood to be naughty."

"Thought so," Berta replied without looking up.

I wondered what she'd meant by it, but wasn't sure I wanted to know.

"I'm having the chow mein." Berta laid down her menu. "So, how's that search for what you want outta life coming along?"

I knew there was no use trying to pass a fluff answer off on Berta.

"I've made a little progress. I know now for sure that leaving my husband was the right thing to do."

Berta raised an eyebrow at me. "Yeah?"

"After fifteen years together, we were just zombies going through the motions. I want more than that. I want to *feel loved* when I'm with someone. Am I asking too much, Berta? Maybe I'm just nuts."

"You know what I tell people who think they're nuts?"

"What?"

"That they probably are."

Berta grinned at me until I smiled back.

"Val, dragging up the past is only good for one thing—feeling like crap. What's done is done, kid. Learn from it, but don't dwell on it. Or you'll end up trapped like a gerbil in a wheel, spinning around and around, but going nowhere. Now lighten up and enjoy yourself. Doctor's orders."

"You're right. I'm sorry." I apologized to the woman who didn't believe in apologies. "What do I owe you for the therapy session?"

"After dinner, you can buy me one of those crappuccinos."

"It's a deal."

I WAS IN BED ASLEEP when I heard the door open. I cracked one eye and watched Clarice tiptoe into the room.

"Are you awake, Val?" she whispered.

I heaved myself up on one elbow. "Yeah. How'd it go? Did you say 'yes' to Dr. No?"

Clarice giggled. "Yes. Val, I did the nasty with him in the garden outside the casino!"

"Really? How was it?"

"Like magic. It was...a *fairytale*."

"That guy *did* seem a little too good to be true."

"I know, right?" Clarice said. "As I got closer to the casino, I started to think that I'd made the whole thing up. Then, like a mystical prince, there he was, wearing a smart, tailored jacket and tight, designer jeans. You know I'm a sucker for a man in tight jeans. Anyway, Marcello looked even better than he had this morning, if you can believe it!"

"No, not really. So, what happened?"

"He took me by the arm and led me down the garden path—"

"Ha! Tell me something I *don't* know."

Clarice frowned. "Do you want to hear this or not?"

"Yes, yes. Sorry."

Clarice sat on the bed next to me. "So we walked along this old stone wall. The garden was full of white roses. They glowed like tiny ghosts in the moonlight."

"The ghosts of virgins past."

Clarice wacked me. "One more crack and I'm done here!"

"Okay! I promise!"

"So I had to stop and take it all in...not a word, Val! When I did, Marcello pulled me close and began nibbling my neck. He said my beauty was 'far more than the flowers'. Then he led me to a bench. I took a picture of him on it. Look!"

She showed me the picture on her phone. The glare blinded my sleepy eyes.

"Yeah. That's him all right. Smokin' hot!"

"You aren't kidding. That face. That body! I'm telling you, Val, he's gonna star in my erotic fantasies for years to come."

"Mind if I borrow him for mine?"

Clarice laughed. "You wish. And Val? Marcello told me that he's good friends with the captain of the King Kavanaugh. I kind of invited him aboard tomorrow for a second helping, so to speak."

"Here? In our cabin?"

"Yes...but I promise to keep the festivities to my bed."

"Dang. So near, and yet so far."

Chapter Twenty

I couldn't decide if I was suffering from rejection or envy as I lay by the pool, banished from my room while Clarice enjoyed round two with Marcello. I only knew I felt as if I were missing out on something I wasn't even sure I wanted.

I spent the afternoon re-reading *Sex in Sorrento* and drinking outrageously priced margaritas until I was sure I'd be penniless when the bill came due. I was just about to give up and call Berta's cabin when I spied Clarice walking up to me, wearing a bikini and a Cheshire cat smile.

"How'd it go, hot tramp in the city?"

Clarice grinned. "Polite women don't kiss and tell. But, he asked for my number!"

"But he lives here in Monaco. Do you really think you'll ever see him again?"

"Who knows? I hope so. The world can be a very small place, you know."

"You're right, Clarice. It can be. With all the 'stuff' going on with you and Marcello, I forgot to mention that I ran into a friend of mine yesterday. She's traveling alone. Would you mind if we invited her to join us for dinner?"

"Not at all! Another person I can brag to about Marcello! Goody!"

Waddling under the influence of margaritas, I went to the pool-side bar and rang Berta's cabin. We made plans to meet at The King's Court at seven.

FOR STICK-FIGURES, Berta and Clarice could both put away some chow. We'd lucked out and gotten a table by a window. Clarice and Berta were both enjoying The King's Court King Crab extravaganza, and, surprisingly, each other. They'd hit it off like old friends. I smiled and watched the crab legs disappear from our table as Monaco disappeared from the porthole.

"So, I heard you had an adventure last night, Clarice" said Berta. "How'd it go with Mr. Romeo?"

Berta pulled a long strip of meat from a crab leg, dipped it in butter, and shoved it between her dentures. Clarice giggled and blushed.

"Pretty dang awesome, actually. But I feel kind of...I don't know...*dirty*."

"Why? Because of the actual dirt?" I asked. I turned to Berta. "You know she did it with him outside, in a garden."

"Really?" Berta said without surprise or judgment. "Good for you. Got a picture? Of him, I mean."

"I sure do!"

"Good. I always say, when it comes to lovers, pictures beat out STDs as souvenirs every time."

Clarice laughed. "Val said you were a hoot, Berta. She was right!"

As Clarice handed Berta her phone, I noticed two waiters looking at us and whispering. When they saw I was watching them, they quickly looked away and snickered. *Strange.*

Berta peered at the phone screen. "So this is the infamous...Marcello, was it?"

"Yes, that's him," Clarice said proudly. "What do you think?"

"Well, I hate to break it to you, kid. But he looks a lot like Markus, my cabin steward."

"What?! You've got to be kidding me, Berta!"

"Nope. That's him all right. Most devilish eyes I've ever seen."

"Berta! He tricked me! He...he pretended to be something he wasn't!"

"What did he pretend to be, Clarice? Handsome? Horny? Husband material?"

"No. Not exactly."

"And who were *you* pretending to be?"

Berta's question made Clarice angrier than a wet hornet.

"At least I used my real name!"

"Hey look!" Berta said cheerily, ignoring Clarice as she studied the photograph. "The plaque on the bench.... Ha ha! Clarice, it looks like you lost your head in *Princess Antoinette* Park. Now *that's* funny!"

Clarice wasn't laughing. Berta looked up and finally caught on that my duped friend was far from amused.

"Okay. Well...was he at least good in bed. Or should I say, the *flower* bed?"

Clarice's face grew grim. Berta patted her shoulder.

"Sorry, kid. Was he good in the sack?"

"That's totally beside the point," Clarice argued.

"You enjoyed yourself. What was the harm?"

"You're not from the South, are you Berta?"

"No."

"Then you wouldn't understand."

I kicked Clarice's shin under the table. She closed her mouth into a pouty frown and folded her arms over her chest.

"Okay, then," Berta said calmly. "Moving on. You two missed a hell of a show last night. Wait a minute. What am I saying? I'd have traded places with Clarice in a New York minute. But, I mean, at any rate, the magician was pretty good."

"A magician?" I asked. "I hope he was better than the old codger from the night before. Vinny Victrola or something like that."

Clarice rolled her eyes. "He and his jokes were older than dinosaur dirt."

Clarice sat up and unfolded her arms.

"Hey," she asked, "is it my imagination or is that waiter over there giving me the evil eye?"

Berta looked over. "I'd say it was the eye, but not the evil one, if you catch my drift."

Clarice leaned over the table. "Berta! I'm serious. My reputation on board has been...*compromised!*"

"Compromised? Ha ha! I haven't heard anybody say that since 1957."

"What am I going to do?"

"Nothing, Clarice," Berta answered. "Who gives a flying turd what these people think? In a couple of days, you'll get off this ship and never see them again. Lighten up, kid. I tell you what. Why don't you two meet me at the Kaptain's Klub for a couple of drinks before dinner tonight. I think I can sneak you a few freebies."

Clarice looked around sullenly. "I could use a drink *right now.*"

"What's the show tonight?" I asked Berta.

"I think it's that guy you were talking about. Vinny Cannoli. Back for an encore performance. Either him or the piano bar guy."

"I'd be surprised if Vinny was still alive after that last performance. I'm afraid Clarice and I are a half-century too young to appreciate his jokes."

"They weren't *that* bad, were they?" Berta asked. "*I* liked them."

I shrugged. "I tell you what. Get me all liquored up and I might change my mind."

Berta looked at Clarice, then back at me. "Geez. Given the state she's in, I'm not sure there's enough liquor on this ship to do the job."

CLARICE WAS ON THE warpath. She'd pried Berta's room number out of me, and now that she knew which part of the ship Markus worked in, she was plotting her revenge. Her first order of business was to get herself dolled up to the nines.

"Every good payback begins with looking your best," she instructed me, her green eyes squinted into devilish slits.

"What are you gonna do?"

"I'm going to ambush his sorry ass!"

"And then what?"

"I'm gonna...I'm...I don't know. I'll think of something when the time comes. Nobody messes with Clarice Whittle! I'm going down there right now. Come with me."

"Are you kidding? This is your battle, Clarice. Not mine."

"Come on. What else have you got to do?"

"Uh...preserve my dignity?"

Clarice shot me a look that would have penetrated solid steel *and* one of those mystery meat cutlets at the Hotel Bella Vista.

"Okay already."

An evil grin crept across Clarice's angelic face. I had a feeling this would not end well.

WE SNUCK DOWN TO THE third floor and tucked ourselves away in a cubbyhole niche carved out of the narrow hallway. Voices echoed louder as they came down the hall. I started to speak, but Clarice shushed me. A silhouette appeared in the hallway. Clarice held her breath....

"Hi, dearies," said a grandmotherly woman in a polyester house dress. "Are you two lost?"

"No ma'am," said Clarice. "We're just...waiting for someone."

"Oh. Well, don't wait too long. Life is short, you know!" She smiled at us cheerily and waved an envelope in her hand as if to emphasize her point.

"Yes ma'am," we said simultaneously.

We watched the old woman stop midway down the hall and slip the envelope under a door. A few minutes later, another old woman came sauntering by and stuffed her own note under the same door.

Curious, I took a few hesitant steps down the hall while Clarice stood lookout. A third woman brushed past me and dropped an envelope on the floor, then pushed in under the door with her shoe. I looked up. A plaque read; No. 332. *Berta's cabin!*

I looked down at the floor. The corner of one of the envelopes stuck out from under the door. I looked both ways down the hall. Clarice motioned that the coast was clear. I tried to kneel, but I couldn't in my high-heels. I got down on all fours, butt in the air, and fished the envelope out. I carefully opened the envelope. A simple notecard inside read:

Meet me at the Portside Bar after the show. I'll be the lady in red.
Margery

I checked the cabin number again. It was Berta's all right. *Wait a minute. Was Berta a lesbian? Maybe she'd actually screwed Giuseppe's wife and not him? Is that really why she'd had to leave Brindisi in a hurry?*

I put the card back in the envelope and sealed it again. I felt horrible. I'd just committed a gross invasion of Berta's privacy. I looked over at Clarice and shook my head. I was going to keep my trap shut on this one. Clarice, bless her heart, had the discretion of a dog in heat. I shoved the envelope back under the door. I was still on the floor, butt in the air, when I heard a voice behind me.

"Ma'am, are you okay? Have you fallen?"

A young cabin steward looked at me with concern.

"Do you need a wheelchair or something?"

Geez. Did I look that old? "No thanks. I...just...dropped an earring. I found it!"

I scurried over to Clarice. She'd been loitering in the cubbyhole, looking the other way, as if she didn't know me. As soon as I got close enough, she grabbed me.

"What did the envelope say?"

"That people should mind their own business. Let's go. I'm ready for that drink with Berta now."

Chapter Twenty-One

I was washing my hair in the phone-booth-sized cabin shower, wondering how Mr. Bacon and Sideshow Tent Lady managed to squeeze their giant butts in here to bathe. The unwanted visual that flashed into my mind nearly made me wretch.

Thankfully, it wasn't hard to switch thoughts this morning. I was churning with curiosity about what Berta had been up to last night. Clarice and I had met her for drinks at the Kaptain's Klub, then she'd told us she had other plans and promptly disappeared. Had she met that lady in red from the notecard?

I stepped out of the shower and dried off. I slathered on some deodorant and stepped out of the steamy bathroom.

"Your turn, Clarice."

"Does my hair look all right?" she asked, her confidence still suffering from the Markus mash-up. "I washed it yesterday, but I'm just not sure."

"Look. You're gorgeous. With me standing next to you for contrast, you can't lose. Hurry up. Berta's holding a table for us."

"Okay, already!" Clarice raced around and got ready in record time for her—forty-three-minutes flat.

WE FOUND BERTA IN THE King's Court, seated at the same table by the porthole window, slurping a cappuccino. Today Berta sported blue capris and a white top with a blue collar and twin, blue breast pockets. She looked as if she'd just finished her soda-jerk shift at a drugstore, circa 1943.

"I was beginning to think you two fell overboard," she said.

"Sorry. My bad," Clarice apologized.

"Did you two catch the show last night?"

"No," I said, and shot Clarice a look. "We had an adventure, instead."

Berta flashed her perfect dentures. "Oo-la-la."

"I wish." I sat down and leaned in toward her. "And how about you? Any traction on getting some action?"

Berta shrugged. "Nah. No one on board my type."

My eyebrows raised involuntarily. I never thought about Berta having a "type." I hadn't even been able to figure out whether she liked men or women.

"So, what's your type?" I asked.

Berta set her cup of cappuccino back in its saucer and looked me in the eye.

"Dearly rich and nearly dead. What about you two? Tall, dark and then some?"

Clarice sniggered despite herself. "Don't remind me."

"Not for me," I said. "I'm not sure I'm a 'fling' kind of gal."

"Why not?" Berta asked.

"Because there's no future in it."

"And you found a future with those guys you married? Hello, kid. Wake up!"

"Hey, be nice," Clarice said.

"Sorry. I just hate to see Val stewing her guts out over this. You don't have to marry every guy you sleep with, kid. I thought you knew better by now. I mean, Friedrich and all."

"I guess I've still got a bit of a learning curve."

We all three sighed at once.

"Don't we all, kids. Don't we all."

THE KING KAVANAUGH was docked off the stunning Italian town of Portofino this morning. Clarice and I'd thought about going on a tour, but decided to be lazy and read a book by the pool instead. I still hadn't gotten to the sex part of *Sex in Sorrento*.

I donned my white one-piece suit, a sheer floral cover-up and a pair of gold sandals. Clarice put me to shame in a gold bikini with fake jade beading that brought out the shine in her eyes. When we stepped out onto the open air pool deck, a panoramic view of Portofino splayed out in front of us.

Portofino looked like an older, wiser, and perhaps a tad more re-laxed version of Monaco. Her cliff-top buildings didn't glitter like her younger sister's skyscrapers, but the city itself *did* glow with something I could only define as satisfaction. Portofino seemed per-fectly content to be exactly what she was—an elegant grand dame on the Ligurian Sea.

Clarice and I had thought it would be hard to find two chairs to-gether. Every time we'd passed by the pool area before, it had been crowded and noisy and chaotic. Like a colony of penguins, the white, round sunbathers had been squawking and shuffling and vying for tiny patches of territory on which to build their nests with towels and sunscreen and the latest paperback romances. Today, however, the pool area was nearly deserted.

From across the pool I saw someone waving. I squinted against the sun and realized the arm belonged to Berta. If Portofino was the grand dame of the Ligurian, Berta was the grand disaster. She had on a neon-orange one-piece, floppy orange hat and orthopedic flip-flops. She looked for all the world like an Egyptian mummy on some tacky, touristy summer vacation.

Clarice and I padded over to her. Berta pulled down her sunglasses long enough to show us a curious scrunch of eyebrows.

"What are you kids doing here? I thought you were going on an excursion."

"We were, but we changed our minds. How about you?"

"On port days, the ship's half empty. It's the only chance an old bat like me has of getting one of the good seats for a change."

"I know that's—"

"Aww, crap," Berta interrupted. "I forgot my sunscreen."

"You're all settled in," I said. "Just stay where you are, Berta. I'll run get it for you."

"Thanks kid." Berta looked around cautiously, then cupped her hands around her lips and mouthed the words, "Room three-three-two." She fished her room card out of her orange-clad bosom and covertly slipped it into my hand like a five-dollar tip.

I kept a poker face, but I was more curious than ever. *What's up with all the secrecy?* I had her room key, and I was going to find out.

WHEN I OPENED BERTA'S cabin door, I had to step over an envelope on the floor. It had a heart drawn on it in red lipstick. *Should I pick it up? Should I pretend I never saw it?*

I did a quick scan of the bathroom and found the sunscreen on the counter. Next to it was a bottle of men's aftershave. *Strange.* I checked the shower. There was a men's cheap plastic razor in the soap holder. *What was going on here?*

I opened Berta's clothes closet and rifled through the Skittles rainbow of garish clothes. At the back I found a few men's trousers, a man's dark suit and several men's shirts. On the floor of the closet was a collection of orthopedic sandals and shoes...and a pair of men's black-and-white spats.

OMG! Berta's shacking up with Vinny Cannoli!

A flood of shame washed over me. *Oh crap! All those bad things I'd said about his jokes!* Then I thought about all the notes shoved under the door by those other women. What was up with that? *Should I tell Berta he's a philanderer? Or should I keep my mouth shut?* Berta was no dummy. Surely she must already know. Maybe that's why she never told us she was with him. She was ashamed!

Poor Berta! I'd been cheated on before, and it sucked! *What's wrong with men when a smart woman like Berta has to settle for a two-timing lout like Vinny Cannoli?*

I wanted to help her, but what could I do? Then a thought struck me. *Berta said Vinny was going to perform again tomorrow night. Well, he's going to get a performance from me! I'm going to wait for him in the hallway and give him a piece of my mind!*

I tried to fix everything back like it had been before I rifled through it. I closed the closet. I tiptoed over the envelopes and pulled the cabin door closed. For the time being, I would act as if nothing happened. I would hand her the sunscreen and.... *Oh crap! I forgot the sunscreen!*

WHEN I GOT BACK TO the pool, Clarice was gone. I spotted her waving at me from the pool. I tried to act nonchalant as I handed poor Berta her sunscreen.

"Here you are, dear."

"*Dear?* What's gotten up your ass, kid?"

My heart thumped. "Oh. Nothing! You...you said Vinny Cannoli is playing again tomorrow. Are you going?"

"I wouldn't miss it. You should give him a shot, kid. He's not that bad."

Not that bad! Should I tell her he's a cheater? Maybe she doesn't care. Maybe he's the nearly-dead, dearly rich guy of her dreams. He cer-

tainly seemed to have one foot in the grave. Either way, it was none of my business.

I shoved my thoughts aside. "Why do you like him so much, Berta?"

"Vinny? I don't know. He makes me laugh. We're both from the same era. Made of the same dough, if you know what I mean."

"You're both crusty, New York bagels?"

"Ha ha. Yeah. Something like that."

"Have you ever met him? Talked to him...I mean?"

"Why do you ask?"

My heart thumped again. *Watch it, Val.* "Just curious. I don't get what you see in him."

"Back in my day, people appreciated subtlety. A joke didn't have to be profane or degrade somebody to be funny. Hell, when I was growing up, cuss words were practically *illegal*. Nowadays, that's pretty much all you hear on the comedy stage."

"I guess you're really into comedy, huh?"

"Some stuff, yeah. Like Vinny Cannoli. He's old school. Gives people of my generation a taste of the sappy old stuff we were weaned on. There's comfort in nostalgia. You'll understand that someday. But enjoying the good old days doesn't mean we don't know the score, kid. We just choose to play the game by a different set of rules."

Lying? Cheating? Deceiving? Sounded like the same rules to me.

"So your generation doesn't go in for dirty jokes. Keep it squeaky clean, like in the old movies."

"Don't underestimate us septuagenarians, kid. We've had sex, you know. People like you are living proof."

I blew out a laugh and shrugged. "Yeah, you're right. I guess every generation thinks they somehow invented sex."

"Bingo, kid. But jokes about sex don't have to be raunchy to be funny. There's intelligent ones, too. The kind that make you think."

"Like what?"

"Okay. Let's see.... What do you call the really dense, hairy part at the base of the penis?"

"I don't know. What?"

"The man."

Chapter Twenty-Two

Clarice and I had signed up for a bus trip to Sorrento this morning, and a drive along the Amalfi Coast afterward. This was the same area of Italy we'd seen together last fall. In my small view of the world, if there was any place on the planet worth seeing twice, this was it. Monaco was the playground for the rich and glamorous. The Amalfi Coast was the playground for Mother Nature. She'd toyed with its landscape like a biscuit recipe, trying to find out just how high she could get jaw-dropping beauty to rise.

I felt bad that Clarice was going to miss it all. She'd had to beg off this morning. She'd complained of loose bowels last night after dinner. This morning I woke to find her in the bathroom sleeping next to the toilet. She'd told me she'd felt better, but wasn't sure she should come along. She didn't trust her body not to let her down. I'd helped her back into bed and promised to take lots of pictures and drink a lemoncello in her honor.

From my window on the King Kavanaugh shuttle bus, the Tyrrhenian Sea splashed blue and foamy at the base of beige cliffs that jutted a thousand feet into the clear, blue sky. Dozens of birds soared against the craggy stone backdrop, teasing fishermen in the boats below. In every little village we passed, the homes and shops were cozy and immaculate, like something out of *Better Homes and Gardens*. Even though I knew what to expect, the Amalfi Coast still took my breath away. Its beauty and perfection bordered on simply unbelievable.

I'd wanted to look international for the trip. I'd worn a short, loose-fitting blue halter dress patterned with white Greek symbols. Strappy sandals, a floppy white hat tied with a blue ribbon, and my trusty straw tote from Italy finished off my ensemble. I'd planned a leisurely day of café sitting, people watching, shopping, and general tourist gawking.

About halfway through the bus ride to Sorrento, however, I realized I was feeling a bit off. By the time we arrived at the city center, I barely wanted to get off the bus. I struggled out of the vehicle and searched for a place to sit down. Thankfully, both corners of the intersection we'd been dumped off at had outdoor cafés. I spied an empty table for two at the one on the right. It looked like a little oasis amid the café's lemon trees and pots of gardenias. I made my way over and took a seat.

While I waited to be served, a ghostly white woman of around fifty with dull, black, shoe-polish hair came and sat down in a chair next to me. The chair didn't belong to my table or to the one next to it. It just floated there, random and alone, like the strange woman perched on it like a nervous dove. She had on so much makeup I wondered if she might be traveling in disguise. I didn't have nothing against someone making the most of what they had in the looks department, but if this woman got caught in a rainstorm, her face would've melt off.

"Excuse me, do you speak English?" the woman asked. She had a British accent.

"Yes, I speak English."

"Could you take my picture, dear?"

Dear? Now I knew how Berta had felt.

"Sure."

The woman handed me her phone. "Just push the button here."

"Okay. Smile"

The woman grinned, proving what they say about British teeth. I snapped a couple of shots and handed the camera back to the woman.

"Prego," said a man's voice. I turned to see the waiter had arrived.

"Uno cappuccino, per favore."

At hearing me speak Italian, the waiter brightened up perceptibly. He smiled warmly and disappeared.

I turned back to talk to the black-haired woman, but she stared straight ahead, as if I were of no further use to her. I sighed and looked away, just in time to see a lovely man walk by and give me a thumbs up. I perked up and smiled. He was tall and slim and dressed in a dark blue suit. He carried a motorcycle helmet in one arm. With those smoldering brown eyes and dark, wavy hair, he just *had* to be the real Italian deal.

He changed directions and came to sit at the table between me and the Brit.

"Where are you from?" he asked.

"Glastonbury," said the other woman. She smiled at him like a hungry wolf.

Not missing a beat, the handsome stranger said, "And you, miss? Where are you from?"

"Florida," I said, slightly ashamed of not being European.

"And how long are you here?"

I waited a moment to see if the British woman would answer. She didn't. She was too busy gathering her things to leave.

"Just a few hours. I'm on a tour."

"What a pity. You are so beautiful. I would like to get to know you."

Come on! This is unbelievable. Where are all these men back in Florida? He must be a gigolo!

"How sweet," I answered.

"May I join you for a...what are you drinking?"

The waiter arrived with my cappuccino. In an Italian microsecond, the two men exchanged a quick succession of hand signals. Whether the motorcycle man had ordered a drink or the two had just sized me up, I had no idea. But I didn't have the presence of mind to care. My stomach had begun to gurgle and boil like Uncle Jack's moonshine still right before it blew.

"I am Roberto," said the devil in a blue suit as he joined me at my table. He took my hand and kissed it. "You are a lovely woman."

My stomach gurgled louder. I laughed to cover the noise.

"Thank you. I am...Megan," I lied.

What was the point in being honest? I'd never see him again. Maybe that was the whole point to these crazy encounters.

I began to break out in a sweat. My stomach gurgled again. I needed a toilet—and *pronto.*

"Excuse me, Roberto."

I walked slowly and carefully until I was out of his line of sight, then I ran inside the restaurant.

"Toilette!" I nearly screamed at the waiter. He pointed upstairs. I leapt like a gazelle up the stairs and grabbed the handle on the ladies' room door. It was locked. I tried the men's room. The door opened right before my bowels did. I pooped my underpants a little. There was no time to be ladylike and line the seat rim with toilet paper. I sat my butt on the bare toilet seat and shot a jet stream of diarrhea into the bowl. *Whew!*

I did a courtesy flush, then waited to see if there would be an encore performance. After a minute or so, I was pretty sure I was done. I stepped out of the crappy panties between my feet and looked around for a place to throw them away. Most ladies' rooms had a container for sanitary discards, but this was the men's room. *Oh crap! There wasn't even a garbage can!* I couldn't just leave the panties lying there on the floor. I couldn't flush them down the toilet, either.

What if it clogged? Oh, I didn't even want to think about it! *Oh no! What if someone was waiting right outside the door?*

I was about to panic when I spied a small window about eight feet up on the wall. *I could fling them out the window!* I tried tossing them up, but missed and narrowly escaped them falling back into my face. *Yuck!* An idea hit me. I took a pen from my purse and used it like a makeshift slingshot. I stretched the elastic waistband over one end, pulled it tight, and catapulted the poop-stained panties out the window on the first shot. *Finally, one of my country skills paid off! Good riddance, nasty panties!*

I washed my hands with half the soap in the dispenser, then cracked open the door cautiously and took a peek around. The coast was clear. *I'd gotten away scot-free! Yes!*

I felt loads better and about a ton lighter as I tiptoed down the stairs and out of the café. As soon as I stepped outside onto the sidewalk, I heard a commotion. I peeked around a lemon tree and saw a couple yelling at my waiter. I recognized the man. It was blowhard Frank from the WOW vacation group. His pink-haired companion was Botox Val.

Frank was waving his arms wildly, pointing at the sky. I followed his finger upward to a small, square window in a wall. I followed blubber-lipped Val's eyes over to their table. My gut went limp. *Oh my gawd!* My poop-stained panties had landed right in the middle of their dinner! They were hanging off of their water carafe like a crap-filled flag of surrender.

I snorted with laughter. Frank looked my way. I yanked the brim of my hat down over my face and turned hard on my heels. I scooted away as fast as humanly possible in a short dress and no panties, but I kept doubling over with crazy laughter that teetered back and forth between bitter horror and sweet revenge. I dove inside a tacky tourist store about a half a block away, next to the shuttlebus bus rendezvous point. I spent the next hour holed up in there like a fugitive from justice, smirking and lurking behind bottles of lemoncello and racks of laminated placemats.

FIRST DOMINIK, THEN Friedrich, now Roberto. Three strikes. I was out. But for the moment, it didn't matter. After what had happened with Frank and Val II today, I felt like I'd just hit a home run. The universe had conspired to help me settle an old score. It was rooting for my side at last! Even Sung-Li wasn't around to shame me when I re-boarded the King Kavanaugh. *Yes!*

Clarice wasn't in the cabin when I got back. I hoped that meant she was feeling better. She still hadn't returned after I'd taken a long, hot shower and donned a fresh set of clothes. I left again to check my emails. I hadn't bothered for a couple of days, for two reasons. First, shipboard Internet cost about $300 a minute. Second, I still hadn't decided what to say to Friedrich.

The Internet Café was empty when I arrived. Not even one surly teenager was skulking about. I picked a cubicle by the window and logged on. The email Friedrich had sent two days ago glared at me. I clicked on it and read it again.

Dear Val,

I tried to forget, but my heart aches for you. Please meet me at the port in Naples on Friday. I have something I want to give you.

Friedrich

I was out of time. Friday was tomorrow. I hit the reply button and froze. *Should I or shouldn't I?* I thought about deceitful Markus and two-timing Vinny. Friedrich was freaking Prince Charming compared to them. He might be the one. Or at least, the best *I* could do. If I didn't go, I'd never know. I took a deep breath and blew it out. I didn't want to sound too desperate...or frightened. I typed.

Hi Friedrich,

That sounds like fun. Meet you at 8:30 at the dock.

Val

My finger hovered over the "send" button like a mosquito over a naked butt cheek.

"Hey, it's you!"

The voice startled me. My finger jabbed send. I turned around. It was the teenager who'd helped me a few days ago.

"Hi, Charlotte."

"Hi. Hope I didn't scare you."

"No. It's all good."

"Are you done now?"

"What?"

"With the internet."

"Oh...yes, I guess."

"Then log off. Quick!"

"Why?"

"Just do it!"

I did as I was instructed. A message popped up informing me that my cabin account would be charged $18.37 for this internet session.

"Wow!" Charlotte exclaimed. "You coulda bought a pizza for that! I'm glad I'm on our family plan. If I did what you just did, I'd be in big trouble."

"SO, ARE YOU GIRLS GOING to catch Vinny tonight?"

For a second, I wondered how Berta knew of our diabolical plan to shake down Vinny and Markus after dinner. Then I realized she was probably just asking if we were going to the show.

"I'm planning on it," I replied.

"Oh yes! Wouldn't miss it!" Clarice said too cheerfully.

Yep. If everything went according to Clarice's and my plans, both Vinny Cannoli and Markus the Manipulator were going down in flames tonight.

Clarice and I took our seats at the dining table alongside Berta.

"You two look like you're feeling better."

"And she looks *thinner*, too. It's just not fair," I complained.

Clarice shook her head and put a hand to her tummy. "Let me tell you, Val, this is *not* the way anyone wants to lose weight."

"I know. I had a bout with it, too. But my stomach still looks like a basketball."

"You're crazy. You look fabulous. Doesn't she, Berta?"

Berta's eyes had been scanning the room. "Uh? Yes. You two look fabulous. I like the sparkles, Val."

I had on a loose-fitting, short dress made of dark-blue material that glittered like sequins.

"This old thing? It's my camouflage dress. You can't make out anything under all this shiny."

"Well, you both look fine," Berta said. "And I'm glad you're all dressed up. I've got a treat for you kids. I swiped an invitation to the Kaptain's Klub cocktail party tonight. It's right after dinner."

Berta handed Clarice an envelope. She opened it and pulled out a gold-lined square of cream-colored paper.

"No offense, Berta," I said. "But who are *we* going meet there? Everyone on board is old enough to be—"

Clarice smiled and waved the card at me. "It says here, 'Free Drinks.'"

I smirked. "Well, in that case, I'm in."

Berta laughed. "I'm not."

Clarice's brow furrowed. "You're not coming?"

"Nope," Berta said. "I gotta do something first. I'll meet you girls at the show."

AFTER DINNER, CLARICE and I took our fancy, gold-lined invitation and swaggered smugly down to the Kaptain's Klub's exclusive cocktail party. I sucked in my melon-belly, opened the swanky wooden door, and sauntered in with Clarice. *Let the party begin!*

Electronic candlelight cast a bluish-yellow glow over the room. Across one wall, a full liquor bar was lined with people perched on high-top stools, buzzing with tipsy conversation. The rest of the club was dotted with clusters of three or four upholstered chairs encircling tiny tables of dark-stained wood. The Klub looked like a typical cocktail lounge, but still, something seemed off. I blinked twice and looked around again. It hit me. In the dark, the guests' deeply tanned skin, bleached-white teeth and silver hair gave them the appearance of...*film negatives.*

"This is weird," I said to Clarice.

I turned to see her reaction, but she was already bent over the bar, ordering drinks while dirty old men ogled her rear-end. Another inch shorter and she'd have offered them an embarrassing Southern exposure.

I blinked again and scanned the room for a second time. That's when I saw him. Markus. He was dressed in a neat, charcoal-colored suit, white shirt and a crisp red tie. He held a drink tray in his hand, and was chatting up a woman whose face I couldn't see.

"Got you a Tanqueray and tonic," said Clarice. "The old man at the bar called it a TNT! Funny, huh? Actually, he said, 'Here's a TNT for a bombshell.'"

I took the drink from Clarice and scowled.

"Leave it to a man to turn a compliment into an act of war."

"Gee, Val. Lighten up."

Why do people say that? It never works.

Clarice elbowed me, spilling my drink. "Let's have some fun!

"You mean like those two?"

I raised my drink in the direction of Markus. He was busy chumming it up with a woman in a cozy corner for two. Clarice's mouth fell open. She dropped her glass of champagne. It bounced silently on the carpet and spewed white foam three feet into the air like a miniature volcano with rabies.

The two-timing cabin steward must have felt her burning stare. He glanced up from flirting, gave Clarice a quick, dead look in the eyes, and returned his attention to the other woman. She was somewhere between fifty and sixty, and pushing two-hundred pounds. Why would he ditch Clarice for *that* lady?

Before I could say a word, Clarice made a beeline for Markus. I scrambled to catch up to her.

"Hello Markus," she said sarcastically.

"Hello, Ms....?"

I had to hand it to him. This guy was a pro at being a jerk-off. I think Clarice blanched. I think she half-believed she had the wrong guy. But no, there was his blasted nametag. Markus. Markus the magnificent, manipulating man-child.

"It's Whittle, Markus. Clarice Whittle. You lying piece of crap!"

"Excuse me, Madame." Markus genteelly kissed the older woman's hand. "Uno momento, per favore."

He got up and led Clarice by the elbow to an empty corner. I followed, hot on their heels like a reporter from the *National Enquirer*.

"What's the deal, Markus?"

"The deal is fifty dollars," he said coldly.

"What!?"

"You heard me. Fifty dollars. That's my rate. I gave you a sample. Then the second time you didn't pay me. Look lady. If I don't get paid, you don't get laid."

"What! I never!"

"No, of course not," Markus said smugly.

Clarice Whittle blew her top. She snatched Markus by the hair on the top of his arrogant head and marched him, arms flailing, over to the group of ladies who'd been admiring him from the corner.

"See this douchebag, ladies?" Clarice wiggled her pinky finger in the air. "Not even this big. A totally lousy lay. Fifty dollars? He's not worth fifty cents!"

Clarice let go of Marcus. He jumped back and sneered at her, then slid back into his sleazy gigolo face. He smiled at the ladies, but they weren't buying it anymore. They turned their noses up and scattered like buckshot across the room.

Clarice turned to me and grinned like a devil on the loose.

"One down. One to go."

IT WAS VINNY CANNOLI'S turn at bat.

We skulked around in the hallway near Berta's cabin. An older lady in a beautiful silver cocktail dress walked by, looked Clarice and me up and down, and shot us a dirty look. She had an envelope in her hand. I realized I was still holding the envelope with the Kaptain's Klub invitation.

The elegant woman slipped her envelope under the door of Berta's and Vinny's cabin. She passed by us again and muttered, "How are we supposed to have a chance when you young trollops keep giving it away?"

Her comment got me fired up. *Clarice and I were catches. Why would we settle for a scrawny old two-timer like Vinny Cannoli?*

I was getting ready to bang on the cabin door when it opened. Out stepped Vinny in his top hat, tuxedo and spats, just as I'd hoped. I slapped the invitation in Clarice's hand and pounced in front of him like a ninja in heels.

"How could you treat Berta that way, you dried up old dirt bag!" I yelled in his face.

Vinny flinched and put up his arm, as if to ward off a blow.

"She deserves better than you, you philandering old piss-wad!" Clarice yelled.

Vinny put his arm down and looked me in the eye. He started to speak, then stopped.

"All those invitations from other women?" I said angrily. "Do you deny it, you two-timing jerk-wad?"

Vinny studied us both for a second. He blew out a breath and spoke.

"Aww, flapdoodle, kids. It's me, Berta."

Chapter Twenty-Three

I was too jumpy to sit still, much less try to eat breakfast. I was supposed to meet Friedrich soon, and had worried myself silly over
the possibility of having a repeat performance of my comic-tragic
Italian opera, *The Poop-and-Run Skank of Sorrento*. It was just as well
I didn't have an appetite. Another millionth of an inch and I
wouldn't have been able to button my jeans. On the bright side, if I
happened to start bleeding internally while in Naples, I was already
wearing a denim tourniquet.

Clarice, on the other hand, was gloating and enjoying her breakfast of champions. By the time Berta joined us, she'd already downed
two apple Danish and a pot of tea, and was just warming up.

"Good morning, Vinny," I said to Berta as she slid into the chair
beside me. "Going tranny today?"

Berta grinned. "Hiya, kids."

Our waiter appeared.

"Crappuccino?" Berta asked. Clarice and I nodded. "Make that
three, please."

The waiter lumbered off.

"I still don't get it," I said. "What's with the whole Vinny charade?"

"I didn't have time to explain last night," Berta began. "I had to
get to my show. But like I told you before, I work on the ship so I
can travel for free. I've been doing it for years. I usually do the lecture

circuit, but it was already taken for this cruise. All they had left was a spot in entertainment. I used to do an improv act back in my college days. So I came up with this shtick on the spot."

"That's pretty brave, Berta," Clarice said.

"It's more than that," Berta said. "It's genius! With the Vinny Cannoli gig, I get to travel *incognito*. Nobody knows me. That means nobody's hassling me after the show. And I don't have to keep up that nicey-nice polite bullcrap for the customers. As far as anyone else knows, I'm just that old bat Berta in cabin..."

Berta hesitated and looked around before whispering, "three-three-two."

"I get it," I said. "But what's up with the cloak and dagger act? The secret cabin number?"

"And all the notes slipped under your cabin door?" Clarice asked.

Berta sighed. "That's the crap end of this shtick, kids. I have to watch my back with the jealous old ladies."

"What do you mean?" I asked.

"You see, I get a better audience if they think I'm—I mean *Vinny*—is single. I get a bonus for packing the house. If the old broads found out that Vinny was sharing a cabin with *me*, I could lose customers—not to mention get stabbed to death with the daggers in those old ladies' eyes."

"But what about the envelopes?" Clarice asked.

"Okay. Stick with me here. So, the old broads think Vinny's single. But they never see him wandering around the ship. One day, some old lady spots Vinny going into a cabin. The news spreads like wildfire over the old biddy grapevine, and these gals start slipping love letters under the door for the old geezer. 'Let me buy you dinner.' 'Have a drink with me.' Blah blah blah. I tell you, girls. Times must be tough if women have to fight over a washed-up old Vaudeville act like Cannoli."

"But he makes me laugh," I sighed wistfully.

Berta cracked a wry grin. "Yeah. I guess there *is* that."

The waiter arrived with our cappuccinos. "And what would the ladies like for breakfast?"

"I'll have the eggs Benedict, half a grapefruit and a stack of pancakes," Clarice said.

"You know, that sounds good," Berta said. "Make it two."

"Nothing for me," I said.

The waiter looked stunned. He recovered his composure and said, "Very good."

Berta glanced around at the plump patrons eating after-breakfast parfaits.

"I'm guessing he's never heard that line before," she laughed. "What's up with you, kid? Still not feeling well?"

"No. I'm fine. It's just that...well...I'm meeting Friedrich in an hour. I'm too nervous to eat."

"Oh."

There was that blasted syllable again. The one that said everything and nothing at all.

"You don't approve?"

"Not for me to say, kid. But if you don't mind, I think Vinny wants to weigh in."

"Really? What are you, some kind of comedian?"

Berta scrunched her eyebrows together and lowered her voice an octave. "Yes ma'am, I am. So, tell me, young lady. What do women and brick sidewalks have in common?"

I shrugged. "I dunno."

"Lay 'em good once and you can walk all over them for years."

Clarice hooted with laughter. I winced. Vinny's joke had hit way too close to home.

SUNG-LI LOOKED PISSED and bored and sullen as she swiped my ship card and wished me a nice day with all the cheerful insincerity of a late-night telemarketer. I walked down the gangplank and along the chain-link fence separating the port from the city streets. I'd replied so late to Friedrich's email, I wondered if he was going to show up. The thought made my stomach flop. At the exit gate I spied a blond man with a square jaw, thin lips and a set of sea-blue eyes.

The expression on Friedrich's face was a strange mixture of pleasure and pain. The corner of his mouth didn't curled upward, but his eyes registered hopefulness tinged with fear.

"Val. You came."

"Of course I came. I said I would."

Friedrich gave me a short nod of acknowledgment, but didn't seem convinced. I wondered who, in his past, had not kept their word.

"Goot. Shall we walk?"

Friedrich fumblingly grabbed my hand and we set off down the cobblestone street. It felt awkward to see him again. But good, too. Familiar. Still, I didn't know what to say. I guess he felt the same. Soon, both of our palms were drenched in sweat. *What were we doing here?*

We walked down a busy sidewalk lined with bakeries, florist shops, butchers and green grocers. Laundry flapped in the breeze high above our heads, strung out on lines between apartment buildings built centuries ago. Cats lazed on terraces filled with bicycles and potted plants. And, true to form, Italians honked their horns and drove like madmen along the street.

"Have you hunger, Val?"

I was ravenous. But my jeans were so tight, I was afraid to sit down, much less eat. I shrugged.

"Napoli...uh...Naples is the home of pizza," Friedrich said, stumbling for words. "That's what they claim. But I think the truth is that pizza was invented in America."

I stared in a shop window displaying large, round pies covered in cheese, pepperoni and mushrooms. My stomach didn't give a flip where pizza originated, as long as it ended up in my mouth.

"Let's get a pizza here," I said.

Friedrich nodded and showed me his half-smile.

We chose a table for three outside on the busy sidewalk. Friedrich slung his backpack on the chair between us and went to join the small crowd at the counter to order. In a sea of dark-haired, suave Italians, I'd almost forgotten Friedrich's sturdy, Nordic charm. His hair was the color of sand, the perfect complement to his sea-blue eyes. If his nose had been a bit smaller and his lips a bit fuller, he would have been an absolute hunk—and totally out of my league.

Compared to the Italians, Friedrich's body language was less animated. He was stiffer, and more reserved. He spoke their language and appeared confident, but his self-assurance came off more like protective armor than a true personality trait. Still, he looked triumphant when he returned holding two glasses of red wine.

"Cheers," he said, handing me the wine. He pointed at his left eye with his left index finger, prompting me to remember the German rule.

"Ah yes. I must look into your eyes, or—"

"Seven years bad sex!" we said simultaneously.

The joke broke the awkward tension between us. We both took a sip of wine, our eyes properly locked. I thought it was funny, but Friedrich appeared to take the whole toasting thing quite seriously. I was about to say something when he seemed to read my thoughts.

"I have something for you." Friedrich dug into his backpack.

"What is it?"

Ever since receiving his email, I'd tried not to think about what it might be that Friedrich had to give me. Still, my mind had time-and-time-again overruled me. After ridiculous thoughts like the keys to a Ferrari or a villa in Tuscany, I'd finally settled on something reasonable. I figured Friedrich was going to give me jewelry. A necklace, or perhaps a promise ring.

"Here, this is for you," he said. He handed me an unwrapped cell phone.

"Oh," I said, borrowing a syllable from Berta.

I reached for it and bumped my glass of wine. It tilted and sloshed a red stain across the white tablecloth.

"Ooops! I'm sorry. I was just so...*surprised.*"

"It is a Technoblast 3800. An unlocked model equipped with an SIM card for Italy."

I didn't understand a thing he'd just said.

"Gee, thanks. But I already have a cell phone."

"With this one, we can keep in touch while you are here."

"Oh."

"Val, I want to stay in touch. Don't you?"

A voice inside the restaurant shouted out something and Friedrich got up and left. I stared at the phone and wondered if I should be disappointed or elated. I felt neither. Just confusion. *What was I doing here with him? What did I want?*

Friedrich returned carrying a whole pizza. Hunger erased my train of thought. The gooey, melted mozzarella dotted with bright-green basil leaves was too much for my famished appetite to resist. I grabbed a slice and bit into it. It burned the skin off the roof of my mouth.

"Ouch!"

I jettisoned the molten-hot bite of pizza. It knocked over a bottle of olive oil and tumbled across the table, leaving behind greasy, tomato skid marks. Combined with the spilled wine, our romantic table for two looked as if it had been trampled by a hoard of pigs.

"I'm sorry!"

Friedrich just shrugged and said, "It happens."

I took another sip of wine to cool my throbbing, seared upper palate.

"So, Val. You didn't say. Do you want to stay in touch?"

I nearly choked on my wine, but managed to recover. I wasn't sure what I wanted. So, I did what I always had before. I capitulated to the other person's wishes.

"Yes."

Friedrich smiled his almost imperceptible smile and gave a quick nod. "Goot." He took out a pack of cigarettes and started to light up.

"But I have to be honest, Friedrich. I don't want to be with someone who smokes. I'm not telling you what to do. But it's a deal breaker for me."

Friedrich studied his cigarette for a moment, then put it back in the pack.

"I will stop."

"Do what you want, Friedrich. But don't do it for me. I don't want to be the one who tells you what to do. I don't want to have to take the blame, or be the bad guy. I don't want you to end up resenting me."

"I want to, for you. I want you."

I nearly swallowed my tongue. "What? You want *me?*"

"Ya. I want you."

"But why?"

"Because when I hold your hand, I can no longer feel my feet on the ground."

I DON'T REMEMBER HOW I got back to the ship. But I must have, because when I came back to earth, I was sitting across the dinner table from Berta and Clarice.

"Crap, kid. You look like you're in deep."

"Oh, Berta. It was so romantic!"

"A pizza in Napoli? I had one, too, kid. Nothing special. Actually, not even as good as what I can get on any corner in Brooklyn."

"No. I mean...the things he said."

"Actions speak louder than words," Clarice said sourly.

"That's just an old saying."

"If it weren't true, it wouldn't have had time to grow old," said Berta.

I pouted. "You guys don't want to hear about it, fine. But don't piss on him without knowing what he said."

"Okay, kid," Berta said. "I'll bite. What did he say?"

"Something totally original. Friedrich told me that when he holds my hand, he can't feel his feet on the ground."

Clarice snickered. Berta started to roll her eyes, then caught herself.

"Look, you two. When I was married to Jimmy, his 'I love you' was meaningless. It was as thoughtless as 'Have a nice day.' Just something said without thinking. Jimmy didn't *see* me. Friedrich is different. He *sees* me!"

"Love is blind, kid."

Clarice snickered again.

"I'm *serious*, Berta! He's *pursuing* me. And I like it."

"Wake up, kid. You're just having an ego trip. A temporary titillation. A fling. Nothing more."

"You weren't there. You don't understand."

"I understand plenty. Don't forget, I've been listening to people spill their guts to me for years. I know infatuation when I see it."

"Infatuation?"

"You're acting different, kid. You're not seeing straight. Women are always twisting themselves into what they think they have to be for a man to like them."

"Amen to that!" Clarice agreed.

"I'm not acting different."

"Kid, the only thing recognizable on you is that hairdo."

"I already told him I'd spend the weekend with him in Rome."

"Aww, kid. Don't you know by now? You should never stay in touch with people you meet on vacation."

Chapter Twenty-Four

The cruise was over. I hugged Clarice goodbye as she boarded a shuttlebus to the airport. I'd be back in Florida with her in a few days. Berta was staying on board for another tour as Vinny Cannoli. According to her, business was good.

"Where else can an old woman like me get paid to tour the world, laugh my butt off, and be the envy of every other woman onboard?"

"You have a point, there. But this time, let's stay in touch, okay?"

The two of us exchanged emails and phone numbers.

"I'll miss you, Berta. You've helped me more than you know.

I thought I saw a tear in the tough old lady's eye.

"I'll miss you, to, kid. Don't do anything I wouldn't do."

FRIEDRICH GREETED ME at the port in Civitavecchia with a short kiss and a long-stemmed, red rose. I took the flower in my hand, and suddenly felt completely alone. A strange déjà vu feeling swept over me. I watched, disembodied, as Friedrich placed my suitcase and carry-on carefully in the back of his tiny Peugeot.

"What's wrong?" Friedrich asked.

Frightened, I broke out in tears. "I...I don't think...." *If you don't stand up for yourself now, Val, you never will.* "This red rose. I...I prefer yellow ones."

"Oh. Is that all?" Friedrich took the rose from my hand and threw it onto the street. He smiled. "Okay. From now on, yellow roses. I can do this."

I looked at the rose laying in the gutter. I took a deep breath and dried my tears. Then I smiled hesitantly and climbed into his car. I let my worried thoughts blow away in the wind as Friedrich whisked me along in his silver convertible.

"Which direction are we going?"

"South. Along the coast. Toward Sorrento."

My stomach gurgled at the thought of Sorrento. I don't know why I didn't tell Berta and Clarice about it. Maybe it was just too embarrassing. Every time I thought of Frank's blood-red face as he pointed at my panties, I cringed and smiled.

The day was bright and clear and glorious. My white, floppy hat danced in the breeze as we sped along. We both said little, content to take in the sights and the fresh, salt air. Friedrich managed the narrow, winding road like a pro, shifting gears instinctually, his eyes intent on what lay ahead.

By the time we arrived at the beach town of Santa Marinella, my shoulders shone pink against the straps of my white sundress. I wanted to search my purse for some sunscreen, but I couldn't drag my eyes off the incredible scenery.

Ornate, pastel-hued shops lined one side of the road. A dusky-sand beach beckoned from the other. The narrow strip of beach was decked out with two long, neat rows of white sunning beds. Just a few yards from the sparkling ocean, beachgoers lounged lazily upon them, protected by the shade of huge green and blue umbrellas.

Along the shoreline, sun worshipers strutted, displaying their tans and designer bathing suits. In the surf, heads adorned with bright-colored hats bobbed in rhythm with the waves. Clusters of beachcombers gathered at one end of the beach near a square, castle-like fortress that stood guard like a boxy Sphinx.

"Oh! Let's stop for a moment! I want to take a picture!"

Friedrich found a spot and pulled over. I snapped a few shots, then we went for a walk on a blunt, uninspired concrete promenade. It jutted out into the clear blue water like a narrow, dead-end road, supported by buff-colored boulders on either side. We walked to the end of it and peered into the water. A gust of wind blew Friedrich's sandy bangs into his eyes. I reached up to brush them back and he flinched.

"Why don't we have a coffee," he said absently, as if wanting to change the subject on a discussion he'd been having with himself.

"Okay."

He took my hand and led me to a tiny, outdoor café overlooking a harbor. The inlet itself was made of flesh-colored sand, giving the effect of a pair of sandy arms wrapping around perhaps fifty small boats that had found refuge within them. As I took a snapshot with the camera on my phone, Friedrich's arms wrapped around me. *Would he prove to be my sanctuary, or just a port in the storm?*

"Beautiful, ya?"

"Ya."

Friedrich laughed. "Speaking German already."

"Yes. I've mastered Italian. I figured it was time to move on."

Friedrich's right eyebrow shot up, forming a triangle with no bottom.

"To something even better. Ya?"

I smiled. "Ya."

We sipped our cappuccinos, then took off again, following the ocean road. A half an hour later, our trip along the coast ended in Fiumicino, a less glamourous, more business-like city on the outskirts of Rome. Fiumincino's lone, narrow beach held no umbrellas, but its quaint harbor rivalled San Marinella's for beauty. As we turned away from the shore and onto the highway toward the eternal city of

Rome, I watched a four-passenger plane come in for a landing at a small airport.

All roads had always led to Rome. Now, even the skies did, as well.

MY HOTEL IN ROME WAS actually an air B&B just outside the walls surrounding Vatican City. Despite the traffic chaos and jumble of confusing street signs, Friedrich had no trouble finding the place.

"I've been to Rome a few times," he explained. "Let me be your tour guide. What do you want to see first?"

"The Vatican? I mean, it's right there." I pointed to the nondescript concrete wall. In a city full of beauty, the thick, blank barrier was ugly and foreboding. It appeared to have been built to hold in prisoners rather than to protect a pope.

"You don't really want to see that, do you? Look. See the lines of people wrapping around the wall? They are all waiting. It would take hours to get in."

"Oh. Okay. Well, I guess not."

"Buy the picture book. It's on every street corner. You know that you can't take photographs in there, don't you?"

"No. Why not?"

"There's no money in it for the church."

"Oh. Well, then. Where would you suggest?"

"You've seen the Colosseum, ya?"

"No."

Friedrich's lip curled smugly. He took me by the hand and said, "Let's go."

I had to admit, it felt good to relax and let someone else be in charge. Friedrich led me expertly along the streets of Rome, pointing out statues and fountains and ornate carvings on buildings. He seemed to know so much about the world it left me feeling a bit naïve and inadequate. I bought the picture book of the Vatican, as he suggested, and two pairs of stained-glass earrings as mementos for me and Clarice. The thought of her made me suddenly miss her badly. Rome had seemed a lot more fun with her last fall.

By the time we arrived at the Colosseum, my feet were killing me. I ducked into a tacky souvenir shop and bought a pair of cheap flip flops. The only ones in my size were dayglow orange. I thought of Berta and smiled. I carefully peeled the straps of my sandals off the backs of my hamburger ankles and inched into the flip flops. They looked atrocious with my white dress and hat, but hey, these were desperate times.

I followed Friedrich around the corner. In my white dress and orange shoes, I felt like a pigeon-toed goose.

"We are here," he said.

I looked up and sucked in my breath. Peeking out from above the treetops was a roundish wall of open arches, soaring thirty feet above the foliage. On top of the arches, climbing even higher, was another story that looked like a crown, with square openings offset from the arches below them. The effect was like windows looking into the heavens above.

"Wow! That's amazing! Should we take a tour?" I asked.

"No. You don't need it. I can show you everything."

We bought basic entry tickets and joined the crowd milling about the ancient structure. With the view no longer obstructed, I realized that the Colosseum actually had three full stories of arches stacked one upon the other, the last row topped with the square-windowed crown. The ancient structure was enormous—as big around as a football field and as tall as a ten or twelve story building. It wasn't built to a normal human scale. I felt as small and insignificant as a chipmunk scurrying about in its presence.

Over half of the third row of arches and top crowning stories were missing. Still, the oval Colosseum hadn't lost any of its power to

impress. Made of the same buff-colored stone as most of Italy's archi-
tectural treasures, from the outside, the Colosseum could have been
mistaken for the discarded, broken bracelet of a giant, immortal goddess.

Compared to the outside, inside the structure was somewhat of
a letdown. It made me think of a rundown, overcrowded graveyard.
The unearthed rows of seats and headstone-like structures poking up
from the ground reminded me of the sun-bleached, skeletal remains
of a deer I once saw in the woods as a child. Sections of the ruins
were still half buried under dirt and debris, their excavation stalled
for some future date.

"I don't get it, Friedrich. How did something so incredibly magnificent end up ruined and half buried in muck?"

Friedrich shrugged. "Neglect."

His reply caught me off guard. A drop of water hit my face. I
looked up at the sky. It had turned grey.

"You have seen enough, ya?"

The ominous rain clouds amplified the uncomfortable feeling
that had crept over me. I suddenly felt as if I were walking around in
a tomb, gawking at the dead dreams of strangers. A shiver went up
my spine.

"Yes. I've seen enough."

We wound our way through narrow streets and alleys on our way
back toward the B&B. Rain showers sprinkled us intermittently as
we walked along the tree-lined *Fiume Tevere*. The river-like waterway
that ran through Rome was walled both sides. Local artists had been
unable to resist the long, blank canvas. From the cover of maple trees,
we sheltered from the rain and studied the beautiful works of graffiti
adorning the dusky stone walls.

The heaviest rain held off until we were a few blocks from the
Vatican. Then it came down in buckets. Friedrich grabbed my hand
and we ran like naughty children, ducking under awnings and trees

where we could. Two blocks from the B&B, my right flip-flop blew out. By the time I hobbled into the building where my room was, we were both soaked to the skin.

We tromped up the stairs and I fumbled the key into the lock. The rain had turned my hair into dripping ringlets. My innocent white dress had turned transparent in the rain, revealing opaque hints of the sexy, peach-colored bra and panty set I'd bought in Brindisi. I could feel Friedrich's warm, electric presence behind me as I struggled with the key. My back arched and the hair on the nape of my neck stood on end.

The door finally opened and I stepped into the room, leaving a puddle of rainwater where I'd stood. Friedrich followed me in, closed the door and turned the deadbolt. The click echoed in my mind like the sealing of a vault. My pulse began thumping in my ears.

Friedrich took me in his arms and kissed me hard on the mouth. The steamy heat of his wet body against mine triggered an unstoppable, primal urge within me. I wanted to feel his bare skin on mine. I wanted to rake my nails across his back. I needed to feel the hard, thrusting heat of him inside me.

I was wild with desire. If Friedrich was, too, he hid it well. He turned me around and unzipped my dress. I stepped out of it. He disappeared into the bathroom with it. He returned a minute later completely naked. He stood behind me again and unhooked my bra, then pulled down my panties. Again, he stepped into the bathroom and returned a few seconds later.

"You want?" he asked.

I nodded.

Friedrich took me by the hand and led me to the bed.

"IT IS DIFFERENT WITH you this time," Friedrich said as we lay spooning in the bed, listening to the rain.

"What do you mean?"

"In Brindisi, you were not sure you wanted me. But this time, you welcomed me."

Friedrich was right. About my body, anyway. Unlike our time in Brindisi, today I hadn't had to battle with my conscience. I'd wanted him and I'd not given a friar's flip about the consequences.

"You're right, Friedrich. I'm glad you came to Rome. I'm glad we had this last chance to enjoy each other."

"Ya. Me too. Even though you are a lot of work in the bed."

I laughed and Friedrich smiled. Then his face suddenly changed.

"I have an idea," he said.

I don't know if it was fear, afterglow, or the small kernel of hope I felt growing inside me, but I decided to take Friedrich up on his crazy idea. Before the rain had stopped and we'd dressed for dinner, I'd cancelled my Monday flight from Rome to Tampa. I'd also given the B&B notice that I'd be vacating my room in Rome a day early. Friedrich had to be back at work in Brindisi on Monday morning, and I was going with him.

Chapter Twenty-Five

Arriving back at the Hotel Bella Vista was a bit surreal. In fact, the whole next week was like a drunken ride on a merry-go-round. I kept snatching glimpses of things I'd seen before, but I never had time to grasp their details, let alone their significance.

Elegant Antonio was busy tending the front desk when Friedrich and I shuffled in at half past ten Sunday evening. He seemed happy to see me, but not surprised. He shot Friedrich a look that made me curious. Had Friedrich brought other women back to the hotel with him? Chances are, I wasn't Friedrich's first American rodeo. I hadn't really asked him much about his past. Partly because I didn't feel like divulging mine. If I wanted to let my bygones be bygones, I had to give him the same courtesy.

As Friedrich showered, I sat on the couch in his room and watched the strange stack of electronic gadgets blink their indifferent greetings at me from their dark, dusty corner. I suddenly felt caught in a time warp. It was as if I'd dreamed up the whole cruise and everything else I'd experienced since the last time I was here, lying in Friedrich's bed. But this time, things *were* different.

This time I had no other room to run off to. And no other place to go.

WHEN I AWOKE MONDAY morning, Friedrich had already left for work. I suddenly realized I didn't know the rules. Could I go downstairs for the hotel breakfast? Was I even *allowed* to stay in his room? I checked the clock. It was quarter to nine! I really must have been beat last night. Friedrich, as well. When he'd come to bed, he'd given me a peck on the lips and flopped over onto his pillow. He'd started snoring three seconds later.

I dressed and waited my turn at the cranky elevator. It jerked to a stop. The doors opened. Standing before me was Jersey girl Tina.

"Hey Val. Saw you get in last night. Having a nice ride?"

I smirked and joined her inside the tiny elevator.

"What do you mean, nice ride?"

"Come on, Val. Don't play coy. I knew you were screwing Rick Steves. Hand over the gory details."

"Geez, Tina. I haven't even had a cappuccino yet."

We both laughed. The elevator jerked its doors open to reveal the hotel lobby.

"Join me for breakfast?" I asked.

"Sure." Tina sauntered along behind me as a surly young man in a suit led us to a table. When he dumped our menus at a small table for two and left. I turned to Tina.

"Where's Giuseppe?"

"Vacation. His substitute is a real gem."

"I can see that. So, what about *your* gem. What was his name? Jessy?"

"Jonny."

"That's right. How's it going with you two?"

Tina's gaze shifted to the table. "Okay, I guess."

For this tough girl, that was almost a confession of undying love.

"Do I detect a hint of *amore* going on?"

Tina shrugged and smiled.

"There *is* something about this place, isn't there," I confessed. "It's like... one big stage for romance."

"Yeah," agreed Tina. "If you're not in love in Italy, you're wasting your time."

"Exactly! So, are you in love?"

"Maybe. Are *you*?"

Even though I'd pondered the question privately, being asked it point blank took me by surprise.

"I...I don't know."

"Why not? Being in love is easy. The trick is to not make a big, hairy deal out of it."

I wasn't sure if the girl in front of me was a naïve idiot or an enlightened sage. But I *did* know that for the past few days, everything around me had seemed lighter and fresher. Colors were brighter. Food tasted richer. Everyone seemed nicer—except for our new waiter. Did that mean I was in love? Or was I just finally learning to enjoy the moment? Was it amore, or something I'd yet to define?

FRIEDRICH CAME THROUGH the door with a stunned look on his face.

"What's wrong?" I asked.

"Nothing. It's just that...I've been called back to Germany."

"Is that good?"

"The project here is finished. The company wants me to report to the main office on *Donnerstag*."

"Donners Tag?"

"Oh. Excuse me. Thursday."

"*This* Thursday?"

"Ya. We leave tomorrow."

"Tomorrow!"

"Yes. We take the train."

"What about your car?"

"I cannot take it to Germany. Not yet. My divorce is final in a few weeks. I come back and get it then."

"Your *divorce*? I thought...I don't understand."

"If I take the car to Germany, I have to register it and claim it as assets for the divorce. In a few weeks, it is all over. Then I come and get it."

"What? I...I mean...I thought you were *already* divorced."

"It is only paperwork left. I haven't seen her since I took this job in Brindisi."

"Oh. What will you do with all of your things?"

"I pack them. I put some in the car. Then you and I take the train to my apartment in Landau."

"Where is Landau?"

"Near Karlsruhe."

"In Germany, right?"

"Ya. Of course."

I knew nothing about Germany. But at the moment it didn't matter. Friedrich needed my help, and we had too much to do to waste time pondering anything else. I got caught up in the whirlwind of Friedrich's urgent mission. He disappeared for half an hour and returned hauling several large, metal trunks he'd retrieved from somewhere in the bowels of the hotel. He packed his electronic equipment while I wrapped his kitchen things in newspaper and stuffed them into a crate. By midnight, we had everything packed away.

I made some grilled cheese and sausage sandwiches with the contents of his fridge, accompanied by the last of a bottle of white wine. We chewed tiredly, said little, and collapsed into bed.

The next morning, Friedrich woke me, a cup of cappuccino in his hand.

"For you, *mein Schatz*," he said.

I smiled, sat up and took a sip. There was no sugar in it, but the bitterness seemed to give me strength. It perked up my exhausted body enough that I could haul it out of bed. I looked around at the room. It was empty except for the hotel furniture and a couple of suitcases.

"Where are the crates?" I asked.

"Stored away with the car. Now get dressed, mein Schatz. We have a train to catch."

A MILLION HOURS LATER, in the middle of the night, we got off yet another train.

"How long before the next connection?" I asked, too tired to really care.

"No more trains. We are here."

I looked around, but all I could make out was the yellow blur of street lights.

"This way," Friedrich said. He turned and started walking, pulling two suitcases behind him in the street.

I grabbed the handle of my suitcase in one hand, my carry-on in the other, and followed him like a tired, lost kitten, down the dark, empty street.

Chapter Twenty-Six

Just like that, my Italian vacation was over and I was living with Friedrich Fremden in Landau, Germany.

During our long journey from Brindisi, Friedrich had kept me awake and entertained with stories about his family and interesting tidbits about Landau, the city where he was born and raised. In its heyday, Landau had been touted as the garden city of Southern Germany. But, according to Friedrich, the city's glory days were far behind her. The flower beds in her once attraction-worthy parks were bare now, but neat and well maintained. Though many shops were empty, others still bustled with business.

Friedrich told me the region, known as The Pfalz, could be compared to the American South. People there lived slower-paced, more rural lives than most of Germany. At one time, tobacco had been king. After its demise, the locals had turned to farming apples and wheat and rapeseed for oil. They also raised pigs and chickens and the occasional cow. But mostly, the people of The Pfalz cultivated vineyards for making wine.

The entire, hilly outskirts of Landau were lined with row upon row of carefully tended grapevines. According to Friedrich, every fall, the fruit would be harvested and pressed and fermented into good-quality bottles of Riesling, Chablis and Dornfelder. At the first frost of the season, grapes intentionally left to freeze on the vine would be harvested and pressed into the coveted, regional specialty—ice wine. The Pfalz was an important part of The Southern Wine Route, a string of picturesque villages that lived and died by the grape harvest and the tourist dollar.

AFTER TWO DAYS OF NON-stop travel, we'd fallen into bed exhausted and bleary eyed. Today, in the morning light, Friedrich's quaint little apartment had turned into an outdated, dusty hoarder's hovel. While he went to fetch us coffee and buttered pretzels for breakfast, I had a look around the place.

Books and boxes filled with junk lined the living room and bedroom walls. Every cabinet and drawer I opened was stuffed to the brim with chipped cups, dead fountain pens, socks with holes in the toes and other useless junk. *How could he live like this?* Then I remembered he hadn't lived here in years.

Friedrich's two years in Brindisi explained the dust. But what about all the junk? Being both a woman *and* from the South, this was a situation beyond toleration. His filthy bachelor pad was in desperate need of a good scrubbing. I decided to surprise him and clean it up while he was away at work. I couldn't help myself. It was in my DNA.

I heard the door open and I tucked my thoughts away for the moment.

"Here is your coffee, mein Schatz." Friedrich's blue eyes sparkled to match his half smile.

"Thank you. I mean, danke."

I took a sip of the coffee and was immediately disappointed. It was a poor imitation of an Italian cappuccino. In fact, it was really nothing more than rusty water disguised as coffee.

"*Bitte,*" said Friedrich.

I took another sip. "No. Not bitter. It's too weak to be bitter."

Friedrich looked confused for a moment. "Ah. Not bitter. Bitte. It is how you say 'you're welcome' in German."

"Oh. Danke is thank you. Bitte is your welcome."

"Precisely. You will be speaking fluent German in two years, I am sure of it."

I nearly choked on my coffee. *Two years?* I haven't even been here *two days*. I had no idea yet if I wanted to stay. But, truth be told, there was something comforting in knowing that Friedrich had said, in a way, that he wanted me here.

"I must go to work. Did you try the pretzel? It's from the Fuss family bakery. They make the best in Germany."

I took a bite. It was soft and buttery and gooey. "It's delicious."

"So, I should be home by four or five o'clock. What will you do today?"

"Um. Eat pretzels and learn German. Maybe take a walk into town?"

Friedrich nodded, but I could tell he wasn't listening. His mind was somewhere else. He gave me a peck on the lips and disappeared out the door.

I chewed my pretzel and looked in the cabinet under the kitchen sink. It was stuffed with old rags and shoe polish containers and used-up sponges. I found an empty plastic bottle that looked as if it had once held household cleaner. There was some dried up yellow crust in the bottom, and a date stamp of 1989. I found a piece of paper and wrote down the name on the bottle's faded label. I fished around a little deeper and found a few other containers and wrote down their names as well. I got dressed and was ready to hit the pavement.

I stepped out the entry door to Friedrich's apartment and turned left. I followed the road toward the center of town, in search of a store to buy the cleaning supplies. There may have been shops much closer by on another street. But given my horrible sense of direction,

I was afraid to make a turn and end up lost to the annals of history. *American skeleton holding list of misspelled German cleaning supplies found in rural cornfield.*

So I limited my trek to the shops along *Felder Strasse.* In the daylight, Landau didn't look half bad. Several ornate, three-story houses made of the region's yellow sandstone still looked regal and charming, kind of like the antebellum homes near Greenville. I noticed a sign over a doorway of one house. It displayed the date 1888. I smiled. Somehow, these old beauties had found a way to coexist with the small shops sandwiched between them. Maybe there was a space for me here, as well.

I shuffled by small, family-run bakeries, boutiques and butcher shops that appeared to still be eking out a living despite the chain-store grocers and discount clothing shops. I peeked in a storefront full of books. I stopped in and bought a German phrasebook. I looked up the word for cleaning. *Putzen.*

I trudged onward, my confidence reinforced by my newfound German word. Another half mile or so down the road, I found a grocery store called *Rewe.* I tried to free a grocery cart from the line of stacked ones, but it wouldn't budge. An old lady in an unintentionally vintage dress from the 1970s stared at me like I was a degenerate. She took out a silver coin and placed it in a slot near the cart handle and slid it back and forth. The cart released the chain binding to the others.

I watched her disappear into the store before I fished around my change purse for a one-euro coin. It fit right in the slot. I slid it back and the chain fell free. *One small victory for me!* I suddenly realized that living in a foreign country would be a lot harder than I'd thought. *Geez! I couldn't even grab a grocery cart without a lesson!*

I entered the small *Rewe* store and wandered around until I found an aisle stocked with bottles of stuff that looked inedible. I smiled at a young woman who was shopping with a baby and showed her my list. She stepped back and glared at me as if I'd held out a handful of feces for her to eat. What was left of my confidence fell into shattered bits onto the floor. I ducked my head in shame and spent the next half an hour shifting my eyes timidly back and forth from my list to the containers, trying to match the words with the items on the shelves.

Having grown up around country people myself, I thought I would fit right in here in The Pfalz. After all, I had all the right skills. I was independent, good-humored, smart and hard-working. But having never lived abroad, I hadn't counted on the whole culture and language barrier thing. From the reactions of the people I'd encountered so far, I'd arrived in Germany with the social skills of a newborn goat.

WHEN FRIEDRICH HAD first mentioned The Pfalz to me on Sunday, to my American ear it had sounded like The Faults. Given the rudeness of my first two encounters, I now secretly found that amusing. The Germans I'd encountered on my shopping adventure had left me with the impression that they would rather be rude than wrong. It made sense. Friedrich had warned me that most Germans, even though they learned English in school, would refuse to speak it with strangers for fear of making a *fehler*—a mistake.

I wondered why they didn't see their own rudeness as a mistake.

BY THE TIME FRIEDRICH arrived home carrying a bag of groceries, I was wiped out both mentally and physically. The kitchen was gleaming, and the delinquent bathroom had survived its first come-to-Jesus meeting with a Southern woman with OCD—obsessive cleaning disorder.

"Very impressive," said Friedrich. "I give you the greatest compliment in Germany. *Du bist fleissig.* You are a hard worker, ya?"

"Danke," I said. "Now you take me to dinner."

Friedrich nodded that charming, quick nod of his. He carried the groceries into the kitchen and started laughing like a hyena. I realized it was the first time I'd ever heard him really, truly laugh.

"What's so funny?" I called from the living room.

"Come in here."

I walked to the kitchen. He held up a jug.

"Is this what you cleaned with?"

"Yes."

Friedrich burst out laughing again.

"What?!"

I was tired, cranky, and in no mood to be laughed at. The look I shot him needed no translation. Friedrich's laughter stuttered to a halt.

"Let's go. I explain you on the way."

Over schnitzel and beer, Friedrich told me that I'd cleaned the windows with fabric softener, scrubbed the bathroom with flea powder and washed the kitchen down with an industrial-size, vinegar douche. At least that explained the *Rewe* cashier's weird expression when I'd picked up my bag of supplies, said the word *putzen,* and pointed a thumb at myself.

It was obvious I was going to have to learn to speak German *and* to find way around Landau. I'd been in town *one single day*, and already the only grocery I knew how to get to was now a place I could never show my face again.

Chapter Twenty-Seven

Over the weekend, I met Friedrich's mother and made my first German friend. It wasn't her. We went to visit Frau Fremden on Sunday after she got home from church. Besides the fact that she would turn eighty in December, Friedrich had told me almost nothing about his mother. As we approached her front door, it opened and a short, plump woman as black as ebony stood smiling at us. She hugged Friedrich and turned to face me.

"Friedrich! This must be your Val! Come in, my child!"

"Val, this is Tamela Pango."

"So nice to meet you, Miss Pango."

The woman eyed me kindly, but warily. "Call me Tamela. I take care of Mrs. Fremden. I'm originally from Tonga."

Tamela ushered us into a dimly lit parlor. Every wall was lined with tall, heavy-looking curio cabinets and bookshelves overburdened with a bizarre assortment of mementos. They appeared to document a life that had survived two world wars, three children and two grandkids.

My eyes fell on a nicely framed, black-and-white photograph of a young man and woman posing by a car parked in front of a bombed-out building. A bright-yellow plastic Spongebob figurine rode the antique frame like a rodeo cowboy.

"Friedrich!"

Startled, I turned toward the voice. In a dark corner sat an old woman. She glared at me through watery, blue eyes. The skin on her face looked both leathery and paper thin, ghostly pale save for a smattering of age spots. Her lower jaw protruded unnaturally to the left, and when she spoke again, she revealed a mouthful of yellow, neglected teeth.

"Frau Jolly, ya?"

"Ya," I answered. "*Freut mich.*"

I used the new phrase I'd practiced nervously on the way over. Basically, it meant "Happy to meet you." But I wasn't. Just the opposite. She scared me, and I began our relationship with a lie.

The old woman turned her attention back to Friedrich, dismissing me as if I were of no further interest. She began speaking angrily to Friedrich in German. Every syllable that came out of her mouth sounded like a cussword to me. Friedrich's voice in German sounded no better. I shot an uneasy glance at Tamela. She pursed her lips and shrugged. I guess this was their version of normal.

Frau Fremden's body was as contorted as her voice. She sat, twisted, in an ugly, floral-patterned armchair circa 1970s. Each of her gnarled, liver-spotted hands kept a tight grip on the knobby wooden ends of the chair's arms. Despite her attempt to sit up straight, her spine was noticeably curved to the right. I could also tell that underneath her light-blue polyester pants she wore an adult diaper. I felt trapped in the nursing home that time forgot.

Friedrich and his mother kept talking—or arguing—or whatever they were doing, until Frau Fremden started to cry. This appeared to tick Friedrich off. He looked over at me.

"It's time to go."

I approached the old woman to say my goodbyes. She grabbed my hand in hers. Her boney fingers were surprisingly strong. She pulled me down until I was face-to-face with her. She planted an unwanted, wet kiss on my mouth. It was a Herculean effort to smile, but I managed it.

"Freut mich, Val," she said and released her vice grip. I sprung up and stepped back. As I did, the old woman began blasting a stream of what sounded like complaints at Friedrich.

"*Bis bald, Mutti*," Friedrich said dismissively.

"Goodbye, Mrs. Fremden," I said, and gave a weak wave.

Friedrich grabbed my hand and tugged me toward the door. I hadn't felt so relieved to leave a place since my last visit with my own ungrateful, guilt-slinging mother. When we stepped outside in the fresh air again, I hadn't realized I'd been holding my breath. I took in a big gulp of air.

"Sorry, Val. My mother can be...what you say, *manipulator*."

"Really?" I said, trying to feign surprise. Then I lied again. "She seemed sweet."

Friedrich studied me with a look of suspicious disbelief. Then his face shifted.

"You have met the beast. You deserve a reward. I know what it will be."

I smiled with delight. "What?"

"You see in a minute."

WHEN FRIEDRICH PULLED up to an appliance store, my heart sunk. I'd had enough "gifts" of vacuum cleaners, can openers and toaster ovens to last five lifetimes. My jaw locked and my face grew red with anger. Friedrich didn't seem to notice. He got out of the car and closed the door. I sighed and did the same. I followed him begrudgingly into the store. When he showed me what he wanted to buy me, my anger dissolved into delight. I kissed Friedrich and watched eagerly as he and the salesman demonstrated to me how to use my new German friend.

It was a boxy contraption of grey plastic and chrome that made cappuccinos at the press of a button. It was love at first sight, and I named him Otto. He cost a fortune, but Friedrich said he would be worth it. When I fed him fresh water, Italian coffee beans and whole milk, he returned the favor with a hot, foam-topped cappuccino that truly did rival the ones I'd come to love in Italy.

When we got back to his apartment, Friedrich set Otto up on the freshly douched kitchen counter, and, for the first time, I didn't feel so alone in a sea of Germanity.

WITH NO TICKET BACK to Florida, I didn't feel compelled to live each day like a ticking countdown to the end. Time snuck by unnoticed, as it's prone to do for new lovers. Every morning, Friedrich would bring me a cappuccino in bed, then fetch fresh, buttered pretzels for breakfast. While he was at work, I cleaned and organized his apartment, strolled around Landau, and shopped for food and accessories to brighten the place up. In the evening, I made dinner or we went out. We talked, we drank wine, we got to know each other, and we made love. A lot.

One day Friedrich took me to meet his sister, Olga, a younger version of his mother, and her husband, Hans. They'd invited us over for dinner at their place next to a vineyard. It was a beautiful house, but followed the family theme; cluttered and unappreciated. Every windowsill and bookshelf was crammed with no-longer noticed pictures, figurines, travel mementos and, oddly, chunks of rose quartz.

Hans spoke English quite well, but Friedrich's sister didn't. Despite this fact, Olga domineered the conversation, demanding to know every word spoken. After ten minutes or so of tedious interpreting, the three of them fell into speaking only German. She won. I lost.

I wandered outside to escape the growing feeling of isolation. The backyard held things I could understand. A fish pond. Raspberry bushes. And a huge cherry tree—a true novelty to a native Floridian like me. Being a bit north of Italy, the fruit in Germany was just now ripening in the gloriously warm, dry July weather.

It was after 8 p.m., but the sky was still blue, lit by a low-hanging, persistent summer sun. I explored the side yard next to a vineyard and discovered a vegetable garden. Tomato plants heavy with fruit spilled onto the ground next to zucchini the size of my calves. I suddenly felt homesick for my grandparents' farm in Greenville, where I'd spent so many summers as a child.

I went back inside and helped clear away the dishes. After a meal of meat and potatoes, I was bloated and tired. Olga seemed content to let me do the lion's share of the clean-up. When I'd finished loading the dishes into the dishwasher, I returned to find that Hans had set the table with four small glasses and a large wine bottle full of clear liquid. Hans opened the bottle. The strong smell of alcohol struck my nose on impact.

"This is kirshwasser, made from our own kirsh—uh, *cherry* tree," Hans explained. He poured some into a shot glass. "Sit. Try it."

I obeyed. I took a sip and choked. The cherries had all died of alcoholism. This was pure, German moonshine. I looked over at Friedrich. He seemed amused.

"No! Don't sip," Hans instructed good-naturedly. "Like this." He poured himself a shot and tipped the whole thing down his throat.

I followed his example. The strange brew burned all the way down my throat and inside my stomach.

"Very goot!" encouraged Hans.

Friedrich poured himself a shot and threw it back. "I think it's time you had your first *real* German lesson." He refilled our shot glasses with the hundred-proof hooch.

"*Und mir?*" Olga asked sulkily from the kitchen doorway.

Friedrich filled Hans's glass and poured a fourth for Olga. She sat next to me and winked in a way that made me squirm inside. Or maybe it was just the kirshwasser.

"A toast!" said Friedrich.

"A toast!" echoed Hans and Olga.

We raised our glasses and clinked them together. Everyone was careful to make eye contact.

"*Hau weg die Schiesse!*" the three said at once.

We downed our shots and Hans poured another round.

"Hau weg die Schiesse!" I said along with them.

Olga poured another round.

"Hau weg die Schiesse!" I slurred at the strangely cracked-looking faces.

I poured the next round.

"Hau weg die Schiesse!" I think I managed to say.

WHEN I WOKE THE NEXT morning, Friedrich was sitting beside me on the bed, holding a beautiful cup of cappuccino. My head thumped like a palsy-ridden jackrabbit.

"Guten morgen, mein Schatz," he said. His face looked pleased with me.

"Guten morgen. Oh, yes. Danke."

I took the cup and started to take a sip, but then I thought I would make him proud and use the new German phrase I'd learned.

"Hau weg die Schiesse!" I toasted.

Friedrich laughed. "You know what this means?"

"No."

"Roughly translated? Get rid of this s*%t."

THE MONTHS OF JULY and August were glorious. Not hot and humid like in Florida. On weekends and some evenings after work, Friedrich and I would go walking through forests and farmers' fields ablaze with bright-yellow rapeseed blooms. Every day, I added a few more German words to my repertoire. I discovered that Schatz, Friedrich's pet name for me, meant treasure. I was his treasure! It made me feel special.

It was a lovely, intoxicating way of life, and I did my darnedest to enjoy it. I had no pressing reason to return to the States. No one was waiting for me there. No one, that is, except the immigration officials. Friedrich reminded me one day that my ninety-day visa was almost up. It was time to go home.

I COULDN'T QUITE LABEL my feelings as I stood at the gate in Frankfort airport. What could I say that would be appropriate? See you later? I had a great time?

I'd made no promises to Friedrich. I hadn't wanted to lie. I'd enjoyed my time with him immensely. But did I belong with him in Germany? I still didn't have a solid answer to that question. Besides, we hadn't discussed what would happen next. I was grateful that neither he nor I had made false pledges. I guess we both wanted to see how we felt when we were apart. Would absence make the heart grow fonder, or would newfound freedom reign?

"You are the best what ever happened to me, mein Schatz," Friedrich said. "I am not good at goodbyes."

He kissed me on the cheek and turned and walked away. I watched him go, hoping to blow him a kiss, but he never looked back. A couple beside me were also saying their goodbyes.

"Bis bald, mein Schatz," said the man to the woman.

He kissed her and she walked toward the gate. Another older couple let go of each other's hands. It was time for them to say good-bye as well.

"Aufweidersehen, mein Schatz," said the woman.

"Aufweidersehen, mein Schatz," said the man.

I turned and walked toward my gate thinking that maybe Schatz wasn't such a special name after all.

Chapter Twenty-Eight

It was nice to see a friendly face at the airport in Tampa. Clarice was there to greet me with a smile and something I hadn't even realized I'd missed—a good-old, cornpone Southern accent.

"Val! Girl, ain't you a sight for sore eyes!"

I studied the face of the woman who'd been my friend and confidant since we'd met at a party eleven years ago. She was still as cute as ever, with her sparkling green eyes and blonde hair cut in a not-too-fussy bob. She was dressed in Florida summer survival gear: a short-sleeved, loose-fitting cotton sundress and thin-strapped sandals.

"No, Clarice. *You're* a sight for *my* sore eyes! What did I miss while I was gone?"

"Nothing but ninety bad-hair days in a row. The humidity this summer's been brutal!"

Over two months had gone by since the cruise, but Clarice and I picked up as if we'd seen each other at breakfast. For me, that was the sign of a good friend. Being raised by a family that had doled out approval in small, hard-earned dollops, I'd always felt a bit insecure. Making friends had never been easy for me. When I'd met Clarice, she'd been a godsend. She was worth her weight in gold to me.

"*Nothing's* happened since I left? Not even a bad date?"

"Nothing compared to your summer romance! I want to hear all about it. Leave no juicy stone unturned!"

"It wasn't *that* juicy."

I spied my luggage and pulled it off the conveyor belt.

"Who do you think you're talking to, girl. I can read you like a book. And your face has erotic romance written all over it."

"Oh. Do I need a napkin?"

Clarice blanched, then doubled over with laughter.

"Val, you're the absolute queen of one-liners. That one alone was worth hauling my butt over here to pick you up. Have I said it yet? I'm *so* glad you're home!"

I swallowed a lump in my throat.

"Thanks. Me too. And thanks for letting the 'one-liner queen' stay with you for a few days. I really appreciate it."

"Are you kidding? You can stay as long as you want. Your rent is to be paid in tales from your trip. I live vicariously through you, you know."

"Yes, I'm well aware of that fact. It may be cheaper for me to stay at a motel."

Clarice swatted my arm. "Just for that, you can load your own bags, missy."

She clicked a button on her key fob. It beeped and the trunk lid flew up on her beat-up Ford Focus. I hefted my heavy suitcase into the trunk. The weight reminded me that I'd brought back *every single thing* with me. I hadn't left a stitch at Friedrich's apartment. Not even a pair of sexy panties to remember me by.

IT FELT WEIRD TO WAKE up with no cappuccino—and no Friedrich—waiting for me. Clarice had gone off to work and left me alone with Melvin, her orange tomcat. He stared at me accusingly as I fumbled to the kitchen and fiddled with the Mr. Coffee machine. Clarice had left half a pot of black brew on the warmer for me. I poured a cup. It tasted like burnt mud. I poured it down the drain and clicked off the machine.

I looked around the kitchen. It was bright and cheerful, just like Clarice. Even though I'd been to her house many times before, today it seemed different somehow. Strangely, I felt like an intruder, as if I didn't belong. Restlessness ran up my back like a daddy long-legs spider. *What was I going to do all day?*

I petted Melvin and gave him the last two treats from a jar on the counter. That seemed to win the fat, fuzz-ball over. He sauntered off to lay in a sunny windowsill.

I looked at the clock. It was 8:45 a.m. Clarice would be home in...*eight hours! What should I do now?* I washed the coffee pot. That killed off two minutes. I picked up the *St. Petersburg Times* on the coffee table. One quick glance at the headlines made me lay it down again. Same crap. Different day. I could call my mother. *Oh my gawd! Was I really that desperate?*

I went to the garage in search of more cat treats. I found my car instead. I'd forgotten all about it. *Duh! I could go for a drive. Pick up some cat treats and dinner!* I calmed down. I was okay now. I had a mission.

I dressed in shorts and a t-shirt, said goodbye to Melvin and stepped back into the garage. Only fifteen minutes had passed since I'd discovered my car, but the summer heat had already raised the temperature in the garage a good ten degrees. I sighed and braced myself for the coming blast. I clicked the button to open the garage door, and was accosted by a wave of thick, hellish air. That was something I certainly *hadn't* missed while I was in Germany.

I drove my Ford to Publix, my favorite grocery store. Even though I'd been there thousands of times before, when I walked in, I nearly had a panic attack. During my time in Europe, I'd forgotten how bright the florescent lighting was, how hideously colorful all the packaging was, and how ridiculous the number of choices were.

I pushed my cart to the pet aisle. It was a bloody warzone! All those brands screaming for attention. Did a cat really need thirty-two different kinds of treats to choose from? I thought I would re-member the name of Melvin's favorite treats, but so many similar names caused the words to vanish from my memory like disappear-ing ink. I settled on a bag with the image of a cat on it that looked a lot like Melvin. Meowy Yum Yums. *WTF.*

I'd planned on cooking a nice, healthy dinner of salmon and greens, but the smell of fried chicken from the deli broke both my will and my willpower. I followed the aroma to a display case and placed a box of chicken in my cart. Next, I headed to the produce section and picked up a bundle of collard greens and some potatoes. At least I could still claim I cooked the side dishes.

I searched the wine section and settled on a German Riesling from Saarbruchen, just north of Friedrich's stomping grounds. The thought of him made me suddenly want to rush home. *I'd forgotten to check my emails this morning!* I got in line behind a plump, sweaty man in a Rays jersey and ball cap. His shorts hung down past his knees and he had on shower shoes. He was buying a case of beer, a box of chicken wings and a box of donuts. He looked me up and down briefly, then looked away.

"Having a party?" I asked, trying to be friendly.

"No."

"Oh. I'm sorry. I didn't...."

"Look. You're not my type. Just let it go."

The man paid for his groceries and left, never looking back. As I bought my groceries and hurried home, I felt that old veil of un-desirability closing in on me. I set the groceries on the counter and clicked the computer's power button. I gave Melvin a Meowy Yum Yum while I waited for it to boot up. Melvin sniffed the fish-shaped nugget. It was the color and texture of a chunk of half-dried brown clay. He looked up at me in disgust and waddled away.

I logged in and checked for emails. I sat up straight. There was one from Friedrich. I clicked on it.

Dear Val,

I hope you had a pleasant trip. Let me know you arrived well. I miss you, and so does Otto.

With heartfelt greetings,

Friedrich.

Attached to the email was a photo of the cappuccino machine. Friedrich had stuck a picture of a sad face on it. The frown made my lips smile and my heart ache.

I WOKE UP ON THE COUCH. Jet lag had gotten the better of me. Before I'd passed out, I'd emailed Friedrich with a simple note letting him know I was okay. Then I'd eaten a piece of fried chicken. That was a lie. Then I'd eaten the entire box of fried chicken.

I looked at the clock. It was 4:33. Clarice would be home in less than an hour. I grabbed the cardboard coffin of chicken bones and headed for the car. I made it to Publix in less than ten minutes. I stuffed the skeletal remains in a garbage bin outside the store and ran inside. I bought another box of chicken and a packet of antacid, and scurried back to Clarice's house. I was mashing the potatoes when Clarice walked in the door.

"Mmmm! Smells like Southern cookin' in here!" she called from the front door. "Either that or something died up in the attic."

"It's collard greens. Get washed up. I'm putting dinner on the table!"

I heaped Clarice's plate high with collard greens, lumpy mashed potatoes and a fried chicken breast and wing, her favorite pieces. My own plate got a modest portion of potatoes and lots of greens. As I poured the Riesling, Clarice came in and took a seat at the table. She took a bite of collard greens.

"How can something that smells like a dead skunk taste so good?"

"It's one of those mysteries of the cosmos, I guess."

Clarice laughed, then looked at my plate. "What? You're not having any chicken?"

"I'm trying to watch my weight."

"You look fine. Don't go turning into a skinny, whiny twerp on me!"

"Okay. I'll have a leg."

I went into the kitchen and took the smallest leg from the box. I wondered why one leg actually *was* smaller than the other. Was this some kind of mutant, fiddler-crab chicken?

"What should we toast to?" Clarice called from the dining room.

I walked back to the table. "To friendship."

Clarice picked up her glass and started to take a sip.

"Wait! You have to look me in the eye!"

"What? Why? I already took a sip while you were in the kitchen."

"Oh."

"What's the big deal?"

"Nothing, really. Friedrich says if you don't look each other in the eye when you toast, it's seven years of bad sex."

Clarice stared at me for a moment. "Well that explains it. Now I know the *real* reason why American men are such lousy lovers!"

I laughed and turned scarlet. My embarrassment didn't go unnoticed by Clarice.

"What? Shut my mouth. I'll be darned! He's *good*, isn't he?"

I looked down at my half-eaten chicken leg and smirked.

"Dang it! He's *really* good. That does it! I want details!"

"I can't give you details!"

"I know. I was just fooling. But tell me this. You really like him, don't you?"

"Yeah, I do. It's funny, Clarice. I've lived here nearly all my life, but today was totally weird. Maybe it's because I don't have my own place, but I feel...*lost*. Like I don't belong here anymore."

"Maybe because your heart belongs somewhere else?"

"I don't know. I only know that things seem... *pointless* here. *Empty*."

"Girl, why is it so hard for you to just admit you're in love?"

I *was* in love. I must have been. I could see it in Clarice's eyes.

I shrugged. "You're right."

"So what are you going to do about it?"

"I don't know."

"Girl, you're on my last nerve! Write that boy and tell him! Then get your butt on the next plane out of here!"

"That's easy for *you* to say, Clarice. Your butt still fits in a coach-class seat."

THAT EVENING, I WROTE Friedrich asking when I could come back. He wrote a one-word reply. "Yesterday." I booked my ticket to return in two days. I passed the time playing with Melvin, gossiping with Clarice, and writing my very first love poem.

Good Conditions

"I need a holiday,"

I said. To erase the fragments of a life no longer wanted.

Off to Italy to volunteer.

Teaching English without baggage.

I just had to laugh.

"Your luggage will be here tomorrow,"

the hotel manager said, for four days in a row.

"Mi dispiache.

Let me buy you lunch."

I graciously accepted.

"I will take her to lunch,"
the stranger said, looking dumbstruck by his own words.
Thus began a conversation
that took us both by surprise.
I climbed into his convertible.
"Let me show you Alberobello,"
he said. Then drove through postcards of Italy,
swapping war stories with me
like two strangers on a plane.
I forgot about lunch.
"I must take you to Matera,"
he said, ignoring the sweat pouring from my palms.
We made plans to meet again
the following afternoon.
I could hardly wait.
"I feel like Sophia Loren,"
I said, waving at the other volunteers
from the passenger seat of his silver Peugeot.
Sure beat the tour bus they were in.
I couldn't believe my luck.
"Your feet are in goot conditions,"
he said, peering at me from under a Gilligan hat.
His compliment delivered poolside, in a red Speedo.
He tried to dive into my eyes.
I would not let him in.
"Let me make you dinner,"
he said. He cooked! He cleaned! Cappuccino and foot rubs!
He told me he liked me
just the way I was. I think he meant it.
I got more than I bargained for.
"You are the best what ever happened to me,"
he said. I tried to believe I was worthy of his praise.

I felt my soul quicken.
Liquid hope filled my eyes.
I let him in.

Chapter Twenty-Nine

When I landed in Frankfurt on Saturday morning, Friedrich greeted me with a hug, a kiss, and a surprise. He was working for a new company.

"An opportunity came up at a nearby power plant," he said. "I had to take it."

"That's great! When do you start?"

"In a few weeks. I am finished at my old job. I am in between now two weeks. We have some time together."

He put his arms around me again and hugged me tight. The way my body reacted, I knew I was ready to spend some time with him, too. He took me back to his apartment. It felt like home. He took me back to his bed. It felt like home, too.

We spent the next ten days in that soft, twilight place only new lovers can dwell. His apartment became our love nest. We lay in bed half the day, talking, cuddling, napping and making love. We had food delivered and drank wine and dined by candlelight. We meshed into each other. We bonded. We fell in love.

Only when we thought we might succumb to scurvy and scoliosis did we finally venture out of bed. One fall day we went to a wine fest being hosted by a tiny village nearby. We joined the crowd milling about along the barricaded main street. Closed to traffic, the road had been transformed into a marketplace. Stands selling trinkets and wine and snacks lined the sidewalks. Pedestrians clogged the street.

We stopped at a vinegar stand and sampled the goods on offer. The stand was in front of a house nestled in the middle of the festivities. Friedrich took a shot of strawberry vinegar, then looked up and stared. I followed his eyes upward. Behind a six-foot tall, wooden gate stood an old winemaker's house. Carved into the plaster above the door was the date 1786. The house was in disrepair, but it had the bones of a real beauty.

"That is the kind of house I want," Friedrich said, then folded his arms across his chest and stared at it.

I tasted a sample of the walnut vinegar. *Yuck!* Leave it to a German to make an aperitif out of *vinegar*. I had to catch my breath and clear my throat before I could speak.

"*That* house? Really? It needs a lot of work."

"I'm an engineer. I like a project," he said. "That's why I like you."

"Gee, thanks," I laughed. But Friedrich's remark got me wondering. "Tell me the truth. Why do you *really* like me?"

Friedrich turned his head in my direction, but kept his arms folded. "Because you are an elegant woman. You are not just looking to get off the street."

I'd been fishing for a compliment. I'd ended up with a flounder.

"What do you mean, Friedrich?"

"You have your own money. You are not trying to live off me like a parasite."

I had been hoping for something more romantic than not being a leech. My face fell so far he actually noticed.

"I do not mean that I am trying to get your money," he backpedaled. "When we are married I will sign a prenuptial contract. You keep what is yours."

"When we are married?"

"Yes. That is why you came back to me, no?"

"Are you...*proposing* to me?"

"Well, I suppose so. Yes."

I stared into his serious, unflinching blue eyes. "I...I don't know what to say."

"Say nothing. I give you a week to think about it."

I tried to speak. My mouth opened, but no words came out. Friedrich winked at me playfully, and I hit him on the arm.

"I'm serious!" I said.

"So am I. Let's get married. Will you be mine, Val?"

"I...I. I thought I had a week to decide."

Friedrich's face registered concern and a tinge of hurt feelings.

"Why don't we go to a spa for a few days? We can relax and you will have time to think what you want for your life."

"Okay."

WE DROVE EAST TOWARD the Black Forest. As we drew nearer, the land turned hilly. Rocky outcrops began to peek through the verdant, grass-covered slopes. Soon, the foothills turned to small mountains, and we stopped for lunch at a roadside attraction called the Pioneer Village.

Scattered over a couple of acres of land, a dozen or so old houses and other structures stood resolute, grey and weatherworn. According to a placard, each building had been carefully disassembled, moved to the site, and reassembled into a full-scale, working model of a sixteenth-century village. I kind of knew how they felt.

We stretched our legs and toured the wonders of bygone German engineering. A watermill used the power of a small stream to turn a huge, round, grinding stone. A blacksmith shop displayed simple tools and strange, mechanical devices made of metal.

Further down the path, sturdy wooden homesteads built half into the hillside featured ovens adorned with colorful tiles designed for cooking and heating. A man dressed in period clothes cranked a handle on a boxy contraption made of wood, demonstrating that the centuries-old device could still separate kernels of wheat from the shaft.

But the real star of the show was at the attraction's restaurant. *Schwartzwalder Kirshtorte*—Black Forest Cake. It was a calorie-worthy splurge of booze-soaked chocolate cake with cherry filling and whipped cream topping. I found it to be the perfect finish to a meal of *schnitzel* and *pommes* (pan-fried pork and French fries). *Hmm. Maybe Germany really was starting to rub off on me....*

We arrived at the spa ready for a swim. We checked into our room and quickly changed into our bathing suits. I headed for a pool outside. Friedrich grabbed me by the arm.

"We go this way," he said, and tugged me toward a different door.

"Why?"

"The other is for naked only. You want it?"

"Oh. No. I don't want it."

We spooned and hugged in the "not-naked" pool like two otters in love. I giggled and laughed like a schoolgirl, but not everyone appreciated my good humor. An old woman wearing a rubber swimming cap from the 1940s shook her finger in my face and said, "*Ruhig.*"

I turned to Friedrich, not for an interpretation, but for comfort. I'd just been scolded and told to keep quiet. I looked around at the other dour faces. *Geez! If you can't be happy on vacation, when can you be?*

I decided if I couldn't laugh, I could at least smile. I beamed my pearly whites at everyone. Out of thirty-odd bathers, I got one smile back.

"Look, Friedrich! I cracked a German face!"

Friedrich smiled and raised my score to two. The old man who'd played my game waded over and asked Friedrich something in German. Friedrich shook his head.

"Nein. Americanerin. Mein Val."

My Val. *I was his Val!*

MY WEEK WAS ALMOST up, and despite two divorce decrees bearing evidence to the contrary, I still didn't know if I was the marrying kind. I was waiting for a feeling that would make me absolutely certain it was the right thing to do. When the feeling didn't come, I began to question whether such a feeling really existed. Was stone-cold certainty about love just a fantasy perpetuated by fools in novels and silly romantic movies?

The feeling never arrived, so I quit waiting and said yes. Friedrich had smiled, kissed me lightly on the lips, and made a phone call. A few days later, we went to a lawyer and drew up a bunch of papers in German. I'd signed them.

Afterward, Friedrich announced we would get married at his sister's house. That had sounded okay to me. I'd already had a big wedding. I didn't need another. I certainly wasn't going to drag any of my friends or relatives across an ocean for a five-minute ceremony. So, I sent them all an email instead.

On a Sunday in late September, underneath the cherry tree in Hans and Olga's backyard, they, along with Friedrich's mother and Tamela from Tonga, witnessed Friedrich's lawyer say the words that turned Friedrich and I into husband and wife.

I thought I would feel different after the ceremony. More settled, perhaps. But I didn't. To be honest, nothing had changed for me except my legal status.

On Monday, Friedrich went off to his new job, and I was left to wander the streets of Landau alone, dependent entirely on the kindness of the rare, random stranger willing to throw me an English bone. After a few days of this, a gnawing, empty feeling made me face the facts. If I was going to live in Germany, it was time to get busy learning German.

THE FIRST FEW MONTHS were all about vocabulary building. It felt akin to moving a mountain of dirt (*Erde*) with a bent teaspoon (*Teelöffle*). By the end of October, I'd beaten about two hundred words into my head. They rattled around up there, useless, until, like a bingo ball, someone actually chose one of those exact words when they spoke to me. Even then, by the time I recognized and translated the word, the person had already said a dozen more words by then and I was left holding a blank card.

One day, I read on the Internet that I would have to have a vocabulary of at least five thousand words to even consider carrying on a conversation. That didn't include grammar or verb conjugation. I got so frustrated I wanted to pitch the whole idea. *Maybe it would be easier to teach all the Germans English....*

I'd started with the niceties. Please. Thank you. That was delicious. Nice to meet you. You're welcome. These phrases had come in very handy for the first few seconds of meeting someone. After that, I'd said, 'Hello, my name is Val.' After that, I faded to the status of a useless dolt.

Each time we visited Friedrich's mother or his sister Olga, I would listen intently to their conversation, trying to make out one word from another. It was like living a bad childhood dream—the one where I had to take an oral exam that I'd forgot to study for. It was exhausting. After an hour or so, I'd give up and go sit alone in silence.

"You can't just throw her in a corner," I heard Hans tell Friedrich one day. "You need to help her out."

But even when Friedrich tried, I simply couldn't learn German just by hearing it. My brain needed to see it written down, and to repeat it about ten million times. If I heard a word or phrase often, I'd ask Friedrich what it meant and how to spell it. I'd write it down and try to memorize it.

By November, both the weather and I had turned grey and were prone to shed droplets sporadically throughout the day. I gave up on learning German. I spoke English with Friedrich at home. Given the crummy weather, I didn't even want to leave the house. I lost myself in denial and Raymond Chandler novels.

I wasn't used to German attitudes or weather. In fact, I'd never experienced a real winter before. When 'winter' came to my hometown of St. Petersburg, Florida, I usually just stayed in that day. By the time I'd found my one and only sweater, the danger had passed. But here in Germany the cold and grey drug on for months at a time. I couldn't get a job, either. It was against the law until I'd established residency. Besides, no one would hire me if I couldn't speak German.

Eventually, I ran out of novels and novel excuses. After taking in the Christmas markets, I perked up and decided to give German another try. It was then that I realized learning a new language was a lot like death. They both involved five stages of coping. I'd already been through denial and anger and bargaining. I'd just spent a good month in depression over it. That left the final phase—acceptance. I was teetering like a see-saw on the edge between the last two phases when something happened that shifted my whole focus.

I went out to the garage and caught Friedrich smoking.

He'd laughed when he knew he'd been caught. I was so shocked, I didn't know what to do. I'd laughed half-heartedly along with him. But there was no denying it. I had caught my husband in a bald-faced lie.

Chapter Thirty

I'd detected cigarettes on Friedrich's breath many times before, but he had explained it away as second-hand smoke from hanging out with guys in the breakroom at work. I'd believed him. I had no reason not to—until the day I caught him in the act.

To my mind, there were three kinds of lies. There were the white ones we used to spare others' feelings. There were the grey ones we employed to deceive ourselves into thinking a fabrication was in the best interest of someone besides ourselves. And then there were the out-and-out, bald-faced ones designed to get us off the hook and escape the consequences of our unsavory deeds.

All three had the same thing—deception—at their root base. Was one kind better than another? I couldn't say. But I knew I would rather someone "cheat and tell" than deceive me behind my back. The past had taught me all too well that lies eroded trust, betrayal corroded confidence, secrets destroyed connection, and deception obliterated respect.

I now knew that Friedrich was capable of committing direct, unflinching, straight-faced deception.

Part of me was angry to the core. Part of me thought maybe I deserved what I'd gotten. I wondered if I was being taught a lesson by the karmic deity of relationships. I mean, who was I kidding? I'd told my own share of lies. Mostly white. But I'd have been telling a grey one to say that I'd never, ever told a bald-faced lie.

Nevertheless, I'd argued bitterly with Friedrich about *his* lie. He'd promised not to do it again. But was he telling the truth *that time?* I would never be able to be absolutely certain again. I slept on the couch for the next two days, sorting through my feelings and trying to devise a way to give us a clean slate again.

The next day Friedrich came home with a big eraser. I was in the kitchen making dinner when he sprang it on me.

"Val, we buy a house."

"What?"

"Remember the house we saw at the wine fest? The one we liked very much?"

"Yes, I think so."

"It is *zu verkaufen*. For sale. Let's go look, ya?"

My anger disappeared. "Okay. Ya."

EVERY GREAT DECEPTION calls for a great distraction, and I was up to my elbows in mine.

I spent the rest of the winter and all of spring scraping moldy, yellowing wallpaper off ancient, plaster walls and trying to direct the remodeling activities of two Polish-speaking men I suspected of being perpetually half-drunk. While Friedrich was at work, the three of us knocked down walls, built new ones, hung doors, installed sinks and tubs, and laid down new tilework and flooring. In the evening, Friedrich and I spent our time together pouring over plans and quotes for plumbing, heating, windows and kitchen designs.

We'd both put down a sizable deposit on the house. Friedrich said he would pay the mortgage and I would pay for the renovations. That had sounded good at first. But even though we did a lot of work ourselves, my money drained out of my bank account faster than I could transfer it from the US to Germany. Before I knew it, spring was gone and so was a hundred thousand euros—about a hundred and fifty thousand US dollars of my savings.

But most of the downstairs was done. I loved my new country kitchen and the beautiful, wood-burning oven I'd designed myself. It took pride of place in the sunny living room, and kept us toasty on even the coldest days. Through the custom, wooden windows I could see purple and yellow crocus and red tulips begin to show their lovely faces amidst patches of bare mud and melting snow.

The roof was replaced in May. We still had the upstairs bedrooms and baths to go. After that, we would start on the house's crumbling exterior, the barn, and the overgrown gardens. With renewed resolve, I set my jaw firmly to work mode and marched upstairs. I peeled more wallpaper, scraped away more grime and sanded and polished ceiling beams.

By June, I'd become a brainwashed, zombie slave to the house. Its needs were never ending. I slogged through each day, blind to everything but the task at hand. By evening, I was too tired to do anything but argue with Friedrich when he came home from work. One day, I was scheduling an appointment with a plumber when I noticed the date. It was the twenty-second of June. I'd met Friedrich exactly thirteen months ago on the twenty-second of May. I'd meant to mark the anniversary with a special evening. Where had the time gone?

I booked the plumber and shooed the Polish guys out of the house. Friedrich and I couldn't keep going on like this. We needed a break. We were living like ships passing in the night. How long before we got torpedoed?

I showered, styled my hair, put on a dress and made up my face for the first time in months. I pinned a note to the door for Friedrich to find when he came home from work, then I walked to a small, Italian café we had nicknamed our Little Alberobello.

Dear Friedrich,

A year ago, you found me in the Hotel Bella Vista and said, "I'll take you to lunch." You drove me to a café in Alberobello, Italy. Today, it's my turn to say, "I'll take you to dinner." I don't have a silver Peugeot, but it's just a short walk to Little Alberobello. Come and find me again, mein Schatz. Let's start another wonderful year together.

Your Val

I WAS DRINKING A GLASS of wine and trying not to fall asleep when a familiar voice whispered in my ear.

"It was more than a year ago."

I turned my head. Friedrich kissed me on the cheek.

"I know. Thirteen months. But thirteen is a lucky number in Germany, ya?"

Friedrich smiled. "Ya. And I'm a lucky guy."

We did find each other again that evening. We talked and laughed together like we used to. It felt almost like it had before we'd bought the house. At the apartment, we'd always had time for each other. That evening we made time for each other again, and made love for the first time in what seemed like ages.

Chapter Thirty-One

Our vintage winemaker's home turned out to be a mirage. The end of the renovations seemed to be drawing ever nearer, only to turn out to be a cruel, costly illusion. Every time we solved one problem, two more sprang up in its place. Another year went by, along with another hundred thousand euros from my bank account. But it was okay. Friedrich made enough money to pay the bills, and he had a good pension. We would be okay.

It had been Friedrich's idea to hire the Polish workers. Technically, they had been illegals, and theoretically, they were supposed to have worked cheaper. But it had been me who paid the price for this school of hard knocks. Late in the game, I discovered that much of their work had to be redone to pass inspection. It took another year to tear out and redo their poor workmanship. I could scarcely believe that three whole years had gone by, lost in the 'twilight renovation zone'. I was dipping into my last hundred grand in the bank. But that still seemed like plenty. After all, my money was the icing on our financial cake.

That's what I told myself, anyway. But deep down, I was worried. Not so much about the money, but my utter reliance on Friedrich for everything. During my first year in Germany, I'd tried to learn the language and fit in. But then the house had consumed my every waking moment for the next three years. So, even after four years in Germany, the borders of my world hadn't stretched very far beyond the gate to our old winemaker's villa. I had worked night and day on the house, leaving little time for a social life. Besides riding my bike to the shops or going out with Friedrich, I'd become a simple hausfrau leading a very isolated life in a small village of less than a thousand people.

In Florida, I had always been confident and independent. But here in Germany I was totally reliant on my husband. He was my interpreter, legal representative, tax accountant, bill payer, and my only friend. That was a lot for him to take on. After all, the typical man versus woman barriers were hard enough in a relationship. Add to that our cultural differences, language barriers, and the fact that I was an artist and he was an engineer, and we were left with a lot of checks and not much balance.

I usually spoke with Clarice on the phone once or twice a month, but over the years our connection had faded due to the distance between us. Our lives were no longer similar, and that caused us to soon run out of things to say to each other. I hadn't seen her in four years, and the thought of her slipping away panicked me. As my world had shrunk and shriveled over the years in Germany, Clarice had become my only American friend—my only woman friend. I didn't want to lose her. Now that the villa was beginning to look more like a house than a construction site, I felt I could finally invite Clarice for a visit. Friedrich was fine with it, so one evening I sent my best old friend an email. The next morning, I awoke and ran to check my computer. There was a reply. Clarice had accepted with a hearty, "Hell, yes!"

"Clarice is coming!" I announced to Friedrich. He stood in the doorway of the bedroom we'd dedicated as a home office. He held a cup of cappuccino in his hand.

"I think this is the first time I find you out of bed before I bring you coffee," he teased. "I take this as a good sign."

"It is!" I beamed. She can come next month. June third! That's okay, ya?"

"Ya. Sure."

I hugged Friedrich, nearly spilling the forgotten cappuccino in his hand.

I WAITED ON PINS AND needles to catch a glimpse of Clarice's smiling face as it came through the arrival gate at Frankfurt. I'd taken a train to meet her. I still hadn't found the time to get my driver's license. I'd been too busy with renovations, then with making everything perfect for my friend's visit. I'd spruced up the guest room with new, white sheets and a cute floral bedspread. I'd taken the train to France and stocked the fridge with some of my favorite delicacies to share with her.

The electronic board displayed that flight 844 had landed. Clarice was here at last! I waited impatiently, searching each passenger's face for those sparkly green eyes and cute, button nose. But I couldn't find her. After the last passengers walked by me, I asked a member of the flight crew if they had seen Clarice on board.

"It's a big plane. I couldn't say," said the female flight attendant. "Why don't you check at the reservation desk? Follow me."

The woman led me to a clerk at a reservation window. My worried look must have given her all the confirmation she needed of my sincerity.

"Could you please check the passenger list for flight 844? Clarice Whittle?"

The clerk eyed the flight attendant, then tapped on her computer screen. "She's on the manifesto, but a note here says she never boarded."

"That's strange," I said. "Does it say why?"

"No. Sorry. That's all it says."

I checked my phone. No texts or calls. Not knowing what else to do, I took the next train home. When I arrived, I checked my emails. Nothing from Clarice. But there was an email from an Edmund White. I clicked on it.

Dear Ms. Fremden,

The family of Clarice Whittle asked me to inform you that she was killed in a traffic accident on the way to the airport. My deepest condolences for your loss.

Sincerely,

Edmund White, Esq.

I FELL ON THE FLOOR and sobbed uncontrollably. I was still crying an hour later when Friedrich walked through the door and yelled up the stairs for me.

"Hallo! Val? I'm home, mein Schatz. Did your friend have a good trip?"

I tried to answer, but I couldn't speak. I stumbled to the head of the stairs. Friedrich took one look at me and climbed the steps to meet me.

"What happened?" he asked, holding me by the shoulders.

"Clarice," I said between sobs. "She's not coming. She's been killed. She's dead."

"I'm sorry. You know, I made a party for her at the pub."

"Yes. I know. We have to cancel it."

"It's too late for that. I go."

I looked up at Friedrich. Was this customary in Germany? I didn't know. He hugged me, then went back down the stairs.

"I'll be back soon," he said, and disappeared out the door.

I collapsed onto the bed and cried. Another two hours passed before I heard Friedrich come in. He climbed up the stairs and crawled in bed with me. He was drunk.

"Let's make love," he said. He put his hand on my breast. I shot up out of the bed.

Who was this man I thought I knew? Clarice, my best friend, had just died!

In that moment, something died inside me, as well.

Chapter Thirty-Two

I'd been wrong to compare death to learning a new language. Coping on my own with the loss of Clarice had proved much harder. Now that she was gone, my ties to the US dwindled considerably, along with my blind devotion to Friedrich.

To be fair, *his* ardor wasn't what it used to be, either. As we marched through our fifth year together, Friedrich's morning cappuccino delivery lost its way, replaced with a quick, perfunctory kiss goodbye before he left for work. I'd been reduced to just another item on his morning check-off list. Find wallet. Get keys. Kiss wife. Start car. Drive to train station.

And, to my dismay, those old, 3 a.m. demons from the past had begun to make sporadic appearances, waking me up to whisper, "There has to be more to life than this."

I wondered if Friedrich felt the same. I could sense his interest in me slipping away. How could I blame him? I was boring. Had no life, and therefore nothing interesting to say. It was high time I broadened my own horizons. I needed to make a life for myself here in Germany. So I made a plan.

A few weeks into July, I took the train to Karlsruhe to attend a meetup group for English speakers. At that very first encounter, I met Rita Rudeburg, a tall, thin, neurotic lawyer. She reminded me of a praying mantis in a mannish suit and a frizzy brown wig. At the time, I didn't have the luxury of being picky. She would have to do.

264

Rita was seeking a partner with whom to practice English. I needed someone to help me learn German. We were a match made in...Karlruhe. We agreed to meet once a week. I returned home excited for the first time in ages. I'd shared the news with Friedrich. He'd told me he was glad, but his words had lacked enthusiasm. He'd just taken another job and was preoccupied with sorting out problems with his new boss. He mentioned something about mobbing, but I hadn't understood what he meant, and he didn't want to explain.

FOR ME, LEARNING A new language and culture required just as much letting go of the past as it did embracing the new. It proved to be a long process that didn't happen overnight. Nearly every Wednesday afternoon for the next year and a half, Rita and I met at a café near her office in Karlsruhe. I would take the train into the city, have lunch, and do a little window shopping. At precisely 3:15 p.m., I would go to the café, order a coffee and wait for Rita's pointy, narrow face to poke through the door.

Rita was smart and accomplished, yet she was almost completely devoid of both confidence and empathy. It made for an odd combination of skills. Whenever we practiced German together, I could count on her for blunt, merciless corrective criticism on my choice of words and pronunciation. But whenever we practiced English, I had to coax the words from her like a scared puppy, employing lots of praise and encouragement at every step.

Rita's *kaffee klatch* lessons, along with my own endless hours of study and practice, finally began to pay off. Toward the beginning of my sixth year in Germany, my conversation skills started to bloom.

One day, in April of our second year of meeting together, Rita did the unthinkable. She invited me to her house. Up until that point, I had been merely a *bekannte* to Rita—an acquaintance on probation, so to speak. The German lawyer had been deliberating the verdict on whether I would be deemed worthy of friendship status. The invitation to Rita's home meant I'd made it. I was no longer on trial.

Rita lived on the outskirts of Karlruhe. I'd finally gotten my driver's license, so I dropped Friedrich off at the train station that morning and borrowed the car for the day. The car had a built-in GPS, so I only got lost twice along the way. Given my sense of direction and the Germans' unflinching expectations on punctuality, I'd left myself plenty of room for error. I arrived ten minutes early and waited in the car.

I rang the doorbell at precisely noon. Rita opened the door before the chime finished sounding.

"Hallo, Val. You are, what you say? Right on the time."

"Hello, Rita! These are for you."

I smiled and handed Rita a *mitbringsel*—a small hostess gift of a bouquet of flowers. It was considered rude to arrive empty-handed. That was one lesson I didn't need to repeat.

"Thank you. Please, come in."

Rita's house was clean and orderly inside and out. The interior was typical of the scant handful of German houses I'd been invited into over the last six years. Basic, brown-wood furniture from the 1970s filled her living room, along with shelves loaded with figurines and what-nots. But Rita's house held something I hadn't seen before. In one corner of the living room stood a massive bar made of heavy, dark wood.

Rita played hostess and stepped behind the bar. She took two small bottles of aperitifs from a cabinet and set them on the counter. I hoped they weren't the horrible, brown Amaro that Friedrich liked so much. I picked up one bottle and started to open it. Rita snatched it from my hand.

"Only for looking," she scolded.

"Oh. Sorry."

Rita put the bottles away and led me to her kitchen. There she'd set up a modest but nice lunch spread of assorted sandwiches and fruit salad, along with a pot of coffee and two strawberry tarts. I started to take a seat, but hesitated. I wasn't one-hundred-percent sure this wasn't "just for looking" as well.

"Please, sit," Rita offered. "Shall we have a lesson as we eat?"

I smiled and started to take a seat.

"Not there. This one."

I traded places with Rita and sat down. "Well, this looks lovely."

"Thank you," Rita said. She reached for a sandwich with a long, thin mantis arm. "You first."

She obviously wasn't talking about the sandwiches. She must have meant the lesson.

"Okay. Rita, what's the German word for happy? It's not in my translation book. I've looked everywhere but I can't seem to find it."

"There isn't one," she said matter-of-factly. She poured herself a cup of coffee. "Glücklich is the closest. But it really means lucky. In Germany, you are lucky if you are happy."

Boy, no one had to tell me that.

"Well, what about frohe?"

"That means...merry. Like merry Christmas."

"And freud?"

"Freud is joy, not happy." Rita took a bite of a sandwich, chewed it twice, then swallowed it. "Like shadenfreud. You know. The joy of watching another suffer."

Geez! No word for happy, but a word for enjoying someone else's pain?

"How about compassion, Rita?"

"No. No German translation."

Hell, that explained a lot. I learned more about the German psyche in that five-minute conversation with Rita than I had in the prior five and a half years I'd spent living there.

BEING A GERMAN'S FRIEND involved a lot of obligations. Friends were expected to call at least once a week. They also had to make their very best effort to attend every event to which they were invited. They were expected to remember every name of every family member or significant person ever mentioned in conversation. And, upon dread of excommunication, a friend was obligated to never commit the unforgivable sin of forgetting another friend's birthday.

Weirdly, it was absolutely *verboten* to wish someone a nice birthday *before* their big day. No birthday gifts were expected. In fact, the birthday person usually paid for the drinks and other festivities. But, at all costs, a friend *had to* call or write to wish the birthday guy or gal a good year ahead.

Despite the responsibilities involved, my friendship with Rita wasn't without its rewards. I finally had someone to talk with besides Friedrich. I also had someone who could read the impossibly complicated notices and letters I kept getting in the mail. I'd shown them to Friedrich a few times. He'd said they were nothing but advertisements. But something in my gut told me they were more serious than that.

One Wednesday in late September, I brought some of my mail with me to our little *kaffee klatch*. When I arrived, Rita was already there. I checked the clock and sighed in relief. I wasn't late.

"Hello, Rita. You're early today."

"Yes. My trial ended quickly. The defendant was declared incopren...incomputable."

"Incompetent?"

"Yes. That's it." Rita looked away, disappointed with herself.

"I thought we might do something different today." I spoke cheerfully, trying to appease the self-scolded puppy.

Rita looked back toward me. She was still chewing on her mistake. "What?"

I dumped three letters on the table. "I thought you might teach me how to read my mail."

Rita shrugged and picked up an envelope. "May I open it?"

"Of course. Open all of them."

Rita opened the first letter. "It is an advertisement from a furniture store. They want to make you a special offer."

I laughed, relieved. "I bet they do."

Rita didn't get my joke, which was no surprise. The German sense of humor was as incomprehensible as the Germans themselves. Rita set the advertisement down and opened the next envelope.

"Ah. This is from the car mechanical. You must make a *termine*...uh...appointment for service."

"Oh. Okay."

Rita opened the last envelope. "This is from the *Finanzeampt*. How you say it? I don't remember."

"I don't know. What do they want?"

"They say you don't pay your taxes. You are being...charged with tax...what is the word? Elevation? No. Ah! *Evasion*. Tax *evasion*."

Rita straightened her back proudly. She'd correctly remembered the English words. She sat back and allowed herself the small indulgence of a self-congratulatory smile.

Chapter Thirty-Three

I was both livid and terrified. I'd trusted Friedrich completely. I'd had no choice. Yet under his stewardship, I'd watched my fortune drain into the pockets of German *handwerkers* and drunken Poles. My cash was gone. I had fifty-eight thousand dollars left in my once-healthy retirement fund. And now I was being charged with tax evasion.

Friedrich had always taken care of filing our taxes. But he hadn't done them right. Now, for some reason, *I alone* was being investigated. The thought of being charged with a crime in Germany scared me to the core. I'd never even had so much as a traffic ticket back home in Florida. A nagging feeling in my gut told me that solving this wouldn't be cheap *or* easy.

That evening, I waited out on the front steps of the villa for Friedrich to return from work. When I heard his key rattling the lock on the wooden gate, I stood up and nervously brushed the creases from my skirt. As soon as he came through the gate, I rushed up to him.

"Friedrich! I'm in trouble. Rita says I'm being charged with tax evasion!"

Friedrich's square jaw tightened. His sea-blue eyes warned of a coming storm. He faced me, but looked over my head as he spoke.

"You need a lawyer, not me."

"But...."

"Listen. I just come home from work. I am tired. I don't have energy to listen to your problems tonight."

"But Friedrich! I need your help!"

"I can't help you. Not with these problems with the Finanzampt. You need an attorney."

Friedrich pushed past me into the house. His face was tired and angry, and he smelled of cigarette smoke. I watched him pass, dumbfounded. I shut my mouth and followed him into the kitchen.

"Look, Friedrich. I'm not trying to start some petty spat. This is tax evasion! For all I know, I could go to jail for this!

"How many times do I tell you? I can't help you. You need an attorney."

Something clicked inside my brain. "How do you know?"

Friedrich's face grew red and angry. He opened the refrigerator and took out a bottle of beer.

"Friedrich, I asked you a question. Did you know about this? How do you know I need an attorney?"

Friedrich stared at me hatefully and took a long slug from the beer bottle. The contempt in his eyes shot fear through me. I couldn't breathe.

"Why can't everyone just leave me alone? I am tired! I don't want to talk to you. Basta!"

Friedrich took his beer and marched out the front door, slamming it behind him. For the first time, I sensed that his problems ran much deeper than just the ones between us. I knew Friedrich's job took a lot out of him. He'd used that excuse to avoid discussions before. But tonight, I'd seen guilt and shame mixed in with the anger on his face. Maybe he had other problems. Or maybe he didn't want to talk to me because he would have to admit he made a mistake. That was something he was definitely not good at. It went against his German nature.

If that was the case, I could understand his reluctance to discuss it. But on the other hand, I had a right to expect Friedrich to support me in this. We were supposed to be on the same team. *But maybe we weren't. Maybe that had just been my delusion.*

Since I'd learned German, I'd had the growing suspicion that Friedrich considered me a second-class citizen. When it came to his family, he refused to take my side on anything. He never took me with him to his company's holiday parties. He talked over me in public. And on the rare occasion we met his friends for drinks or dinner, I felt tossed aside, excluded and forgotten. Even more telling, I wasn't allowed to say anything bad about Germany, but Friedrich was free to criticize America all he wanted.

And now he had abandoned me to deal with this tax dilemma on my own. We'd grown further apart than I'd ever imagined.

ACCORDING TO RITA, I had two weeks to respond to the latest letter from the *Finanzampt,* Germany's version of the IRS. I needed an attorney, fast. Rita offered to help, but her lack of compassion, even for an attorney, was utterly appalling. So, I asked the only other professional I knew. My hairdresser. She recommended a man in a nearby village who spoke perfect English. That had sounded perfectly perfect to me.

I called the attorney's office and made an appointment for the upcoming Wednesday. For reasons I wasn't sure about myself, I decided not to tell Friedrich about my meeting. Not yet, anyway. I told him I needed the car to meet with Rita at her house again. In other words, I told him my first bald-faced lie.

I DROVE ALONG THE COUNTRY backroads of the picturesque Southern Wine Route toward the law office of Mr. Donald Manheim. The name itself was a blend of two cultures. I hoped he would turn out to possess the best attributes of both. I sped past walnut and chestnut trees laden with bumper crops. It had been a pleasant summer and fall, weather-wise. I couldn't say the same, marriage-wise.

I turned left and followed Kleindorferweg to the address I'd scribbled on my notepad. I parked under a maple tree ablaze with fall colors. The patchwork piles of leaves crunched as I shuffled through them in the parking lot. A red one clung to my thick brown leggings. I set it free and stepped inside the door of the modest, single-story office building.

"Frau Fremden?" asked the woman at the front desk.

"*Ja. Das bin ich.*"

"Oh. I forgot! You're English, ya?"

"American, yes."

"Please, take a seat. Herr...Mr. Manheim will be with you in a moment."

I started to sit, but didn't have the chance. A nice-looking man in a well-made blue suit stepped out of an office and came toward me, his had extended.

"Hello! Ms. Fremden? I'm Donald Manheim."

His English was American, not British. So was his handshake. No cold, dead fish. His hand was warm, his grip firm and confident. I felt myself relax a little inside. If anyone could help me, I felt certain it would be this man.

"Come with me," he offered, and gestured toward his office door.

His blue-grey eyes twinkled welcomingly. As I followed him into his office, I noticed a touch of grey in his sandy-brown hair.

"Have a seat, please."

"Thank you. My hairdresser was right. Your English is perfect."

He laughed casually, something I'd witnessed rarely in my six long years in Germany.

"Yes, it had better be. My mother was an English teacher. An American. So, tell me, how can I help you, Ms. Fremden?"

"Please, call me Val."

"Don't you know by now that such informality is verboten?" he teased.

"I have been made well aware of the fact on numerous occasions. But humor me, Mr. Manheim. I could use a friend."

The attorney's jovial smile straightened into a more serious, sympathetic line. "I totally understand. Call me Don. It will be our little secret."

I smiled weakly. "Thanks, Don. I'm having problems with my taxes. I got a letter saying I'm being charged with tax evasion. My husband always filed our taxes. I had no idea how to do it in Germany. It's unfathomable enough in the US."

I pushed the letter across the desk toward him. He read it quickly.

"Yes. That's what it says. Is your husband a CPA, per chance?"

"No. An engineer."

"Why was he doing the taxes, then?"

"Well, he has a penchant for saving money the hard way. He's always trying to cheat the system. You know what I mean? Like not pulling permits. Hiring Polish workers. I guess he thought he could save money doing the taxes himself."

"Oh. Okay. Did you bring your tax records?"

"Yes. Here they are." I heaved a satchel full of file folders onto his desk.

"I should be able to get through them within a week. Is that acceptable?"

I nodded. "And there's one more thing I want you to look at for me."

"What's that?"

"My prenuptial agreement."

A WEEK HAD GONE BY since my appointment with Donald Manheim. I'd passed the time in a nervous twitter. I didn't like keeping secrets from Friedrich, but I also didn't want to bicker with him about uncertainties that could turn out to be nothing. I'd decided to wait until I knew the facts before bringing up the topic again. Hopefully, I would find out today that the tax issues weren't so serious. Maybe the whole thing had been a misunderstanding that could be solved with a simple letter of explanation.

Nevertheless, I'd lied to Friedrich again about why I needed the car. I'd told him I wanted to go shopping in France. I thought about the tangled web I was weaving as I waited in the small reception room in Donald Manheim's law office. I decided they were white lies.

"Nice to see you again, Ms.—oops. I mean, *Val*."

Don greeted me with the same warm smile and handshake as the week before. I perked up. Maybe there wasn't doom and gloom in my future after all.

"Hello, Don. Nice to see you again, too. I hope."

He shot me a sympathetic smile as we walked to his office. He closed the door and sat down across the desk from me.

"What's the verdict?" I asked hesitantly.

"Not good, I'm afraid," he said apologetically. "It looks like your husband neglected to claim your assets on the joint filing statements. As a result, with interest, you owe back taxes of forty-three thousand euros."

"What!"

"On the bright side, the tax refunds you got for filing jointly should more than make up for it."

"What do you mean?"

"He claimed you as a dependent, unemployed spouse, so you earned a ten thousand euro tax refund each year. That's fifty-thousand right there."

"Oh."

The sandy-haired lawyer studied me for a moment. I thought I saw anger flash across his face.

"He never told you about the refund, did he?"

I slunk back in my chair. "No."

"I was afraid of that. Especially after reading the pre-nup."

I sat up straight in my chair and leaned forward. "Why? What does it say?"

"Well, the long and the short of it is, if you divorce him, he keeps all of his personal assets and his pension, and you keep all of your money."

"But we spent all of my money on the house!"

Don Manheim's face grew resolute. "I was afraid of that, too. I have to give your husband credit. He may be lousy at taxes, but he's a great strategist. He set you up perfectly. Legally, you're entitled to half the profits on the house. But I have to warn you, the real estate market here isn't looking good. And values don't go up that much in Germany when you renovate."

"So, I'm screwed."

"Only if you want to get a divorce."

Don leaned over his desk toward me, his resolute face softened at the edges with compassion.

"Is that what you want, Val? A divorce?"

I stared back at Don Manheim, but I couldn't see him. My eyes were too full of unshed tears.

My husband played by two sets of rules. Heads, he wins. Tails, Val loses.

Chapter Thirty-Four

As I drove back toward my beautiful winemaker's house in the vineyards, I realized my once-cozy haven had vanished, replaced with a cold, conniving enemy base camp. I felt betrayed and unwelcome. My gut was hollowed out. I couldn't wrap my head or heart around what I'd just learned. *How could Friedrich do this to me?*

I needed someone to talk to. Someone who could help me understand. But I had no one on my team. I was all alone, and it was my own fault. Without Friedrich, my list of friends had shrunk to one; Rita Rudeburg. How could I possibly explain my feelings to a stick insect? I racked my brain. There had to be someone I could turn to for the clear, straight-talking advice I needed.

Suddenly, the image of a twirling bowtie flashed across my mind. *Berta!*

It had been six long years since I'd last seen the old psychologist from New York. I wondered if she was still alive. And if she was, would she remember me? Berta had given me her business card in Brindisi. I vaguely recalled tucking it into my Italian phrasebook all those years ago. I hoped I could find it the little book that had silently born witness to my dreams of *la dolce vita.*

When I got back to the house, I ran up the stairs like a thief in the night. I rifled through a chest I used to store books and mementos. I found the phrasebook. I turned it spine-side up and fanned the pages. Berta Goodman's business card fell out, along with a brochure for the Hotel Bella Vista. The hotel's cheerful peach color had faded. I wondered about Antonio, Giuseppe, and the others. How had their lives turned out?

I looked at the clock. It was 3:37. Friedrich would be home in an hour. I called Berta's number. It rang six times as I bit my thumbnail to the quick. Then the crusty old woman's unmistakable voice croaked out the sing-song message recorded on her answering machine.

This is Berta. Can't you tell?
I'm not here, so go to hell.
Or if you're not a jerk or creep,
Leave a message at the beep.

Just knowing that both Berta and her sense of humor were still out there alive and kicking somewhere made me feel a tiny bit better. I left her a message with my cell number. I pictured skinny old Berta in her frog-colored outfit and wondered where she was and what she was doing. Was she playing Vinny on a cruise? Or working as a clown in a traveling Romanian circus? With Berta, anything was possible. I smiled tentatively at the thought of her having fun and wondered why in the world I hadn't called her before.

SINCE THE SPAT ABOUT my taxes last week, Friedrich had taken to coming home, grabbing a beer, and ignoring me. In a way, I'd been relieved. I hadn't had to hide my feelings or play pretend house while I'd waited to find out the fate of my tax situation. All week, I'd left my husband alone to stew in his own juices, and crawled into bed only after I knew he was asleep.

But tonight was different. I knew what he had done.

My stomach flopped at the idea I had been duped by Friedrich. As the clock ticked down to his arrival home from work, I began to panic. Should I confront him tonight or hold my tongue? I was afraid. I felt unprepared and alone. As my attorney said, Friedrich had proven to be a great strategist. I'd been completely outplayed.

I didn't know whether it was time to show my cards, or hide my hand a little longer. The trouble was, it appeared that no matter how I played it, Friedrich was holding all the trumps. The only thing I had going for me was the element of surprise.

Before I took Friedrich on, I needed my own strategist. On a more basic level, I also needed access to the car. If Friedrich took that away, I couldn't get to my attorney's office. The train didn't run to Don Manheim's village. I decided to hold off for another evening. I hoped in the morning I would feel stronger, and clear-headed enough to devise a better plan.

YESTERDAY, I PRETENDED to have a headache and stayed in bed all evening. This morning, I pretended to be asleep. The truth was, I just couldn't look at Friedrich without wanting to slap his face. I could hardly wait to hear the door close behind him as he left for work. I got up and made a cappuccino. I tried to drink it, but my hand was too shaky. I was pouring it down the sink when the phone rang. It startled me, and I jumped like I'd been stuck with a hot poker.

"Hello?"

"Hiya, kid!"

"Berta! It's so great to hear your voice!"

"Ha ha! That's a good one, kid. My old, raspy voice? You always were loaded with one-liners. How's it going with that 'do-over life' you were after?"

Do-over life! I'd forgotten all about it. "Oh. Uh...not so good. I think I'm getting a divorce."

"Like Yogi Berra said, it's déjà vu all over again. What's going on, kid?"

"I married Friedrich. The German guy in Brindisi. I've been living with him in Germany for the past six years."

"Oh."

There it was again. That little syllable that spoke volumes.

"Long story short, Berta, Friedrich deceived me. He set me up. Now I'm nearly broke and in trouble with the German IRS. I don't know what to do."

"Aww flapdoodle, kid. That's no good. That's *bull hockey*."

"I knew I could count on you to put things into perspective. How are things with you?"

"Better than with *you*, kid, and I screwed a guy on a cruise ship who neglected to tell me that his wife was the ship's captain. That kind of blew my whole cruise-gig operation, if you know what I mean. Now I'm in the UK entertaining old bats on bus tours. I call it BOBing, for short."

Hearing Berta's voice brought home just how alone I felt. I laughed, causing unshed tears to tumble from my eyes.

"Sounds like a good time, Berta."

"It has its ups and downs. That's life. But kid, you sound terrible. Wanna tell me about it?"

Berta hung on the phone patiently while I cried for five minutes. Then I choked out my story between sobs.

"I screwed it all up again, Berta. Things were good at the beginning. But there were signs, you know? He lied to me about smoking. He cheated his ex-wife out of the money for his car. He had this...*clinical* way about him...like he didn't trust people very much. But I thought he would be different with *me*. Then we bought this old house and I sunk all my time and money into it. I was too exhausted to think straight. I ignored all the warning signs that things just weren't right."

"That's not a crime, kid. Love is blind *and* dumb."

"But the signs were all over the place. Oh, Berta. I don't know what I keep doing wrong! I don't know how to make a man happy."

"You can't make someone happy if you don't have it to give. Sorry, kid. But you sound miserable."

"I am."

"So let me get this straight. Your husband lied to you, bamboozled you out of all your money, and abandoned you when you needed his help."

"Well...yeah."

"And you're still debating about whether to get a divorce?"

"I...I know it sounds stupid. But I feel so wiped out. If I leave I'll have nothing."

"You'll have yourself, kid. And from what I remember, that's a lot."

BOLSTERED BY BERTA'S pep talk, I decided to accost Friedrich right as he came through the door. There would be no time for him to prepare, and no time for me to chicken out. I heard the key rattling in the door. It was time to play my hand. Blinded by anger and dismay at his betrayal, I forgot all about *his* strategy. I forgot the fact that it had been Friedrich's game plan all along to keep his cards close to his chest.

Friedrich opened the door and stepped inside. He put his briefcase down and eyed me warily.

"Friedrich, we need to talk. I found out I owe 43,000 euros to the Finanzamt. You knew it. You saw all the notices. You lied to me and said they were junk mail! Why did you do that? Why didn't you take care of this for me?"

Friedrich flinched. His blue eyes turned ice cold. The tendons in his jaw tightened. His face registered not a touch of surprise. Or empathy. He said nothing.

"And why didn't you tell me about the tax refunds? I'm entitled to half of that money. You took it all, without even telling me. That's not fair. That's stealing!"

Friedrich's face turned red and twisted.

"You attack me! You call me a liar! You say I steal from you. This is why you have no German friends!"

Though his words stung, they were like an antidote for my anger. A strange calmness came over me, and words came out of my mouth that surprised even me.

"*You're* German, Friedrich. Are you not my friend?"

Friedrich turned his back to me and headed for the kitchen. I trailed behind him, haranguing him with my unanswered questions.

"How could you do this to me? You promised to take care of me. I trusted you!"

Friedrich wheeled around, his crimson face contorted with anger. He spat his words at me like a rabid dog.

"You are not a good wife! You never made me feel loved!"

Friedrich didn't say another word. In fact, he never spoke to me again. I slept in the guest bedroom. Friedrich packed a suitcase, took it with him to work the next morning, and he didn't come back.

Chapter Thirty-Five

"When did the bed go cold?"

I stared across the desk at my immaculately dressed attorney. He looked too prim and proper to posit such a crude query.

"What kind of question is that?"

Don Manheim pursed his lips and blew out a soft sigh. "A very German one, I'm afraid."

I was incredulous. "Does it mean what I think it does?"

"Yes, and no. It's just a date in time. To start the clock ticking on your divorce. According to German law, you have to live apart, without relations, for a year before you can file. While we wait, we can get the paperwork ready and sort through the assets. The rest goes pretty quickly after that."

"Oh."

"So, do you have a date?"

I thought back to the last time Friedrich and I had made love. The frequency had dropped off considerably after Clarice's death. His thoughtless advances that night had nearly killed my libido. That had been—*oh my gosh!*—two and half years ago! *Since then? Let me think....*

Don interrupted my mental math. "Like I said, it doesn't have to be an exact date. Just one you'll both agree to."

"I think it was his birthday. March thirteenth. No. It was *my* birthday, April first. Wait. There was another time this summer. After a fest. In August. I don't remember the exact date...."

"That's close enough," interjected Don. "Okay. Today is October thirteenth. Let's just say it was August thirteenth. Two months ago. So we can file in ten months."

"What should I do in the meantime?"

"I imagine we'll be busy getting you off the hook for your taxes. And you might want to look at putting the house up for sale. The market here moves really slowly."

"Thank you, Don. Could I use your phone? I forgot mine. I...I need to call a cab."

"Don't tell me you don't even have a car."

I shook my head, too embarrassed to speak.

"He really did have you trapped in a golden cage."

"Trapped? Yes. Cage? Yes. Gold? Not so much."

"Well, I'm glad you can still have a sense of humor about this."

"I have to. I have a feeling when this is all over, it's the only thing I'll have left."

OVER THAT SIXTH LONG, cold, lonely winter, between Christmas and springtime, my limp sadness transformed into an itchy irritability. I'd gotten two phone calls over the holidays, neither of which was from Friedrich. Rita Rudeheim had phoned to invite me to a party, but I didn't go. On Christmas Day, Don Manheim called to wish me a happy holiday, and, I suspect, to make sure I hadn't hung myself in the attic.

"Merry Christmas, Val," he'd said in a too-cheery voice.

"Thanks. Merry Christmas to you, too."

"No word from the stobex?"

"What?"

"Oh. Sorry. Office lingo. Soon-to-be ex. Stobex."

"Got it. No. I guess that's my gift from him."

"Glad to hear you've still got your chin up. We'll get you through this."

"Thanks, Don. Hey, could I ask you a question?"

"Sure."

"What's 'mobbing'?"

"It's kind of like bullying. It's when a person thinks he's being persecuted by others, whether it's real or imaginary."

"Okay, thanks. Have a great holiday."

"You, too. See you at our appointment in January. I hope to have some good news from the Finanzamt by then. These Germans seem to take the whole month of December off."

"Yeah. Okay, then. Bye."

I clicked off the phone. Friedrich had complained a few times about mobbing at work. And he'd changed jobs four times since we'd been together. That was highly unusual for a German. Had he really been mobbed, or was it all in his head? Had he felt mobbed by me, too?

I looked around the beautiful house we'd wasted so much time renovating. Even though it was full of Friedrich's what-not collections and half-finished projects, my footsteps rang empty in the still silence. I was alone, with only my thoughts for company. My eyes fell on a stack of paint cans by the back door.

"*You can't just toss her in a corner.*"

The words of my stobex brother-in-law popped into my mind. A sudden realization hit me. *This was not my doing.* Friedrich had been a hoarder before I met him. He'd collected things, then neglected them. His apartment in Landau had been an obvious testimony to the fact. I'd been nothing more than his latest obsession. He'd collected me, then neglected me. But, like everything else in his life, he couldn't let me go.

Chapter Thirty-Six

While I waited for the cold, dark winter to end, I tried to resurrect the woman I'd left behind in Italy. Seven years ago I'd dreamt of becoming a human *being*—of creating a new life that savored the simple beauty of living. Instead, I'd gotten sidetracked and created a situation more complicated and unhappy than the one I'd left behind in Florida. Where had I gone off track?

In Italy, life had been all about love. Everyone had been in it to win it. They'd embraced their passions and enjoyed each other like one big, crazy, loving family. Here in Germany, life had seemed all about avoiding catastrophe. People had hidden their true feelings away, fearful of being deemed unworthy. Ironically, their fear of making mistakes had caused them to make the biggest failure of all. They never really took a chance and *lived*.

In a way, I'd been just as guilty. Bit by bit, I'd hidden away parts of myself that didn't fit the expectations of my German husband or his family. I'd folded away so many facets of myself that I'd become as one-dimensional as a cardboard image of myself. A paper-thin silhouette with nothing inside me, and no one to back me up.

It was time to drop this sad charade and do as my friend Berta once advised me nearly seven years ago. I needed to get off my butt and start living.

"AM I THE BAD GUY HERE?" I asked Berta over the phone.

"Listen, kid. Blame is not the name of the game. Does it really matter whose fault it is? There's no badge of honor for being a miserable martyr. Love and marriage are two distinctly different things. Neither come with any guarantees."

I knew what my friend was saying was true. Still, I had so many unanswered questions.

"But why would he refuse to talk to me?"

"Guilty conscience? By keeping his trap shut, he wouldn't have to admit his dastardly deeds."

"You're right. I guess I already knew that. I just wanted confirmation."

"Don't worry, kid. In my book, you're a good egg."

"Thanks, Berta. You're always right. Remember that joke you told me back in Brinidsi?"

"I was in Brindisi?"

"Cut it out! The one about what do women and brick sidewalks have in common?"

"Oh yeah. Lay 'em good once and you can walk all over 'em for years."

"That's the one. I'm the butt-end of that joke."

"Well, that's all right. As long as it's a cute butt."

BY THE END OF JANUARY, I'd talked to Berta a dozen times. She'd reminded me that I was a truth seeker, a champion, and I still had a smoking hot ass. I would never again take for granted the ridiculous optimism of Americans. In my book, they would forevermore win out against the stubborn pessimism of Germans. When Don Manheim called the last day of the month, I realized I'd have to scrape way a lot of rust and muck to find my own bright side again.

"The good news is, the Finanzamt says it will drop their charges of tax evasion against you," Don explained.

"That's great!"

"Yes, but it doesn't get better from there. The conditions for release of charges are that you pay the entire money owed within two weeks, along with a five-thousand euro fine."

"Crap! What does that add up to?"

"Forty-eight thousand euros. Do you have it?"

"Yes, but just barely."

I did the math in my head. After paying the tab, I'd have about eight-thousand euros left.

"Good," Don said. "I suggest you take this route. Fighting it would cost more than the fine they're demanding."

"Okay. Speaking of costs...what do I owe you? So far, I mean."

"It wasn't easy to make your case. I put in a lot more time than I expected."

My stomach flopped. "So, what's the tab?"

"For the tax evasion case, it's nine thousand, five hundred."

"Don, I don't—"

"But," Don said, "I've been corresponding with Friedrich's attorney about the tax refunds he didn't share. I got him to agree to half of it. So that's twelve-thousand, five-hundred. So, in essence, you're ahead three-thousand."

I breathed a huge sigh of relief. I still had about eleven thousand in the bank. But I also still had to pay Don for my divorce, cover my living expenses for the rest of the year, and save enough money to buy a plane ticket home.

"What about the house? Should I list it?"

"I tell you what, I'll get an appraiser over to have a look at it. We can go from there."

"Sounds good."

I hung up and bit my nails to the quick. It hadn't sounded good at all. It had sounded horrible. If I didn't make a profit on the house, I was sunk. I knew the little bit of money I had left wouldn't stretch as far as I desperately needed it to.

IN FEBRUARY, THE HOUSE appraiser came. He measured everything, took pictures of the renovations, scribbled things down on a notepad and left. While I waited for the results, I bit my nails and pinched my pennies.

March thirteenth came, and I called Friedrich on his birthday. It was the German thing to do. He didn't pick up, so I left him a message. When the first of April came and went without a birthday call from my husband, I realized I really was an April fool.

In early May, Don Manheim called to let me know the house had appraised at sixty-thousand euros more than we'd paid for it. It was official. My life's savings had been squandered. Don explained that even if we got a full-price offer, by the time we paid real-estate fees and taxes, I might net a few thousand euros. It would cost me more than that to rent an apartment while I waited for the divorce to be final. At least with Friedrich paying the mortgage, I still had a roof over my head.

I spent the summer helping the neighboring farmers in their vineyards and orchards. I earned enough to pay the grocery and electric bill for May, June and July.

In August, I got another call from Don.

"We can finally file, Val. How are you holding out?"

"Pretty good," I lied.

"Glad to hear it. Look, I've got an offer from Friedrich's attorney about the house."

Incredible! A flicker of hope lit up within me.

"Really? For how much?"

"Well, it's not exactly money. He's offering to take over financial responsibility if you sign it over to him."

The flicker fizzled out. "Oh."

"We could fight this, but it may end up costing more than it would net you. I'm sorry I don't have better news."

"That's okay. I appreciate what you're doing...what you've done. Don, I guess you think I should just agree to give him the house?"

"I'm not saying it's fair, Val. I'm just saying it's not worth the fight. It sucks, I know. I'm sorry."

"Thanks. Okay. Tell him I agree to it. But I get to stay here until the divorce is final. Does that seem doable?"

"I'll make it doable."

"Okay. Do you have any idea of the damages? I mean, your fees? What they'll be when this is all over with?"

"If there aren't any complications, it should be my standard fee. Thirty-five hundred euros."

"And how long will it take? For the papers to be final?"

"Four months, tops."

I did the math in my head. After paying Don's fees and my expenses for the next four months, I would have around a thousand dollars left. Not quite enough for a ticket back home.

THE ONLY CASH COWS I had left to milk were my clothes and the books, household goods and furniture I'd purchased over the years. I couldn't afford another run-in with the law, so I called Rita Rudehiem to find out the rules and regulations about having a yard sale in Germany. To my great surprise, there weren't any. And, also to my great surprise, Rita volunteered to help me hold the sale.

It was a beautiful, crisp Saturday in late October, when tall, stick-thin Rita walked beside short, washed-up me to the main crossroads intersecting my little village. She held out the signs reading *Haushalts Verkauf,* while I pounded their posts into the ground with a hammer.

With my only German friend's help, I'd placed small notices in the regional newspaper and online, advertising the sale. I'd carefully tucked away all of Friedrich's belongings, so as not to confuse potential buyers. Any pieces of furniture or items too heavy to move I had marked with "NZV," the German equivalent of not-for-sale.

When everything was in place, I opened the gate to the tall wooden fence separating our house from the street. I prepared for the flood of customers, but as it turned out, they only trickled in in dribs and drabs.

The antiques I'd collected went first. Then, strangely, dusty old books and furniture from the attic. By the end of the first day, I'd made about nine hundred euros. I took Rita to dinner as a reward. Between bites of schnitzel and fries, she told me she'd enjoyed the day, and wanted to come back the next morning.

On Sunday, we had a steady stream of old ladies stop in on their way home from church. But after two o'clock, we didn't have a single patron for an hour. I told Rita it was time to quit. I walked down to the corner to collect the signs, but they were already gone. I came back and Rita informed me she'd heard my fax machine go off. I went upstairs to fetch it.

The fax was from Friedrich's sister Olga, but I couldn't decipher it. I handed it to Rita. Her eyes grew wide as she read it.

"It says if you sell anything from Friedrich, they charge you with embezzlement."

My knees gave out. I fell on the floor and began sobbing. I didn't think Friedrich could hurt me anymore. But he'd found a way. Rita knelt beside me. She tried to hug me, but her attempt was awkward, as if I were as square as a box. Through my tears, I think I saw a glimmer of compassion in her face.

"Friedrich is what you call *dickhead,* ya?"

Hearing Rita say dickhead made me laugh, despite the horrible heartache inside me.

"Ya," I sobbed.

"He is also horrider. Look at all these things!"

Rita pointed her insect-like arms around at the stacks of clutter. I thought about correcting her English. Friedrich was a hoarder. But then I realized she had made no mistake. Friedrick was horrider. More horrider than I could have ever imagined.

After I settled down and Rita left, I counted my cash. I'd managed to scrape together eleven hundred, thirty-seven euros for my efforts. I blew my nose and wondered angrily, *Would it be enough to cover attorney fees for embezzlement?*

Why hadn't Friedrich sent me the fax himself? Was he that small a human being? Or that big a coward? Why did it come from his *sister*, of all people? They'd been fighting with each other like cats and dogs for the last three years.

An old saying flashed across my mind; *The enemy of my enemy is my friend.*

At that exact moment, I realized that, even after all he'd done to me, I'd still been giving Friedrich the benefit of a doubt of not being a complete dirtbag. I'd been holding onto the idea that I'd failed him somehow, and had caused all this damage. That lingering doubt vanished, along with every other feeling I'd ever had for him.

Chapter Thirty-Seven

Cold, grey November had come and settled, like an unwanted squatter, across the sky and in every corner of the village. I hadn't heard from Berta in two weeks, and was in desperate need of some cheering up. I punched in her number, only to hear a message that the number was no longer in service. Panic stabbed my heart. I got on the computer and googled her name.

The fourth item that came up under Roberta Goodman was a picture of Berta and the first line of her obituary. It read: "Ms. Goodman, aged 87, of New York, died in Glastonbury, England under suspicious circumstances."

I pictured Berta's laughing face and thought about how much she would have enjoyed that last line. *Just what were those suspicious circumstances, my friend? Did you hijack one of those tour-buses and drive it over a cliff? Were you throttled by the hands of a jealous wife?* I loved Berta. Her passing made me sad, but I didn't feel sorry for her. Berta had lived her life to the last drop.

I hoped when I got back to St. Petersburg, I would follow Berta's example and do the same. There wasn't much to go back to, but as Berta said, I'll have me, and that's a lot.

I kissed the tip of my index finger and put it on Berta's image on the screen.

"Goodbye, my friend. I'll miss you."

I PACKED MY SUITCASES and rolled them down the stairs of my quaint winemaker's villa for the last time. Technically, it wasn't mine anymore. As soon as I stepped out the door, I could never return. I picked up the package I'd found hidden away in a closet when I'd scoured the house in search of things I could sell. It was wrapped in Christmas paper, and had my name on it. Friedrich had planned to give it to me last Christmas, but his wall of silence had fallen before the day arrived.

This week, another Christmas had come and gone. I'd intended to open the package on Christmas Eve, but I'd been alone. I was afraid that its contents might shatter my fragile heart and there'd be no one around to pick up the pieces.

I tucked the package into my little, brown-checked carry-on and wheeled it onto the steps beside my big blue suitcase. I closed the door behind me. I dropped the keys in the mailbox, and noticed a postcard inside. I took it out and read it. It was a note for Friedrich, written in German.

Mein Schatz, I am so happy we have found each other. I cannot wait until we are in each other's arms again.

All my love, Christina

I'll never know if the postcard was real, or just one last despicable deed by Friedrich, designed to hurt me. Either way, it turned out to be a gift. After I read the note, my only thought had been; *Thank goodness he's found someone else. He can finally let me go.*

I no longer loved Friedrich. His power to hurt me was gone.

I TRUDGED DOWN THE narrow village road to the train station, my two suitcases in tow. As I boarded the train headed for Frankfurt airport, it began to rain. I fingered the letter tucked into my shirt pocket. It was a notice from Clarice's attorney. He'd been in charge of liquidating her assets after she'd died, and I'd asked him to sell my car in her garage. After complications with clearing the title and his attorney fees, he'd netted me $5,700 for my Ford. That, along with the thirty euros in my pocket, were what I had to begin my life anew, give or take a side of fries.

I thought about my family back home and laughed to myself. *You know, Val, $5,700 is good money for a redneck.* But I wasn't a redneck anymore. I was an international fancy person. And I was back to square one. No, I was further back than that. I was back to absolute zero.

In the company of strangers, I fished the brightly wrapped Christmas gift from my carry-on. I tore off the paper and opened the box. Inside was a strange contraption made of metal and plastic. I held it up to study it.

"It's a walnut press," offered the businessman sitting next to me. "For getting the oil out of the nuts, see?"

He took the press from my hand and twisted the handle. Two cup-shaped cylinders met together like a vice.

"Oh," I said. *Another thoughtless gift from the man who never knew me.*

The man tried to hand the press back to me.

"Oh no. You keep it," I said. "The pair of nuts I'd like to smash with it don't grow on trees."

AS I STEPPED ONTO THE plane headed for Tampa, Florida, a calm resignation swept over me. I pictured Friedrich as I last remembered him; his face red and twisted.

"You never made me feel loved," he'd hissed at me.

In the year that had passed since that moment, I'd learned a lot about what love was, and what love *wasn't*. If I'd had the power to rewind the clock, I would have shared with him a secret I'd discovered. But I couldn't. So I whispered it to myself, instead.

"I couldn't in a million years make you feel loved, Friedrich. That's something you have to do for yourself."

I took my seat next to a little boy wearing a party hat. I suddenly remembered it was New Year's Eve.

"Do you have any plans for the new year?" his mother asked.

"Not a single one," I said.

And I was okay with that, because *I was free.*

DEAR READER,

Wow. I know.

Even *I* cried as I wrote that ending. Val was on top of the world. Now she's at the bottom of the barrel.

But for her hard-knocks-to-happy-ending story to continue, it *had* to be like this.

So here's the bright spot to hang on to; from here on out, Val has nowhere to go but up. True, all she's got left is her dignity and her sense of humor.

I assure you, it will be enough.

Follow along as Val rises—and stumbles—and learns to love herself again. Her self-deprecating spunk and the new friends she meets along the way will help you laugh your *own* cares away—just as a visit with a good friend should.

So I invite you to cheer up, turn the page, and read the first chapter of Glad One. I think you'll quickly see what I mean.

All my best.

Margaret

P.S. I'd like to invite you to come join me on Facebook, and share your own ideas about what makes for a true happy ending. Come join the fun, and find out what other people are saying, at:

https://www.facebook.com/groups/ValTalk/[1]

1. https://www.facebook.com/groups/ValTalk/?source_id=693288710867347

What's Next for Val?

I hope you enjoyed *Absolute Zero: Misadventures from a Broad*. Please do me a favor and click the link below now and leave a review on Amazon. I appreciate every single one!

https://www.amazon.com/dp/B06ZXYK776#customerReviews

Thank you so much! You rock!

Don't miss another new release! Follow me on Amazon and BookBub and you'll be notified of every new crazy Val adventure.

Follow me on Amazon:

https://www.amazon.com/-/e/B06XKJ3YD8

Follow me on BookBub:

https://www.bookbub.com/search/authors?search=Margaret%20Lashley

Ready for more Val?

Enjoy the following excerpt from the first Val Fremden Midlife Mystery:

Glad One: Crazy is a Relative Term!

A Sneak Peek at Glad One

Chapter One

Some people lead lives under a dark cloud. Others, under a lucky star. As far as I could tell, *my* life was under the control of a sadist brandishing a cattle prod and a whoopee cushion.

THE PLANE FROM FRANKFURT, Germany wobbled erratically as it hit heavy turbulence just north of Orlando. My drooping head lurched forward, and I startled myself awake with a piggish snort. I shot an apologetic smile at the man wedged in the seat next to me.

"Sorry. I must have dozed off for a second."

"Right. Lady, that snore of yours could put a jackhammer to shame."

I shrunk back in my seat and groaned. My feet hadn't even touched the ground back in the US, and already I'd had my first rude awakening. What else should I have expected? My whole life to date had been akin to one long, never-ending, rude awakening.

But all that was about to change.

After all, it was New Year's Eve.

I glanced around at the other bleary-eyed passengers around me. They probably had their minds on fresh beginnings, too. As for me, I had no other choice. The past I'd just fled was still too raw and painful to touch. I studied the pale strip of flesh encircling my now-naked ring finger. The ghostly reminder of yet another failed attempt at love sent a hot jolt of desperation racing through my gut.

A puff of jaded air forced its way between my pursed lips, like steam from a relief valve. I needed a good cry. But this was not the time or place for it. To distract myself, I decided to count my blessings.

One decimated pocketbook. Two cottage-cheese thighs. Three maladjusted ex-husbands.... Crap!

Whoever was running the show up there had a wicked sense of humor, and I was getting darn tired of being the punchline. I scrounged around for my powder compact and opened it, intent on repairing my makeup after the nine-hour flight. One glance in the mirror at my worn-out face made me snap it shut.

Why bother?

In forty-five years, I'd accumulated a good portion of wrinkles, a fair amount of belly fat, and, apparently, precious little wisdom. These questionable assets, along with $5,726 and a suitcase full of inappropriate clothes, were all I had left to launch my latest life makeover. I slumped back into my seat. I was bone-dragging tired. Even so, a wry grin snuck across my lips, like a stolen kiss from a stranger.

I was not defeated. Not yet, anyway.

The way I saw it, I still had two viable options. One, I could finally learn to laugh at myself. Or two, I could drink myself into oblivion.

I fished around the bottom of my purse for a coin to determine my fate. I flipped a tarnished nickel into the air. It did a triple gainer, plunged into my coffee cup, and splashed a nasty brown stain onto the crotch of my white stretch pants.

Awesome. Let the festivities begin.

MY LAST LIFE MAKEOVER had begun a little over seven years ago, and had turned out to be a spectacular, downward spiral akin to diving off a cliff with a bowling ball in my pants. Drowning in dullness and fueled by movie-inspired stupidity, I'd ditched a tiresome marriage and lucrative writing career, sold all my belongings, and took off for Europe.

In Italy, I'd met a German and fell in love with the idea of life with a stranger in a strange land. Things had been great for a while. But then the shiny wore off and the cracks showed up...like they always did.

On my arrival back in St. Petersburg, Florida, I'd quickly discovered that seven *wasn't* such a lucky number. In fact, seven years abroad had been just *exactly* long enough for my entire credit history to be erased—just like most of my money. I'd gotten off the plane in Tampa with no driver's license. No place to live. No credit card. No phone. No job. And, worst of all, no friends.

Incredibly, I'd somehow managed to become *a foreigner in my own homeland.*

As a lifelong lover of irony, I'd had to shake my head in wonder at my own warped ingenuity.

How many other people on the planet could claim such a monumental screw-up?

Over the next few weeks, my solo climb back aboard the American dream had required counting pennies and swallowing more than just pride. After that, I'd had to scrounge around for a tire jack and lower my expectations to half a notch above gutter level. That's how I ended up in a "no credit check" hovel of an apartment, living a "no foreseeable future" scrabble of a life.

A few months into what I'd sarcastically dubbed "my adjustment period," I'd been contemplating a *Smith & Wesson* retirement plan when something unforeseeable happened.

I met an old woman named Glad.

I'd been in desperate need of a life coach. Glad had fit the bill perfectly. The fact that she was a crazy, homeless woman had been the icing on the cake.

I could afford her fees.

Keep the adventure going! To get your copy of Glad One, just click the link below:

https://www.amazon.com/dp/B06XTKBMWT

About the Author

Like the characters in my novels, I haven't lead a life of wealth or luxury. In fact, as it stands now, I'm set to inherit a half-eaten jar of Cheez Whiz...if my siblings don't beat me to it.

During my illustrious career, I've been a roller-skating waitress, an actuarial assistant, an advertising copywriter, a real estate agent, a house flipper, an organic farmer, and a traveling vagabond/truth seeker. But no matter where I've gone or what I've done, I've always felt like a weirdo.

I've learned a heck of a lot in my life. But getting to know myself has been my greatest journey. Today, I know I'm smart. I'm direct. I'm jaded. I'm hopeful. I'm funny. I'm fierce. I'm a pushover. And I have a laugh that makes strangers come up and want to join in the fun. In other words, I'm a jumble of opposing talents and flaws and emotions. And it's all good.

In some ways, I'm a lot like Val Fremden. My books featuring Val are not autobiographical, but what comes out of her mouth was first formed in my mind, and sometimes the parallels are undeniable. I drink TNTs. I had a car like Shabby Maggie. And I've started my life over four times, driving away with whatever earthly possessions fit in my car. And, perhaps most importantly, I've learned that friends come from unexpected places.

Made in the USA
Middletown, DE
17 January 2024

47978312R00182